Let Love BE

BOOK 4 IN *THE LOVE* SERIES

Lucy and Evan's story

by Melissa Collins

LET LOVE BE

Copyright © 2014 by Melissa Collins

All rights reserved

ISBN-13: 978-0-9910542-6-8
ISBN-10: 0-9910542-6-1

Cover design and graphics by Sommer Stein, Perfect Pear Creative
Cover Photography by Toski Covey Photography
Interior Design by Integrity Formatting
Edited by Becky Johnson Hot Tree Editing

A Note from Melissa

If you've read Let Love Heal, you'll notice that I've repeated the prologue here in the beginning of Let Love Be. I've included it for those readers who may be picking Let Love Be up as a standalone. When I originally wrote those words for the opening of Let Love Heal, I didn't have Lucy's story completed in my head and since they are such an integral part of her story, they needed to be repeated.

Dedication

For those who are lucky enough to find love...again

Part One

~ Lost ~

September 30, 1995

PROLOGUE
Lucy

The I-beam swings haphazardly in the clouds. Teetering and tottering in the crystal-blue sky, it's the perfect juxtaposition of artificial and natural – steel illuminated by the sun. Over a ton of metal effortlessly cascades through the air on the whim of a crane. It almost looks like a graceful ballet dancer as it swirls and twists, dips and dives. It's mesmerizing, actually.

And then disaster strikes.

A deafening crack of a snapped chain sounds through the once peaceful air. The lively chatter of construction workers and architects instantly morphs into chaotic screams. Everyone runs, seeking cover from the impending doom.

As the massive beam plummets to the ground, people scramble, frantically grabbing others along the way to pull them to safety. It all happens so quickly. In the blink of an eye, it seems as if everyone will escape unscathed.

Until they don't.

The beam changes direction, up ending itself. Head architect, Jimmy Crane, exits the shell of the building. Hardhat on and earplugs in, he's always one to follow procedure to make sure that his work site is safe. His eyes are pulled away from the clipboard of today's itinerary as the shadow of a passing figure flashes before him.

His eyes are drawn skyward. The sun blinds him; his sunglasses are tucked into his front pocket rather than perched across his nose. He doesn't have a second to process anything.

Crushed beneath the massive weight of the steel beam, the last thought that passes through the mind of Jimmy Crane, is of his wife, Lucy and his unborn daughter.

Lucy Crane is consumed with decorating the freshly painted nursery. If ever there was a woman more excited to meet her first child, well, Lucy's jubilance would put her to shame. Purple frills and pink lace don every surface of the room. It's a princess' heaven and a mom-to-be's dream come true.

Lucy sits on the floor, sorting through baby gifts from her shower last weekend. Holding a glittery onesie with an attached pink tutu up against her eight-and-a-half-month pregnant belly, she whispers quietly to her unborn daughter, "Maybe one day you'll be a ballerina…Melody." She tucks a piece of hair behind her ear and taps a finger against her lip as she contemplates one of her husband, Jimmy's, top name choices. "Hmm, no that just doesn't sound right." Still going through baby names, Lucy and Jimmy haven't been able to find one upon which they both agree.

Last night, as they lay in bed, they settled on a short list of names they each liked. Lucy was leaning toward more trendy names – Jessica, Ashley or Emily. Jimmy, on the other hand, wanted his daughter to have a less popular name; she was one of a kind, after all. Well, how could Lucy argue with that? From the moment she'd told her husband of less than a year that she was pregnant, he had absolutely radiated with love and joy. Conceding on his name preference was a small way that she could repay him for how he's taken care of her through the entire pregnancy.

They'd been high school sweethearts, and in the seven years that they'd been together, they'd shared a lifetime's worth of love. When Jimmy would place his lips up against Lucy's swollen belly, and talk to their child, she could swear that her heart would burst at the overly full feeling of love.

On a mission to finish her sorting all of the baby clothes, Lucy snaps out of her happy musings of her husband and their baby. But when she comes across a purple sequined outfit, she can't help put place it across her belly and talk to her daughter once more. "This is going to look absolutely perfect on you…Melanie."

The name rolls off her tongue and sings to her heart. It was one of Jimmy's first suggestions, liking "M" names more than any other. Lucy had originally dismissed it, but now, sitting quietly in her soon-to-be-born daughter's room, the name seems to fit perfectly. Smiling broadly, she says the name once more, "Melanie." Rubbing her belly, Lucy talks to the kicking baby who is rolling around inside of her. "Do you like that name, little Miss Melanie." Another kick and roll.

"Well then, we'll just have to ask Daddy what he thinks when he gets home." Another kick widens Lucy's bright smile. "Okay now, Melly Belly." Lucy chuckles softly at the ridiculous nickname she's just given her daughter. A smile spreads across her face because she knows Jimmy will be pleased with her sudden turn around on his top name choice.

With numb and wobbly legs, Lucy stands to put the piles of clothes away when she hears a knock at the door. Checking her watch, she realizes that it's past four in the afternoon. She's been so lost in her baby daydreams she didn't realize she hadn't heard from Jimmy all day. Knowing that he is extremely busy trying to manage this massive project, she immediately dismisses her concerns. No phone calls during the day means that he is guaranteed to chew her ear off at dinner. The man loves his building, that's for sure.

Brushing her hands over her trendy and modern dark-blue maternity shirt, Lucy flattens out the wrinkles that set in as she was draping onesie after onesie across her belly.

As she peeks through the curtain that hangs across the top window of the door, she smiles cheerfully at her husband's best friend and co-owner of Crane Building Associates, Ray Richards.

"Hey, Ray. What's going on?" Lucy steps to the side allowing Ray to enter into the small foyer. Closing the door behind him, she continues talking. "Jimmy isn't home from work yet, but come on in. Can I get you a beer?" Lucy's bright voice does nothing to lighten the darkness that is cast over Ray's face.

Ray shakes his head, declining the beer. He looks into Lucy's bright blue eyes, and says, "We need to talk, Lucy." His voice is even and curt. Ignoring her stunned reaction to his cold demeanor, Ray walks past Lucy into the sunken den of his best friend's new home - a home to which he'll never return.

Ray sinks into the old, beat-up couch and memories flood his head and heart. This is the couch that they had in their first apartment. It was a rat-hole of a place, but somehow Ray and Jimmy managed to make it work. The couch is a hand-me-down from Jimmy's parents and has survived remarkably well through their college years.

Burying his head into his hands, Ray can no longer contain the sobs that have been threatening to swallow him whole since he pulled in the freshly-paved driveway.

Lucy waddles over to the couch and, not-so-gracefully, lowers herself onto the cushions. Tenderly wrapping her arm around his broad shoulders, she says, "What's wrong, Ray? I'm getting a little worried here."

It's not unusual for Ray to stop over, but usually Jimmy is there getting ready for a golf outing or a ball game. There's something about *this* particular visit that just feels...wrong.

Her concern only makes him cry more. He's crying for the loss of his best friend. He's crying for Lucy, who he's come to love as his own best friend through the years. He's crying for the baby that Jimmy will never get to meet – for the baby that Lucy will now have to raise on her own.

Twisting in his seat, he faces Lucy and wipes the tears from his eyes. Lucy's face pales as all of the blood rushes from it. She can tell that this is not a routine visit on Ray's part.

"Lucy…" Ray's words catch in his throat, stuck behind the ball of emotion that's been lodged there since he witnessed his best friend being crushed by tons of steel.

Lucy covers her mouth with her hands, but her gasp is still audible. "No, no, no, no…." It's the only syllable her brain can manage. She's shaking her head wildly as if it will keep away the horrific news that is so clearly etched across Ray's tanned and youthful face.

Ray wraps his arm around her slumped shoulders and pulls Lucy into a tight squeeze. "I'm sorry. I'm so sorry. There was an accident and…it's Jimmy. He's gone, Lucy."

With those words, her world changes instantly. No longer able to contain her anguish, her chest heaves in sobs as tears pour from her eyes.

How? Why? What? All of these questions swarm her brain, but the bottom line is none of it matters. Bits of Ray's strained explanation filter into her consciousness, but she can't make any sense of it. Something about a beam, about being in the wrong place at the wrong time, about wanting to come here to tell her himself, about not wanting her to have to drive to the coroner's office alone, it's all a garbled mess, because none of it is important. The only meaningful piece of information is that Jimmy, her Jimmy, the love of her life, is gone.

Visions that she will never be able to erase start filling her mind. In a vain attempt to escape them, Lucy shoots up from the couch and begins frantically pacing the room. But she's too weak to stand for long. As pain, anguish and loss eat her alive, she crumples to the floor and wraps her arms around her round belly. Again, the only words she can form are, "No, no, no…"

Unable to let her suffer alone, Ray moves next to her on the floor and pulls her into his arms. Cooing softly to her, he tries to calm her. It's a vain attempt at peace that will never come.

It's always been Jimmy. He was her first friend, her first love, and now he's her first true loss.

Calling on an inner strength that she doesn't truly feel, Lucy tries to stand, but her body rejects the attempt. All she can do is let the sadness swallow her whole, and hope that when it spits her back out, she'll be alive and whole enough to take care of Melanie.

October 2, 1995

CHAPTER ONE

Evan

"You better slow down, old man," Brody puffs out as he powers down the treadmill. Straddling the machine, he places a foot on each side of the belt as it comes to a complete stop.

I swipe a towel over my face, but don't stop my run. "Nah, I still got a few miles left in me. And I am *not* old." My legs are burning, but I can't stop now. There's no way in hell I'm letting this probie lay into me for being old.

Brody chugs down his water as he sits on the bench next to the machines. "You're older than me!"

"Watch it, *kid*. Keep talking like that to an old-timer like me and you'll be scrubbing toilets for a month."

Brody chokes on his water and holds up his hands, surrendering to my empty threats. "Okay, okay, you win."

"Damn straight, I do." I'd laugh, but now my lungs are burning too. He needs to get out of this workout room now so I can slow down without losing my pride.

Just as Brody turns to leave the room, I get a killer cramp in my side. He must see me cringe in the wall of mirrors lining the back of the room where the weights are set up, because he smirks and turns on his heels, heading back to my machine.

Still refusing to let him win, I straighten myself, even though it hurts like a bitch. Casually, Brody leans his elbow up against the front of the machine and takes a look at the speedometer, which is set to seven miles-an-hour.

"Seven, not bad. Let's see if you can handle eight though." He reaches over the control panel and changes the speed.

Prick.

"Oh, it's on now!" My legs pump faster, muscles ripping through the pain, but after a minute or so, I acclimate to the speed and catch my groove. It's not so bad, but if I don't consciously focus on my breathing, I might just keel over and pass out.

"How are those lungs feeling?" he asks mockingly.

Risking any sense of control I have over my body, I ball up my towel and chuck it right at his head. "Fantastic, newbie."

Okay, maybe they burn a little bit, but I'd rather collapse than admit it.

Brody has a smug look plastered to his face as he leans back against the wall, crossing his arms over his chest. "I'm so glad you find this amusing. Hey, didn't Ramirez make you power wash the rigs last month for giving him shit?"

"Yeah, but it's just so easy picking on you, old man. Plus, there are so many around here to choose from." I flip him off, mid stride and he just continues watching me run, shit-eating grin spreading his mouth open wide.

I want to hate him. Hell, we all want to hate him, but his jokes are always in jest. As far as probies, probationary firefighters, go, Brody Callahan is an all right kid. At only twenty-four years old, he's a decade younger than me. With only about two months on the job, I have to admit that the kid knows his shit. Like most of us, he pretty much knew he wanted to be a firefighter from the day he was born. He studied hard and trained even harder, and just this past summer, he graduated at the top of his training class.

Wanting in on all of the action, Brody requested to be placed here at Squad 18, right in the heart of Manhattan. In the twelve years I've been part of the FDNY, I've seen my fair share of new kids. Brody is by far the biggest wise-ass punk we've ever had join our crew.

We loved him instantly.

When I reach eleven miles, and my heart feels like it's about to jump out of my chest, I hit the power button and Brody tosses my towel back at me. His chest is all puffed with pride.

"What're you all happy about over there?" I have to angle my neck up to look at him because I'm currently bent over, hands braced against my knees as I try desperately to seem unaffected by his little game.

"Oh, nothing. It's just that I made you sprint an extra mile. That ought to help your marathon next month." He slaps my back and adds, "See? Maybe a vet like you could learn a thing or two from the new guy."

That gets a more than a chuckle from me. And hell, he's probably right. It sure as shit isn't going to hurt my pace.

I glance up at the clock above the door and finish off my bottle of water. "Day tour is about to start. Better get ready so we can relieve the overnighters."

Standing by the door, Brody props it open with one foot while he extends his hand, allowing me to walk past him. "Age before beauty," he laughs sarcastically.

"I doubt you'll be laughing like that with a toilet scrubber in your hands."

"Ehh, pissing you off is *so* worth a few weeks of bowl detail." He takes a few steps ahead of me and pauses at the bottom of the stairs leading up to the showers. Peering over his shoulders, he says, "I'll race ya, old man!" And then, he's off, taking the steps two at a time.

Even if I did want to prove a point, there's no way in hell my rubber band-like legs could possibly do any kind of sprinting. So, instead of accepting his challenge, I make a mental note to pick up a brand new toilet scrubber when we do the daily meal shopping later in the afternoon.

Holding down the button for the PA system, I call out, "Food's on!"

Mealtime at the firehouse is pretty much like any meal at home. After all, this is our home. We laugh while we eat and catch up on any and everything that's going on in our real homes – new babies, middle school concerts, high school graduations.

The one thing that's missing from our meals is usually manners. It's a first-come-first-served mentality, and since the alarms could go off any minute, you really do need to eat quickly. When the other five men have their plates filled, I scan the room and realize Brody is missing.

"Manny, where's the kid?"

Around a mouthful of mashed potatoes, Manny mumbles, "Studying, I think."

He might be a pain in the ass, but that right there is the reason I can tell Brody is going places. I like that he's motivated, but after our workout this morning and then a long day of running a few drills, he needs to eat.

I use the PA system to get his attention. "Callahan, get your ass down here, kid. The dishes aren't going to clean themselves."

Out of the corner of my eye, I see Brody sliding down the pole. He pops up on his feet when he hits the bottom and pokes a thumb over his shoulder while facing the full dining room. "That never gets old." With a smile of a five-year-old boy who just arrived at recess, Brody fills his plate before sitting next to me.

"Dishes? I thought I was on shitter patrol." He stuffs his face with a chunk of steak, chewing with his mouth open.

See, no manners necessary.

"That was before you were late to dinner." Reaching under the table, I pull out the plastic bag and hand it to him. When he pulls out a toothbrush and a bar of soap, he pulls a 'you've got to be kidding me' face.

While everyone else is laughing in an uproar, I lean in to him and whisper coolly, "That's what you get for calling me old, *kid*."

I laugh a full-bellied chuckle. Besides, thirty-four is not ancient like Brody makes it out to be. He's just a wise-ass twenty-four-year-old.

Our laughter is cut short by the blaring tinny sounds of the alarm bells ringing. Muffled static filters through the room and everyone shuts the fuck up, waiting to hear the instructions.

"Two-alarm fire. Empty warehouse. 2415 Park cross at West Broadway. Squad 18." The loudspeaker cuts out and we all push back in our chairs, racing toward our gear, which is always laid out and ready to go.

Manny, the chauffer, is in and ready to go first as usual. Beeping the horn and wailing the sirens, he slaps his hand on the side of the door, "Giddy up, boys! Let's go. We got a fire to put out!"

Fitzy, the captain slides in next to Manny and gets on the radio to dispatch our ETA. Brody and I sit next to each other in the rear-facing seats behind the front of the engine. Hefting the weight of our oxygen tanks over our shoulders, we slide the masks into place, leaving the oxygen off until we arrive on the scene. Brody hasn't been on too many calls in the two months since he's started. Luckily, it's been a little slow recently.

We twist and turn through the streets of lower Manhattan, speeding as quickly as the traffic will allow us to. On the way over, we hear over the dispatch that the fire has been escalated to a three-alarm blaze.

Another company is called in; more information is called out over the speaker.

When we pull up in front of what's supposed to be an abandoned warehouse, I see a bunch of kids, covered in smoke and soot, off to the side of the building.

"Donovan!" Fitzy calls to me as we both get out of the rig. "Go get those kids away from the building and find out if they know if there's anyone else in there."

"Sure thing, Cap." Grabbing my helmet, I run over to the three boys hunched over, coughing their lungs out.

"You guys okay? Is anyone hurt?" No one answers as a look of fear flits across each of their young and dirty faces. As one of them is about to speak, he starts coughing like crazy, so I hold up my oxygen mask and tell him to take a few deep breaths.

When he stands upright, he seems better – and a little less afraid. "We were just hanging around. I swear. We didn't do nothing." He seems to be about fifteen-years-old, innocent enough, but it's not my job to figure out *how* the fire started.

My job is simple: put the fire out and make sure that everyone is safe.

Now that he has his bearings, the kid scans his group and pales, which is noticeable even through the black smokiness covering his face. "Tony. He's still in there. He was right behind me!" The panic rising in his voice causes him to choke.

I click the button on my walkie-talkie at my shoulder to relay the information to Fitzy. "Cap. There's a kid in there. His name's Tony." I move my mouth away from the speaker to ask the kid where they last saw Tony. "Kid's say he's somewhere on the third floor – that's where they saw him last."

"Ten-four, Donovan," Fitzy's voice calls out on the walkie-talkie. "EMTs are here. I'm sending them over to the kids. Get your ass back to the rig so we can get a move on, now!"

He's already calling out orders as I approach the rest of the team. Brody and I are partnered together. Our mission: find Tony. After Fitzy lays down the rest of the plan for extinguishing the blaze, we all go into motion. Ladders up, hoses out, radios on.

"I lead; you follow. Got it," I direct Brody whose eyes look a little frightened behind the Plexiglas of his facemask. He nods, and when he does, my eyes are drawn to his exposed neck. Reaching out, I adjust the collar of his jacket to make sure all of his skin is covered. For all his bravado earlier in the day, I can tell Brody's more than a little off-kilter right now.

As we crawl up the stairs of the burning building, Brody is never more than a step behind me. The smoke is thick, curling in every corner and crevasse of the hallway. Black and billowing clouds form above us as the heat intensifies. We army-crawl into an open room and my sight immediately falls to a pair of legs stretched out before me. Tony is slumped up against the wall, but even in the dim light, I can tell he's breathing. I call through my radio to let them know that we've found him, but when I turn to look for Brody, he's not right behind me like he's supposed to be.

I crane my neck up to the other end of the small room where there's a door leading into what I assume is an adjoining room. Before I can even call out for him, Brody is testing the door and opening it.

I watch, horrified and in slow motion, as the smoke is sucked back through the seams of the door. "No!" I scream, but it's completely ineffective. He can't hear me over the loud explosion of the flashover. Fire licks at the walls of the larger room as the flames blast everywhere.

With a calmness that belies the frenzied anxiety I'm feeling, I call into my radio requesting back up. Within seconds, Manny is behind me, pulling an unconscious Tony out of the room.

The heat is nearly unbearable as flames begin consuming the room. There's smoke everywhere, making it impossible to see anything. All I know is that I need to find Brody. I need to get him out of here. As I crawl on my stomach across the hot floor, I hear the beams creaking, weakening under the pressure and heat.

Sweat beads in my eyes under my mask. I can barely see. Reaching out and sweeping my hand across the floor, I brush over a pair of boots – Brody's. I crawl up alongside him and somehow make out that he's cradling his right arm with his left.

"Fire threw me back. Busted my arm against the wall." He tells me through the walkie-talkie.

A loud boom crashes through the room as a beam from the ceiling flies through the air. Suddenly, the fire is everywhere. The flashover ignited the entire room and now the structure is compromised.

"We gotta move. Now!" Brody nods, acknowledging my instructions. I get back down on my stomach, but instead of going out first, this time, I crawl behind Brody. I don't want to lose sight of him, so keeping him in front of me is the best way to do that.

Every time he drags his arm on the floor, pulling himself forward one slow inch at a time, I see Brody's body tense, wincing in pain. "Keep going, Brody. You're almost there," I coach, trying to encourage him through the pain.

When my bunker gear gets caught on a spike of wood jutting out from the floor, I grab at Brody's ankle, forcing him to look back. "Keep crawling to the stairs. I just need to get unstuck." Again, he nods before painfully crawling away.

That's when it happens.

The floor breaks away under the heat from below and another huge beam of steel comes crashing down from above. Both Brody and I fall through the open floor. Wood splinters off the walls, cement crumbles on the floors, smoke billows around us as the fire rages on.

My world fades to black as consciousness slips away into the fiery darkness.

October 3, 1995

CHAPTER TWO
Lucy

It's been four days.

It's been ninety-six hours since I last kissed his lips, since I last felt his loving arms wrap around me from behind, since his strong and stubbled jaw nuzzled into my neck.

Numbly — as that's the only way I can do anything since he was killed — I force myself out of bed.

Staring blankly into my opened closet, I become overwhelmed with anger. How the hell am I supposed to pick out something to wear for my husband's funeral when all I can think about is curling up in that box with him?

There's nothing to live for now.

Just as quickly as that thought enters my mind, the sharp kick to my ribs from my unborn daughter reminds me otherwise.

I might not *want* to carry on, but I *have* to.

She'll need me.

I don't even know what I end up putting on, but I'm dressed and walking down the stairs ten minutes later where Linda, my best friend, and Ray, my husband's best friend, are waiting for me.

They look at me with pity in their eyes and I feel the pain weighing like an anvil in my heart. With more sadness than any of us can put to words, we get in the waiting black limo and drive off to the church to say goodbye to the man I've spent my entire life loving.

The only thing that makes me realize that this is not some kind of horrid nightmare is the kicking baby. Holding my hands over my round belly keeps me focused on something other than the priest's words. Counting the rhythm of her hiccups pulls my attention away from counting the minutes since Jimmy was taken from me – from us.

The wind whips outside the church, causing high-pitched whirrs to sound in the knave. The only things holding me up are the hard bench beneath me and Linda's warm comfort at my side.

After a final prayer, I watch the pallbearers carry Jimmy's casket down the aisle in the church.

It's the same aisle that I walked down when we got married. That day, it felt like I couldn't walk toward him fast enough. Now, watching him be carried away from me, I feel time stand still. I want to scream and curse God for taking Jimmy away from me. But, instead, I find that it takes all of my energy to just get out of my seat and follow behind the coffin.

Frozen and incapable of talking through the lump in my throat, the ten-minute drive by our house and to the cemetery passes in complete silence.

My short heels bite into the soft, wet ground. Ray loops his arm through mine and I have to wonder if his intent is to hold me up, or to keep himself steady. I look up into his bloodshot eyes and we exchange a sad smile and nod. "I gotcha, Luce," he whispers and tightens his grip on my arm as he escorts me to the line of chairs arranged before Jimmy's coffin.

Words are spoken, prayers offered up to God, goodbyes are said, but I don't register any of it.

"May he rest in peace." The priest softly closes his bible and I feel fingers close around mine.

The cold and bitter fall air chills me to the bone. Thick, grey clouds threaten overhead. Rumbles of thunder and flickers of lightning are off in the distance somewhere. A thin mist of cold rain hangs all around us.

Somehow, the clouds manage to reign in the water, just as I'm somehow managing to hold back my tears. It's numbness really. You can't cry when you feel nothing. Pain has evaporated and morphed into anesthetized calmness.

Sitting at my side, Linda squeezes my hand again. "It's almost time to go." Her words and the warmth of her hand shake me from my blank stare. What little glimmers of light the sun was just shining have been swallowed up by the blackest cloud in the sky. Angrily, I laugh at how appropriate the scene is.

My light is gone.

Dead.

Buried.

Through the shuffle of people who have come to say goodbye to my husband, my Jimmy, I vaguely feel Ray grip my shoulder. "It's time, Luce."

A fierceness I thought was buried in the ground alongside my love bubbles up in my chest. "No, no, no," I repeatedly whisper, a tiny, fragile sound.

Throwing Ray's hand off my shoulder, I stand as quickly as my almost-nine-month pregnant belly will allow me.

"Easy, Lucy. Come on, let us help you." Linda tries to calm me, pulling me to her side. With all the strength I can muster, I push her away. In the distance behind her, I notice that the crowd that had just left the ceremony has now focused their attention back on the scene that I've just created.

A swift kick to the ribs from my baby girl brings me back to the here and now. I take a few shaky breaths and exhale them raggedly through the sobs closing my throat. Ray and Linda sandwich me between them, afraid that I'll collapse under my pain like I did the other day.

Wrapping my arms around their waists, I squeeze them tightly and try to garner some strength from their support. "I just can't bring myself to say goodbye to him." My chest heaves through the thought of turning my back on him one last time.

Linda grasps my shoulders and pulls me into an intense hug. When she releases me and steps back, holding me at arm's length, I see the pain in her eyes. She smoothes my hair, tucking it behind my ear. "I know you don't want to say goodbye. But it's about to pour and we don't want you getting sick."

On her last word, heavy blobs of rain start falling from the sky. Ray pulls off his jacket and holds it up over my head like an umbrella. "Let's go, Lucy," Ray grits out through the tears he's somehow fought off since Jimmy was crushed.

Looking up into his sad, brown eyes, I break a little more. I force a lame smile, really just to appease them, and ease some of their concerns. "Just give me one more minute with him. Go on to the car. I'll be right there." Ray and Linda exchange a look over my head before stepping away from me.

Inching myself over to the coffin, I reach out a shaky hand. The cold wood finish is glossy with rain and I mindlessly follow the streaks of water as they travel to the seam that keeps the coffin closed.

Thoughts of Jimmy, cold and alone, buried in the ground for all eternity ravage my soul. I'll never be able to hold him again. I'll never curl up next to him in bed.

He'll never hold our daughter.

"I don't know how to go on without you, Jimmy. Please tell me…how." Sobs swallow my words and the rain falls down in sheets through the sky.

The baby kicks once more.

With one hand on Jimmy's coffin and one on my belly – one on my past and one on my future – I say one final goodbye to the only man I have ever loved.

"I'll always carry you in my heart, baby. I love you, Jimmy."

CHAPTER THREE

Evan

The sharp, stinging smell of antiseptic cleaner hangs in the air. I hate hospitals. I hate burn units even more. It's literally hell on earth.

And I'm in it.

Before the others could get up to us, the floor gave way and Brody and I crashed through three stories and sunk right down into the basement. On the way down, my jacket caught on something and tore it straight in half, peeling away the most protective layer in the process. When I landed in the rubble below, I lost consciousness for more than a few minutes. The only thing that woke me was the blaze eating away at my stomach and chest. Ironically, the Kevlar gear beneath my jacket protected me so well that I didn't wake from the burns initially.

The second-degree burns are healing and I didn't need a skin graft. I was lucky. A broken arm and some melted skin, a few days in the hospital and I'm free to go.

Lucky is a funny word, though.

I don't think anyone would consider being stuck on the other side of a three-foot thick cement wall where you hear your partner screaming in pain *lucky*. There's no luck involved in not being able to get to him because you can't move, because you're being burned alive. I don't think anyone would feel fortunate if they were the first to be rescued as the screams on the other side of the wall fade into silence.

"Well, good morning there, Evan. How are you feeling today?" Janice, the day shift nurse, cheerfully carries in my breakfast, smiling as bright as can be.

I try to push myself up in the bed and it hurts like a bitch.

Luck my ass.

"Hey, Jan. I've been better." She places the tray on my side table and helps me get adjusted, propping some pillows behind my back.

"Dr. Tompkins will be around shortly and we'll see about getting you out of this place soon. That ought to cheer you up, huh?" She pushes the bed table in front of me and opens the lid for my breakfast. "You got a few visitors out in the waiting room. Are you up for some company?" She hands me a cup with a few pills in it and I swallow them down with the weak coffee next to my tray.

"Sure, but not for long." I don't need to be reminded of how I failed. Hopefully, the pain meds will kick in before long and I can pretend to need sleep.

Halfway through my plate of eggs and bacon, Fitzy and Manny step into the room, with a cup of real coffee and a box of donuts in hand. I guess having people visit you comes with some benefits.

"Hey, man, you look a lot better than yesterday." Manny hands me my coffee and I manage a polite nod.

I want to say, *"Wanna trade places, see how good it feels?"* but I bite back my sarcasm. He did save me, after all.

"Thanks. Feeling a little better. Nurse said I might be able to go home soon, so there's that."

Fitzy props open the box of donuts and I grab one. Plopping himself down into the chair next to my bed, he looks exhausted. I'm sure these last few days haven't been easy on him either. As Captain of our squad, I'm sure he blames himself for what happened.

I think it's genetic with firefighters. We can't help but blame ourselves when something goes wrong. It's how I'm feeling about Brody.

"How's the kid doing?" No one told me anything yesterday, and if they did, I was so out of it on pain meds, that I don't remember. All I can recall is someone telling me that Brody was here too. Knowing that they got him out of the building was enough for me at the time, but now I need to know what happened to him.

My question hangs heavily in the room for a few long moments. Fitzy drops his elbows to his knees and scrubs his hands over his face. He looks like he hasn't slept since everything happened.

Manny clears his throat and it breaks the tense silence in the room. "He's okay. Still not out of the woods yet, but he's improving by the hour."

"Improving by the hour? What the hell does that mean? How bad is he?" My temper flares as my body tenses. The fucking burns ripple in a flash of pain across my stomach.

He's alive; I have to focus on that, because right now, the look that Fitzy and Manny are sharing is scaring the shit out of me.

"Yeah, he's alive. And he's going to be okay, but they're…" Fitzy is lost for words. Well, fuck that never happens.

"What is it?"

Manny stands beside me and looks over at Fitzy one last time as he nods, obviously granting Manny permission to tell me whatever the hell is going on.

"His legs were crushed, Evan. He survived and that's what…"

"No. Fucking tell me the whole story. What happened?" Pulling the thin blanket covering my legs tightly into my fist, my knuckles go white with tension.

"They saved his life. That's what's important, but they might not be able to save his leg," Fitzy says with more sadness than I've ever heard the man express in the years I've known him.

"Fuck," I curse in disbelief as I slam my hands down into the bed. Pain vibrates through my broken right arm, but the physical pain is the easy part. Knowing what happened to Brody could have been prevented if I would have done my job, if I would have protected him, that's the kind of pain that won't ever go away.

"I wish it weren't true, but it is." Fitzy stands abruptly and jams his hands into his pockets. "Be as pissed as you want to be about it. Hell, we all are, but you're going to have to get that all out now before you go see him."

"I..." In true Captain form, he stops my protest before it can even leave my mouth.

"You can and you will. We're going down there now, give his family a chance to head home for a few hours and get some rest. We'll stop back up and give you an update on our way out."

I nod resolutely as Fitzy leaves the room. Just as Manny gets to the door, he turns back to me. Tipping his chin to my busted arm, which is currently lying across my burnt stomach, a look of guilty anguish washes over Manny's face. "I wish I could have gotten to you sooner, Evan."

I never thought of it that way – that someone would feel guilty about what happened to me. "Don't worry about it, man."

"Yeah, well, I'll see you later."

As Manny walks away, I let the medicated fog fall over me, washing away the pain I feel at letting down Brody, at putting Manny in a position where he has to worry about having let me down.

"Do you need help, Ev?" Tessa's words sound muffled through the bathroom door.

Using my teeth, I tear off one last piece of medical tape and somehow manage to flatten it across my healing skin. "Nah, I got it," I call out dismissively. Stepping out into the hallway, I slide past her and walk into my bedroom.

Rifling through some clothes, I pull out a pair of jeans and a t-shirt. "Why don't you let me help you?" She leans up against the dresser, arms crossed over her chest, legs crossed at the ankles. There's sadness in her eyes and I know more than a little anger. I haven't been all that easy to get along with since I was discharged a week ago.

"'Cause I don't need it. I told you that."

She huffs a sarcastic laugh at me as she watches me wrestle my cast into my shirt. "You sure about that?"

It still hurts like a bitch to move my shoulder through the sleeve, but I'd rather do it myself than rely on someone for something as simple as putting a fucking shirt on. "Yeah, I'm sure," I snap angrily.

I sink down onto my bed, clearly frustrated with…well, with everything. "Tessa, I don't know what you want me to say."

"Then don't say anything. Like you always do," she says. Storming out of the room, I know she expects me to follow.

I give her a few minutes to cool down while I gather my thoughts. We've been together for a little over two years now. It's been good, but I know she's looking for more. More that I just can't give, especially in light of what's recently happened.

Right now, *here* is not what's important. What's important is getting to the hospital to visit Brody after his amputation.

God, the fucking kid lost his leg because of me. If *I* would have crawled out of that room first, then I would be the one missing *my* right leg below the knee. Not some new, fresh twenty-four-year-old probie.

The cabinets slamming out in the kitchen stir me from my thoughts of guilt and shame. I guess I should at least try to calm her down before I leave.

Standing in the arched entryway of the small kitchen, I lean up against the frame and watch her make a cup of coffee.

She is beautiful; that much I can't deny. Long and lean, muscular but enticingly curvy, dark and exotic. The crux – she's needy. Needy as fuck and I don't know how much more of her neediness I can take.

I step behind her, inhale her fruity-mixed-with-vanilla scent and get lost for a minute – just a minute, and then she opens her mouth.

"You've only been home for a few days and already you're going back there." Hell yeah, I'm freakin' going. Damn rookie loses his leg and today's the first day after his amputation – that happened *because* of me – he's allowed to have visitors again. Damn fuckin' straight, I'm going back there.

Choosing not to lay into her, I just run my hand through my hair and reign in my anger. "We've been through this, Tessa."

"Been through what? That you're there for *them* more than you ever are for *me*?" Throwing her arms up in frustration, she stares at me with such contempt. My brain is incapable of understanding how one person could be so selfish. How is it possible to lack so much compassion? Here come the tears.

I can't stand to see her upset, not because I feel bad about my decision. I hate seeing her cry because she does it to make me feel guilty, to get me to give in to her. And I do. "Come here." She willingly walks into my open arms and I press my lips to her unruly, dark brown hair.

The words "I'm sorry" are on the tip of my tongue, but I refuse to say them – this time. I've said them too many times in the past – when I missed her sister's wedding because O'Hallaran needed to swap tours because of his daughter's first ballet recital, when I had to trade vacations with Jones because his son was playing in the state championships.

Holding her against my chest kills – it physically hurts more than I'm willing to express. Burn wounds hurt like a motherfucker, but she wouldn't know. No one knows the pain of those kinds of wounds – no one except my brothers. The ones who are waiting for me at the hospital; waiting for another brother to wake up from surgery only to find out that he's lost his leg.

That's where I need to be.

Not here.

But she doesn't understand that, so I try my best to explain, as carefully as possible.

She leans back from my arms and looks up into my eyes, which I'm sure are shadowed by my conflicting thoughts. "I need to go, but I promise…"

Tessa pushes away from me, causing excruciating pain in my still-dislocated shoulder. "You? Promise? What exactly are you promising, Evan?"

Her arched eyebrow and snarky tone are more than I care to deal with right now. "I can't get into this right now." So much for expecting her understanding.

The nasty laugh that passes by her lips reminds me of every reservation I have ever had about her. I can't deal with her right now, so I step back and grab my jacket from the kitchen chair. Painfully, I pull it over my arm, forgetting about my cast – damn thing. I toss it back on the chair; frustrated and pissed off as I walk toward the door. Just as my hand hovers above the knob, her voice reaches my ear. "Of course you can't deal with it right now. You never have time for me."

I shake my head, not knowing how to move forward – if moving forward is even an option with her. The absolute last thing I want to do it to turn around and look at her disgusted and angry face. "I'll be back later. We'll talk then."

Without a backward glance, I walk out into the chilly fall air, the sounds of the city soothing rather than chaotic. Driving toward my work-family, I can't help but wonder what the hell I'm driving away from.

October 15, 1995

CHAPTER FOUR
Lucy

Two weeks.

That's how long he's been gone from my life.

I've already done the calculations and know the exact number of hours and minutes too.

I've spent the last fifteen days, ten hours and twenty-three minutes without Jimmy. It seems like the only thing that keeps me going is my sick need to watch the clock simply add another minute to my tally.

You'd be surprised how you find ways to occupy your mind in the hauntingly quiet darkness of the night. You'd be surprised how sleep eludes you when you don't have a warm, strong chest to nuzzle into. I find that the only way I can get any rest is if I curl up with his pillow. It still smells like him. The worst minutes are the ones right after I wake up. Still drowsy and unaware of my reality, I think the scent of his pillow, or whatever article of his clothing that I've used as a security blanket to lull myself to sleep at night, is actually him. In those moments of exhaustion and confusion, I allow myself to believe, if only for a split second, he's still alive. That he's still with me.

But then the sun rises and reality dawns.

And it's just a pillow.

Not my husband.

In those hours of darkness, I've also figured out that eleven years, eleven months, three weeks and four days from now, I will have spent more days without him than I did with him.

Counting the days is just another torturous way to keep my mind occupied, but I don't have an alternative, really. I'm existing without him, barely breathing. I find myself still talking to him, especially in the early morning hours when I'm exhausted from yet another sleepless night.

"Oh, Jimmy. I miss you so much, baby. Why …why…why…" My pointless questions get lost in my sobs. The heaving in my chest and the sound of my voice wakes up the baby and I feel a swooshing roll and kick at my side. "Shh, relax, baby girl. Mommy's okay." I rub my hand gently over my just-kicked rib cage and hug my belly through more tears.

All of these numbers play in my head like a grotesque horror film. No matter the minutes, he's gone from my life. I'll never have him back. When the tears subside, more out of simply not having any left rather than no longer needing to shed them, the baby kicks again. I haven't been able to call her by her name yet. I decided on Jimmy's top choice, but every time I move my lips to speak it, a sob chokes me at the thought he'll never be able to say the sweetest name I've ever heard.

She's kicking my ribs through the fit of tears and I find myself suddenly counting kicks instead of minutes.

Focusing on the life growing inside of me, rather than the one no longer with me, gives me the tiniest bit of strength to get out of bed.

The gentle tapping on our − no, wait, scratch that, my bedroom door also forces me to throw back the comforter.

"Hey, sleepy head." Linda smiles as she hands me a cup of tea. "Did you get any rest last night?"

"Maybe an hour or two," I say as I shrug my shoulders, sitting up against the headboard.

For the last twelve years, Linda's been my best friend. We met on the first day of seventh grade and have been inseparable ever since. Basically, all of the memories I have include her.

And Jimmy.

She's been staying with me since Jimmy died.

Honestly, without her, I don't know how I would even get through the day. I don't have anyone else. I'm an only child of parents gone long before their time should have run out. You would think I'd be used to this kind of sadness by now, but nothing could have ever prepared me for this vast, dark emptiness that's consuming me.

"Well, that's better than none, like the other night." A lame, but compassionate smile spreads across her face. She begins opening the curtains, letting in more light than my eyes can handle. I squint and flop down onto the armchair in the corner as I take a sip of my tea.

"Is today my appointment? Or is it tomorrow?" I ask as I blow on the steaming mug to try to cool it.

"It's today at eleven thirty." Linda sits cross-legged on the ottoman in front of me and gently squeezes my knee. "Maybe the doctor will have some good news for you."

"Yeah, maybe." I stare numbly out the window, thinking that good news would be that the last two weeks have been some kind of cruel joke or a nightmare from which I'll eventually wake. But as I feel my belly tighten in a somewhat painful contraction, I realize this is not a dream.

This is my new reality. A reality that no longer includes Jimmy. A reality that will soon include a new baby.

The thought of having this baby without Jimmy at my side, causes a fresh flood of tears to stream down my cheeks. Linda is quickly squeezing into the chair next to me, hugging me tightly.

Softly stroking my hair, she tries to calm me, but it's pointless, really. "It's okay, Lucy. Everything will be…"

Before she can even get the rest of her thought out, I pry free from her grasp and yell, "No! It won't be okay, Lin. It's never going to be okay ever again. Don't you get that?" My outburst takes her by surprise, at least that's what the look on her face conveys. "He's gone. Gone…How am I supposed to… I don't know how to. How do I…" I wrap my arms around my belly but I'm in no way comforted by the rhythmic feel of the baby hiccupping inside of me.

Linda stands next to me and places her hand over mine on my belly. Lacing our fingers together, she stares out the window watching the leaves cascade to the ground with me. Resting her head on my shoulder, I feel her begin to cry; I hear her sniffle and sigh a shaky breath. "I don't know how to move on. I don't know, but I am here to help you figure it out. I'll never replace Jimmy and God knows that I wish he could be here for you." Lifting her head from my shoulder, we exchange a sad smile. "I'm here to be sad with you. And when this baby girl is born, I'm here to be happy with you too. I love you, girl."

Somewhat calmed by her words, I exhale a deep breath and wipe my tears from my cheeks, yet again. "I love you, too. Thank you for …"

"You don't have to thank me for a damned thing. There's nowhere on Earth I'd rather be than here with you." Glancing at the clock, she steps away from me and starts pulling some clothes out of the closet.

"Why don't you get in the shower while I go make us something to eat? Then we can head out to your appointment." Linda hands me an outfit – the only one that still fits and walks toward the door.

"Okay, I'll be down in a few minutes," I mumble toward her retreating back. I notice the shakes that rack her small frame. Saddened by her sadness, I fall back into the over-stuffed armchair and cry, while gazing out into the morning sun.

Another contraction tightens around my belly. I've been having them on-and-off for the last few days, but there's no pattern to them. They're more uncomfortable than painful, and according to my doctor, that's the determining factor in being able to tell if they're "real" or not.

"How are you doing in there, baby girl?" I ask as the tightening subsides. Of course, the only answer I get is another knee to the belly. "I know it's getting tight in there. Any day now, baby."

Another minute clicks by and with thoughts of my daughter's birth in my mind, for the first time in two weeks, I find myself looking forward to something.

"Of course I got the cart with the wobbly wheel," I huff at Linda as I reach for a box of cereal on the top shelf. Monopolizing on the fact that she actually got me to shower and get out of the house, she insisted we go food shopping after my doctor's appointment.

It's not that I have much of an appetite. I honestly can't remember the last time I *wanted* to eat something. But since the baby has to eat, I have to eat.

As my nine-month-pregnant belly knocks about five boxes of cereal off the shelf, Linda stifles a few giggles. "Here, let me get those." She chuckles once more and moves to pick up the mess.

"Right, like I can bend down and get it myself?" That image just makes her laugh a little more and I can't help but giggle at myself. "Seriously, I'm like a beached whale."

Linda hands me a box of Cheerios to put back on the shelf and smiles softly at me. "I know, sweetie. I bet you forgot what your feet even look like."

"Oh, shut it!" I laugh, replacing one more box that I dislodged from its shelf with my belly.

"I can't believe the doctor said I'm still not making any progress. My due date is next week. If she's not out in a few days, I'm going to start sending this kid eviction notices or something." We share another laugh and I run my fingers over the well-known yellow box of Cheerios thinking about the day I'll have to buy them for the baby.

The loud chuckle of laughter that bursts out of my mouth actually feels good.

Hell, it felt good to shower and see the light of day. I haven't been out of the house since the funeral. If it wasn't for Linda moving in with me after Jimmy died, I don't think I would even get myself out of bed.

As we walk out of the cereal aisle, Linda takes the cart from me. Rounding the corner, I toss a bag of chips into the cart. She gives me the side-eye, but I notice her lips curling into a smirk.

"What?" I deflect and shrug my shoulders.

"Nothing, sweetie. It's just nice to see you thinking about food again."

We make our way through a few more aisles and my appetite comes back in full force. Suppressing her laughter, Linda scans the filled-to-the-brim cart. "That's funny. I don't remember cookies, orange sherbet, pickles and tacos being on the list." She waves the yellow sheet of legal paper in my face. Ignoring her sarcasm completely, I toss an oversized candy bar in with the rest of my pregnancy-craving induced purchases.

"Didn't the doctor say that spicy food could help bring on labor?" I eye the taco kit.

"Yeah. So I guess you want those for dinner then?" She bumps me with her shoulder, nearly throwing me off balance.

I take the cart from her, remembering that the doctor also said something about walking to help things progress. Apparently, somewhere in the back of my mind, I latched onto the idea that I want this baby out. Maybe it's something about just needing to focus my attention on something happy and not sad. Maybe it's about walking blindly into the fearful unknown while trying to ignore the pain that is currently my life.

When we make our way back to the refrigerated section to pick up a package of chopped meat, a searing band of heat flashes across my belly. I hunch over in pain, banding one arm around the baby. The other hand holds a white-knuckled grip on the handle of the cart. Linda comes up behind me and rubs my back until the pain subsides.

"You okay?" she asks when I stand upright.

Wiping the sweat from my forehead, I let out a deep breath. "Yeah, but wow, that was strong."

By the time we make it to the front register, another contraction hits me, tightening my belly, back and groin in a blaze of scorching fire.

"Lin, I'm not so sure these are the fake ones anymore," I grit out through a clenched jaw.

She pays the cashier and loads the last bag into the cart. "It's okay, Luce. We've got plenty of time. Let's get this stuff home and we'll call the doctor, see what we should do. Okay?" Her word are cloyingly sweet, like golden honey, but I hear the fearful excitement hidden beneath them.

On the ten-minute drive back to the house – a house I still can't bear to call anything else other than "ours" even though it's really just mine now – I circle back to my thoughts about wanting something to look forward to.

When we hit a pothole, the bump causes my belly to pull and tighten. I'm no longer excited. I'm scared out of my mind. Needing some sense of not being alone, I reach for Linda's hand that's resting on top of the gearshift in the center console.

The feel of my fingers lacing together with hers shakes her out of whatever far-away thought she was just having. She looks over at me in the passenger's seat like she's seeing me for the first time, like I haven't been in the car with her the whole time.

She squeezes my hand in return, and even though I thank God that I have her, I want no one other than Jimmy.

"I don't know if I can do this without him," my weak voices trembles through the pain, both physical and emotional.

Patting my hand, Linda looks over at me; a similar, but different look of pain is etched into her tired face. "Oh, sweetie, I don't either." She pulls into the driveway and races around to my side to help me out of my seat.

When I stand, what feels like a deluge of water crashes to the ground. Standing there, staring at my broken water, both of our mouths are agape at how quickly things are progressing

"So much for those tacos, huh?" We both laugh like hyenas at my ridiculous joke. It's more to avoid the heavy emotional bubble descending upon us.

How is it possible to say hello to the one person you'll love the most in your life, when you still haven't been able to say goodbye to the other half of your soul?

"Come on." Linda wraps her arm around my back and helps me climb the front steps. "Let's get you changed and ready to have a baby."

Her words scare the crap out of me and even though there's a large part of me that wants to – no, has to – focus on the sadness and anger, I push that part down. Focusing on the joy that looking into my daughter's eyes will bring, I decide to just let it be, at least for now.

Thirteen hours and lots of pain medication later and there's still no baby. I had this crazy notion that I would go through this birth naturally, no epidural – just power straight through it. That was before I lost Jimmy. He was supposed to be my strength today, coaching me through my pain. That plan was crushed when Jimmy was. I've had enough pain, more than any one person should have to experience, so the second it was offered to me, I took the epidural. Now, in the early morning hours, through drowsy, but unable-to-sleep, heavy-with-exhaustion eyelids, I make out Linda's blanket-covered form on the chair in the corner.

She notices me moving and walks over to sit at the chair next to the bed. She feeds me some ice chips and we watch the orange sun float up above the horizon. "It's pretty." My throat is scratchy and sore.

"Sure is. A beautiful way to start the day that you'll become a mommy." Linda's words hit me right in the gut and grip at my heart. It's the first time anyone other than Jimmy has called me that.

My God, I'm going to be a mom today. I never envisioned a life where I'd have to be a single mom and the idea of it scares me more than I can say. There'll be no one there to help me through the sleepless nights, no one with whom I can enjoy the milestones. Before I let the emptiness engulf me, there's a light tap at the door.

The doctor comes in, making her early morning rounds. "Let's see how things are going."

Linda moves out of the way while the doctor does her thing. "Looks like that little bit of rest helped, Lucy. You're at ten centimeters. Are you ready to meet your daughter?"

Wordlessly, I nod at her. Linda helps me sit upright, straightening my pillows and feeding me a few last pieces of ice. Everything feels like it's moving in a robotic kind of slow motion, yet at the same time, everything is slipping through my fingers at lightning-quick speed.

I can't speak. I don't want to say anything. I know that if I open my mouth, the only thing that will come out is a sob, a painfully tormented wail of anger. So instead of verbalizing anything, I silently communicate to my unborn daughter.

All right, little girl, it's just you and me, now. Please take it easy on Mommy.

A flurry of activity fills the room. Doctors and nurses dressed in varying colors of scrubs rush around the small space – a perfectly orchestrated vision of chaos. I barely hear the instructions the doctor calls out. Instead, I focus on the one familiar face in the room. In a voice barely above a whisper, I ask Linda for his picture.

I can't look at it; I knew I wouldn't be able to, but I had to have him with me in some way.

"Push," the doctor instructs and I feel Linda holding my leg back, a nurse at the other one.

"You're doing great," Linda coaches as she swipes a cool rag across my face. I still can't say anything in response, not that I have the time anyway as another contraction causes a flood of blinding pressure and burning pain, even through the waning pain meds.

"She's crowning, Lucy." The doctor pats my thigh, trying to encourage me. Her instructions come out rapid fire now. "Push. Stop. Hold on. Let me ease her out. Push again, gentle."

In the midst of all the craziness, I glance down at the picture of Jimmy in my hand. Speaking to him in my mind, I mentally verbalize my deepest fears.

I can't do this without you, Jimmy. I need you. I need you. I need you.

I use my need for him, my fear for the unknown to help me push through the pain.

"It's a girl!" The doctor announces triumphantly, a wide-smile spreading across her face.

When the balloon of pressure eases and the blinding pain recedes, I look down at my daughter who has just been placed across my deflated belly. The doctor cuts the cord, a detail I asked Linda to work out ahead of time to avoid the pang of anguish and bitterness that I knew it would bring up.

The nurses rub the baby's back vigorously, cleaning her of the messy goop covering her newborn skin, but she still doesn't cry.

I gently pat her back, afraid to break her tiny and fragile frame. "Why isn't she crying?" Concerned words float like a thin ribbon through the all too quiet room, threatening to wrap around my neck like a noose. The nurse steps back in place with a new blanket and roughly rubs up and down my daughter's back.

Please let her be okay. Please. I need her.

Huge, grey-blue eyes, the color of stainless steel, stare up at me. In that moment, even though she's still not making a sound, I know she's all right. I feel it in my soul.

"I'm just going to go finish cleaning her up and get her all weighed and measured. I'll bring her right back." The nurse's compassionate caramel-colored eyes reassure me and I hand her the baby.

The second she's out of my arms, her tiny cries fill the room and my heart bursts at the sound. "She's here, Lin. She's really here." I stare up into my best friend's tear-filled eyes as we exchange huge smiles.

"You did real good, sweetie. She's beautiful." Swiping away her tears, she leans down and kisses my forehead.

We hear a few more cries, but within a few minutes, the nurse returns my daughter to my arms. Cuddling her close to my chest, her tiny body swaddled in a sea of soft, pale pink blankets, she smells like a slice of heaven.

The doctor stands next to me and looks down at the baby curled in my arms. "Congratulations. I'll be back in a few hours to check up on you girls."

After a few minutes of oohing and ahhing over my baby, and lots of hugs and kisses, Linda clears her throat. "I'm going to go, too." Linda's words startle me. She can't leave.

She must register the look on my face because she sits on the edge of the bed and smiles at me warmly. "Just for a little bit. I'm going to grab a shower and let you girls get to know each other. You need some rest anyways. I'll call Franny and Lou, and let them know they can come up later."

Jimmy's parents.

I'm not sure I have the strength to face them, but I know I'll have to find it somewhere.

Linda waves from the door and reminds me one last time that she'll be back in just a little bit.

"Looks like it's just us, baby girl." I press my lips to the soft, fire-red tuft of hair on her otherwise bald head. She wiggles her hand out of her blanket and I can't help but count her small, wrinkled fingers.

When they band around one of mine, I lose it. Bringing our joined fingers up to my mouth, I kiss her through the tears.

"Sweet, Melly Belly." I swear she tilts her head to my voice as the words come out of my mouth. It's as if she's piecing together that I'm the one who's been talking to her all these months.

I wonder if she'll miss hearing Jimmy's voice, his lips pressed up against my belly, fuzzy mumbles of fatherly love filtering through the waves of water surrounding her.

Pulling her impossibly close to my chest, I cry through the memory of the last time he spoke to her – the morning that he died.

I press my lips to our joined fingers one more time. "I promise you, Melanie. I will never let you forget your daddy. He loved you so much. I love you so much."

Forcing back my tears, I stare into the eyes of this beautifully, precious, teeny, tiny bundle of love. "She's beautiful, Jimmy." I stare out at the now fully risen sun. The skyline is set ablaze in a glorious kaleidoscope of pinks and oranges. The almost black surface of the lake is speckled with a million dots of light dancing across its surface.

It looks like heaven.

That's where he'll be forever now – in the vast beauty of nature, speaking to us through the flickers of sparkling light that reach us only in our most serene moments.

In the quietly humming hospital room, I tell Jimmy all about Melanie, describing her beautiful red hair and grey eyes, her tiny button nose and plump cheeks.

He might not be there to hold me, but I feel him next to me. I feel him here in my arms where my beautiful Melanie sleeps peacefully.

November 22, 1995

CHAPTER FIVE

Evan

My day shift ran over today. Fine. It didn't run over so much as I *let* it run over. Manny let me know yesterday that he was going to need a few hours this afternoon because his daughter was in a Thanksgiving play at school.

The guy saves my life and he asks me to work a few extra hours so that he can watch his six-year-old in her star role at the head of the first Thanksgiving Day table. Yeah, that was a no-brainer.

I must have lost track of time studying because when Manny claps a hand to my back, it scares the shit out of me.

"You studying?" He reads over my shoulder – nothing all that interesting if you're not a firefighter. Building structures, safety procedures, fire codes.

Closing the binder, I reach for my coffee and take a sip. "Yeah. There's a lieutenant's test in the spring. Thought I'd at least give it a shot."

"Good for you, Donovan. Well, if you ever need any help, let me know." Manny leans back against the counter and pours himself a cup of the freshly brewed pot.

"So how was the play?" I move to the sink, rinse out my mug and hang it on the rack that's attached to the bottom of the cabinets.

Manny smiles widely, a fatherly grin of pride. "It was good. Vikki was more than happy to have the spotlight on her."

"You're going to have your hands full one day."

He chokes on his coffee. "One day? Are you kidding me? They're full now!"

I check my watch. Six o'clock. I'm supposed to meet Tessa for dinner at some fancy restaurant around the corner in an hour. "Well, I'm glad you could make it. Happy to help."

As I walk up to the bunks, I can't help but smirk at Manny and his full hands. I wouldn't mind having to run to work late because of my kid's play. I wouldn't mind knowing that I have a life outside of this place. But, in the weeks following my accident, the thought of having that kind of life with Tessa diminished rapidly.

To be honest, I'm not even sure why I agreed to meet her for dinner tonight. We've done nothing but fight recently. She wants more and I just can't get past her neediness, her complete and total inability only to think about what she wants.

I know I'll never be able to get over how she gave me so much shit for wanting to help out Brody when he was first discharged from the hospital. Me and the guys all helped build a wheelchair ramp up to his front door. His parents live a very simple life and they weren't expecting their grown up son to return back to their home. We did our best to make the transition as easy as possible – for all of them. Brody wasn't all that keen on having to move back home either, but he knew it was what was best for him.

We all saw the depression lingering just beneath the surface. The one thing Brody loved, the only thing he ever thought worthy of devoting his life to, was taken from him in an instant.

All because of me.

Sensing his anger, his sadness, we all made a pact to spend as much time with him as possible when we could. He's still not one-hundred-percent healed – neither physically nor emotionally, but he's getting there.

It was when I would come home from those late night visits, or early morning shopping trips for Brody's parents that Tessa's true colors would show in vibrant form.

"Nice to see you." Dripping sarcasm, her words grated on my last nerve.

Ignoring the bait, I walked past her and into the kitchen. Popping open a beer, I leaned back against the counter and scrubbed a hand over my face. I pinched the bridge of my nose, feeling a massive headache by the name of Tessa taking shape there.

"You said you'd be home at six."

"And?" I swear she brought out my inner asshole.

"And it's eight." Angrily, she pointed at the green flashing lights on the microwave.

"The ramp took longer than we thought. Had to make three extra trips to the store."

"You didn't think of calling?" With her hands on her hips, she stood there, waiting not so patiently.

Yep, there it was. The headache. Not to mention that my arm was fucking killing me. I only just got the cast removed, so it was probably too soon to be doing construction – light though it may be, but there was no way in hell I wasn't helping.

She started tapping her toe, and I lost my cool. Putting my beer down on the counter, with not much gentleness, I stared over at her. Had she once been kind? Had she once been understanding and less self-centered?

If she had, I hadn't remembered those days.

They were apparently long gone.

"No, Tessa. I didn't think of calling. The man can't walk because of a mistake that I made so letting you know that I'd be running a little late slipped my mind." I snagged my beer from the counter and stalked past her, back into the living room where I flopped onto the couch and turned on some random college football game.

When the sounds of her huffing and puffing got closer, I turned up the volume to drown out the fight I knew was coming.

Recalling that fight, and more than a handful that decorated the last few weeks of our dying relationship, I chuckled a humorless laugh looking at the freshly pressed dress shirt waiting for me in my locker.

"Your blue shirt is ready at the cleaners. Make sure you pick it up on your way in to cover for…what's his name?" She handed me the ticket to the dry cleaners as I walked toward the door.

"Manny, and, a dress shirt? Really? Where the hell are we going anyway?" Her idea of the perfect night was some place *"fancy"* – her word, not mine. *Spending an arm and a leg on food I could cook myself, in a restaurant so loud and busy that we could barely keep up a conversation, was most certainly not my ideal date.*

Hmmm, no conversation? Maybe a "fancy" night out isn't such a bad idea, after all.

"Oh, and I forgot to tell you, Marco and Angelina will be there too. It'll be like a double date." She smiled hopefully, knowing full well I would not be happy about that little piece of information.

I bit back my snide remark. No use in starting something I had no intention of finishing. Besides, I needed to haul ass as it was to get to the station in time to cover for Manny – whose name she definitely knew, but just chose to forget, conveniently.

Holding the dress shirt in my hands, I wonder why the hell I feel like I need to keep going, why I need to keep holding out hope that she won't keep getting more and more selfish.

So when the alarm bells sound, the voice over the loudspeaker calling out for a malfunctioning elevator shaft, I gladly slide down the pole.

Mike Jones, the captain on this tour, is waiting beside the rig, a look of surprise on his face when he catches sight of me.

"Thought you left when Ramirez got in?" He slides his boots on and pulls up his bunker pants.

I shrug my shoulders and offer to help out on the fairly routine run.

"Yeah, come on along. I can go over some of your study material about updating service systems."

Watching the blur of Manhattan traffic pass me by, I realize that my fifty-pounds of gear will always offer more comfort than a "fancy" blue dress shirt ever will.

When we get back to the station an hour later, I call Tessa but it goes straight to her answering machine. The thought of going to meet her and her friends at the restaurant is pretty much the least appealing idea I can come up with.

Okay, it was shitty on my part not to get in touch with her. Letting my conscience get the best of me, I call the restaurant and leave a message with the maître d' asking him to let Tessa know that I can't make it. Sure, if I haul ass, I might be able to make it there in time to be bored to death by Marco's stories of how much money he made in the stock market today, or of how Angelina needs to get her nails done. But something about spending the night with people with whom I have absolutely nothing in common is the last thing I want to do.

I need to clear my head. Instead of going to dinner and instead of going home, I walk. There's something calming about walking the city streets that soothes my soul. Some find it too chaotic and loud, but for me, it lets me focus on my thoughts.

In the two hours I spend maneuvering through the foot traffic, I decide Tessa has no place in my future. She's never understood my job — that it's way more than just a job. It's my life, my family. She has always struggled with the fact that my hours are crazy and my safety is not guaranteed.

But looking back over our relationship since I've been injured, I realize what a terrible girlfriend she's been. Even her reaction to seeing me in the hospital was telling. She was more angry than concerned. The fact that I was in pain, that my stomach had been burned and my arm had been broken, were second to her anger at "my stupid job."

Replaying that scene on a continuous loop in my head, I make the decision to end things with Tessa. There's no sense in trying to revive a relationship that's been dead for far too long.

Since I have her key, there's no need for her to buzz me up. It's early yet, so I doubt she's even back from dinner. I walk up the three flights and stare blankly at the 3A on her door. It's not the aftermath that I'm dreading — honestly, I'm suddenly looking forward to being single. What I'm dreading is the hours that I'm going to waste trying to explain myself to her when I know that every single word I say will just fall on deaf ears.

Sliding the key into the lock, I hear muffled sounds from inside. Shit, what if Marco and Angelina came back here with Tessa after I canceled on her? Apparently, I didn't think this through all the way.

I take a deep breath and figure I'm here already — no use is putting it off any longer. Except when I walk into the living room, no one's there. Odd, I swear I just heard voices.

Walking down the short hallway leading to Tessa's room, I figure out where the sounds are coming from.

I crack the door opened slowly, trying my best not to make any noise. The angry and lifeless laugh that escapes my mouth as I watch the scene before me makes me realize just how okay with this I am.

When I clear my throat, the guy at least has the decency to stop drilling into Tessa. "Catch you at a bad time?" I arch an eyebrow and tip my chin at them sprawled out on the bed.

Grabbing for the sheets to cover up, Tessa calls out "shit, shit, shit" in rapid succession. As the guy who was just fucking her stands up, I realize it's Marco – the prick.

As I stalk away from the door, I hear Tessa calling out to me. "Wait, Evan. I can explain."

I turn around so abruptly that she crashes into my chest. "What exactly do you plan on explaining, Tessa?"

"I…it's just… you said you weren't going to make it… and then… things just happened."

"Things just *happened*?" I snarl with more anger than I thought I would have.

She straightens her spine and looks me dead in the eye, venom suddenly replacing her sorrow. "Yes, Evan. Things happened because you weren't there. You're never there. I always come last to you."

I look her up and down, the crisp white of the sheet glowing against her bronze skin. "You sure do." I open the door and stop on the other side to pull my key off the ring. "Here, you might want to give this to Marco."

Without a backward glance, I walk away from the only real relationship I've ever had, without carrying an ounce of sorrow or regret along with me.

The next morning, I wake up with a raging hangover. Turns out drinking away your anger over a cheating girlfriend is only an effective solution in the short term.

I stumble into the bathroom, take two Advil and turn on the shower. The hot water helps clear my head a little, but I still feel like shit. A bagel and some coffee settle my stomach somewhat.

Flipping through the morning news channels, I realize that today is Thanksgiving. "Right, cause I got so much to be thankful for," I snap back at the newscaster talking about the parade taking place in front of Macy's.

The phone rings a few minutes later, and even though I really don't want to talk to anyone, the only person who would be calling me is my younger brother Joe.

"Hello?"

"Hey, Ev. Happy Thanksgiving, man." I can hear his smile through the line.

"Yeah, you too." I rub my hand over my two-day-old stubble. Even though the pounding in my head is receding a little, the screaming wails from the baby through the receiver kills. I hear him shush his newborn daughter and my heart swells more than a little listening to Joe sweet talk his baby girl.

"How is she?" I ask, a smile cracking across my hung-over face.

"She's really great. Sara's been good too," he adds making me feel like an ass for not asking about his wife.

"That's good. I'm happy for you." We get lost in catching up – where they're going for the holiday, how Katie is sleeping and eating, how Sara is keeping up with her medications.

"So are the doctors worried about her depression getting worse?" Sara has always had mental health issues, and the doctor has only recently diagnosed her with mild depression. Afraid that it would only get worse after the baby was born, Joe made her promise to get treatment right away.

I hear a door close and what sounds like Joe flopping onto a bed, the sheets crinkling in the background. "It might be more than depression. At least that's what this one doctor says. So we may have to get a second opinion, but she's actually willing to go, which is a huge improvement from before."

"Geez, Joe. Why didn't you tell me sooner? Is there anything I can do?" I know there's nothing I can do, but I hate feeling useless. He lives a few hours away in upstate New York. I feel like a shit that I haven't even been able to meet Katie yet.

"No, we'll be fine. I just wanted to keep you updated that's all."

Before long, we end the call. Katie needs to be fed and I need to get ready to get in to work for my shift. I'm on at five, but I want to try to get in early to relieve one of the day guys so they can get home in time for Thanksgiving dinner with their family.

I might not have a family of my own, but these men will always be my brothers.

"Food's on!" I yell out through the loudspeaker. A sea of blue uniforms floods the kitchen area. It's almost comical, but at the same time, I'd expect no less. Since it's the hour where shifts are overlapping, there are more people in the room than usual. The volume is louder than that of normal conversation and the laughter fills up the space.

Slowly, the noise fades away as everyone steps to the sides of the room. Since I'm behind the high-top butcher-block counter, carving the last of the turkey, I don't see him right away. In fact, I don't even know he's in the room until I hear his voice.

"Hey, old man!" Brody calls out as he wheels up to the counter.

My gut twists into knots of guilt. I nearly lose it when I see Brody's father standing behind him, his hands resting on the handles of the wheelchair.

"Still a wiseass, I see." I pump his hand and squat down next to him. "It's real good to see you, Brody."

"You too, man." I stand, my knees cracking on the way up. Maybe he's onto something with this "old man" shit he keeps harping on about.

"Mr. Callahan, it's good to see you again, sir." I shake his father's hand and offer him something to eat.

"Kyle, call me Kyle." I nod as he adds, "Thanks, but we're actually on our way to dinner, but we wanted to stop in and pay you all a visit."

He clears his throat, calling the attention of the room – not that he needs to. Everyone's eyes have been glued to both him and Brody since they walked in.

"I just wanted to say thank you," Mr. Callahan scans the kitchen, making eye contact with as many people as possible in the process. "There are no words to express the debt of gratitude that my wife and I owe you for everything you've done for our family," he claps a hand on Brody's shoulder before adding, "for everything you've done for our son."

When the round of applause dies down, Brody speaks up. "Now, I don't want you all to think you're rid of me now. I'm working on something down at The Rock. I'm not making any promises or anything like that, but you might be sitting on the other side of a desk taking notes from me one day."

The Rock is what we all call our training headquarters out on Randall's Island. Right next to a landfill, it reeks of garbage, but that's where we all start out. If Brody could work there, maybe training new cadets, that would be really amazing.

I walk Mr. Callahan and Brody to their wheelchair accessible van parked out front. "It was good seeing you, kid. I…" My apology for letting him down dies on my lips.

"Hey, you still think about studying?" Brody asks so abruptly I can't help but wonder if he doesn't want to talk about it either.

"Yeah, I actually just started last week. There's a test in the spring. Why do you ask?"

"Feel like having a study partner?" There's caution in his words. It's clear he doesn't want to be a burden, but it's inspiring he's not letting his accident get in the way of him moving forward.

"Sure thing. I'll be in touch this week." I shake his hand as he smiles up at me.

It doesn't alleviate all of my guilt, but knowing I can help him in some small way, makes my head swim a little less, makes the knots in my gut loosen just a bit.

December 3, 1995

CHAPTER SIX
Lucy

It's been two months.

I've spent the last sixty-three days, eleven hours and twenty-seven minutes without Jimmy.

But I also started a different count.

It's been seven weeks – forty-nine days, six hours and four minutes - since Melanie was born.

I still sleep on his pillow, hugging his shirt. It's starting to smell less like him and more like Melanie. There's still some cologne left in the bottle on his side of the bathroom counter. It has its own gravitational pull, beckoning me to pick it up and inhale the woodsy, clean fragrance every time I walk past it.

I think Melanie is getting used to the scent as well, falling asleep easier when something of her dad's is next to her.

Melanie's still asleep and like usual, I fought sleep all night long. Waking in the pre-dawn hours of uneasy solitude, I find myself talking to Jimmy, gazing out at the fading stars.

"Your parents moved down to Florida just last weekend. It was too painful for them up here. Even though they said it was about the cold weather, I saw the anguish in your mother's eyes when she held Melanie. She looks just like you, Jimmy." I ghost my fingers over the framed wedding picture on my nightstand. Tracing the lines of his face, I'm already starting to forget the scratchiness of his day-old stubble. "I made Linda move out too. I know, I know. You're probably thinking that I'm being my usual crazy, stubborn self, but I just had enough of her waiting around for me to break."

The real reason was because she was pushing me — too hard, too fast — to do things that I just wasn't ready for at the time. Clean out his closet, donate his clothes, pack up the only remnants I have of my husband — things I'm not sure I'll ever be able to do.

The sun pops up over the horizon, spilling out across the sky, the colors of candied oranges. Melanie wiggles restlessly in her bassinet. Laying my hand across her back calms her. I tuck her back in and decide that I should shower now, while she's still asleep before the day gets away from me.

Glancing out the window one more time, I catch the sun billow up into the aqua-colored sky. "I'll talk to you again later, Jimmy. Love you, babe."

Inwardly, I laugh a little at my coping mechanism. Sure, some might say it's a bit off kilter, a bit crazy, but it's helping.

As the steam from the hot spray fills the room, I test the water and slide the glass door closed. Jimmy's stuff is still in here too — his shampoo and shave gel. I haven't been able to bring myself to throw anything of his out. Like his cologne, I am drawn to the clean, masculine scent of his soap, unable to resist bringing the bar up to my nose every time I shower.

Rubbing it in my hands as I build it into a lather, I wonder how long this bar will last before I open up a new one. How long will the package under the sink last until I add it to the shopping list – buying soap for the husband I no longer have.

Shaking away my depressing thoughts, I finish in the shower and get ready to face my day with Melanie.

Just because I kicked her out, doesn't mean Linda actually stayed away. She just doesn't sleep here now. I guess I should have known better.

But when I hear her car pull up into the driveway and her key twist in the lock, my heart lightens a little knowing I won't be completely alone today.

"Hey, I brought bagels and coffee," she calls out as she closes the front door behind her. When she walks into view, I press a finger up against my lips and point up over to the bassinet in the living room where Melanie is napping after her morning bottle.

We open our bagels and sip our coffee in somewhat stilted silence. It's been like this since I came home from the hospital – awkward, strange, like I'm waiting for something to happen, waiting for someone to tell me that I should do something, *anything*.

"So what's on the agenda for the day?" Lin's got some serious mind-reading skills.

I sigh and lean back in my chair. "I don't know. I mean what am I supposed to do?" I know what she's getting at. She thinks I should be cleaning out Jimmy's things.

She scans the clean, almost sterile living room. "Wanna get a Christmas tree and do some decorating?" The words *"it might help lift your spirits"* are on the tip of her tongue and I love her for taking a sip of her coffee instead.

Ironically, even with all my day counting, I didn't piece together it was time to decorate for Christmas. I also didn't realize until just now that this is Melanie's first Christmas. So, as much as I may have been ready to throw the holiday to the side and continue to mourn, the sense of obligation to give my daughter the Christmas she deserves weighs heavily in my heart. Of course, she won't remember anything, but I don't ever want her to be short-changed because of Jimmy's death.

I surprise the crap out of Linda when I agree to her plan. I know it won't change my mood all too much, but it'll get me out of the house. It'll give me a reason to do more with my day than just cry and take care of Melanie.

We time our trip to the store around Melanie's feedings, leaving right after giving her a bottle and coming home just in time to hear her cries of hunger once again.

"You take her and I'll bring in the rest of the stuff." Linda drops a handful of shopping bags, filled to the brim with ornaments and tinsel, before returning to the car for more.

After warming her bottle and sitting on the couch, I stare vacantly at the lifeless living room sprawling out before me. "Your daddy loved Christmas, you know?" Of course, Melanie doesn't answer. She just slurps away at her bottle, fingers curling tightly around mine.

"Oh, he did. He would already have this place decked out and lit up, having everything just so, perfect, like he was." I nod down at Melanie as if she actually understands what I'm saying.

Linda's hand falling to my shoulder from behind the couch startles me from the conversation with my daughter. "I'm so sorry, sweetie," she says as she slides next to me on the sofa. "I didn't mean to make this a sad day. I just… I wanted to give us something to do, something to distract us *from* Jimmy not being here, not make you think about what it was like when he was here."

"I know you didn't, Lin. But there's no avoiding it. *Everything* reminds me of him, so there's no way around it." We exchange a sad look; her eyes are filled with sympathy.

Hoisting Melanie up on my shoulder, I pat her back a few times. After she burps, I hand her over to Linda. "I might not know how to move on just yet. Hell, I may never know how to move on, but I can't let it hold me back. I have to be there for her." I brush my knuckles over Melanie's baby-soft cheek. "Just because I'm no longer a wife, doesn't mean I can stop being a mother."

"I wish you could still be both," she adds with so much sadness that it squeezes at my heart.

"Me too, Lin. Me too, but this is just how it is." Though there's a hint of confidence in my words, they're really just as fragile as my soul.

I take Melanie from Linda, wrapping her in a blanket and tucking her in for a nap. Thinking about how excited Jimmy would be to decorate for Melanie's first Christmas reenergizes me somewhat. I pop in a holiday music CD, keeping the volume low enough so it doesn't wake Melanie and ask Linda if she wants any hot chocolate.

"I'll make it. Why don't you unpack everything so we can get started?" There's a knock on the door as she walks into the kitchen.

Stretching up on my toes, I look out the window at the top of the door. I'm both happy and surprised to see Ray leaning up against the doorframe, wrapping his bulky winter jacket around his broad shoulders as he shivers against the cold.

A frigid blast of snowy air gusts into the front hallway. "Hey, Ray." I haven't seen or heard from Ray in a few weeks. I think we are both hiding from each other, from the memories we know will come to the surface if we spend any time together. Pushing away those feelings, I pull him from the front porch, through the door.

"I didn't mean to just drop by. I should have called." He looks almost afraid to come in.

"Don't be ridiculous, Ray. You're always welcome here. Come on in. Get out of the cold." He steps beyond my swept-to-the-side hand and into the living room.

He brushes the snow from his jacket and hangs it on the coat rack. As I close the door, I scan the front yard and realize that the snow is really starting to pile up out there. "Linda's making some hot chocolate. Can I get you anything?"

"No, I don't want to intrude." Again, he looks cautious, afraid.

"Stop it," I insist. "You're not intruding." We walk into the living room and he stops at Melanie's bassinet, staring dreamily down at her. "How's she doing?" he asks all hushed and quiet.

"She's good. Eats like a champ and sleeps better than I do." We sit down on the couch and he sees all the bags of decorations. He chuckles as he tips his chin at the boxed, artificial tree. "You know Jimmy would lose his shit if he saw that in his living room."

"Yeah, I know. He hates fake trees, but it was all Linda and I could carry in here." It's sad to say that I thought the same thing when I was paying for the tree. I didn't want to say anything because Linda was trying her best to cheer me up, but the reality is that even something as silly as a plastic Christmas tree reminds me of Jimmy. "Is it wrong to make decisions based on what I think he would do, even though he's not here?" I sink back into the couch and stare at the stupid tree propped up in the corner of the room, just waiting to be assembled.

Ray flops back and sighs loudly, scrubbing his hand over his face, lost in thought for a moment. "Nah, I don't think so," he decides, finally. "I mean, who knows? You might eventually stop thinking about him before you make important choices," he pauses a beat and drapes his arms around my shoulder, "but I know you, Luce. Jimmy will always be in your heart. You'll always think of him."

He's right. I'll never be able, nor do I ever want to stop thinking about Jimmy. Figuring out a way to keep moving forward without leaving him behind is too overwhelming for me right now.

I'm pretty sure Ray is struggling with the same ideas. They were best friends since elementary school, even went to college together. When I lost my husband, Ray lost his brother. We've been stuck in our own worlds of pain.

Linda brings in our mugs as Ray and I stare blankly at the box in the corner. "So you ready to put this up now?" she asks, tipping her chin in the direction we're both staring.

Ray and I share a knowing glance and he smirks at me. "Nope. I'm going to take *that* back to the store and get you ladies a real tree." Ray stands with a sense of renewed purpose just as Melanie starts squirming in her bassinet. Linda gets her as I walk Ray to the door.

"Thanks, Ray." The kindness sparkling in his eyes lets me know I don't need to say more than that. He knows he's doing what Jimmy would want done, what I want done.

A few hours later, everything is done – the pine needles are even cleaned up from the rug. After Ray and Linda leave, I tuck Melanie in for the night. Sitting on the couch, staring at the newly decorated tree, I get lost in memories of all the Christmases I've spent with Jimmy.

"Here you go," he said as he shoved a very poorly wrapped gift in front of me. We were celebrating our very first Christmas together as a couple during our senior year of high school. After ignoring me for two months, Jimmy was finally able to acknowledge his feelings for his best friend – no small feat in an eighteen-year-old boy's mind, or heart for that matter.

I shook the box to see what kind of noise it made and Jimmy grabbed my hands quickly. "No!" he admonished. "Don't do that. You'll break it."

Well, that just intrigued me even more. "Okay, okay. Sorry." I placed a placating kiss on his cheek and all was forgotten.

Carefully, I pulled back the tape. I could tell Jimmy was getting antsy for me to open it already, but I couldn't miss out on the chance to rib him on his wrapping. "What?" I shrugged my shoulders, holding the half-opened gift in one hand. "I don't want to ruin the paper." I arched an eyebrow as he grabbed the present from my hands.

Opening it the rest of the way for me, he held the plain, white box in front of me in his palm. It was a non-descript box. Not small enough to be a jewelry box and not big enough to be clothing, I wondered what the hell it could be.

When I popped the lid, the most beautiful thing I had ever seen shone back at me. Pulling the delicate, hand-blown glass ornament out of the box, I stared at Jimmy in awe.

"Oh, my goodness. This is beautiful. Jimmy…it's just. Wow. Where did you get this?" My words tumbled from my mouth. The love I felt for this boy before me poured from my heart.

Noticing they were shaking, Jimmy took the shimmering piece of glass from my hands and cupped it in his. "My mom's friend is an artist, so I asked her if she could make something for me."

"You mean she actually made this. It's a one-of-a-kind. That makes it even more beautiful." I traced my fingers carefully over the colored globe, noticed tiny bubbles suspended in the surface, focused in closely on what I was sure was a fingerprint melted into the surface.

"Actually, I made it."

All I thought was, thank God, he's holding the ornament, because if it was me, I would have dropped it. "What?" My whispered voice could barely be heard above the crackling fire roaring before us in his den.

"I said I made it." He twisted to face me and kissed my cheek sweetly. "See?" He held his thumb out for me to inspect. "I've even got the blister to prove it." The skin was red and still a little swollen. I remembered just last week when I saw the Band-Aid. I made fun of him when he said it was a paper-cut.

I kissed the pad of his thumb and watched his Adam's apple bob in his throat. "There. All better." His eyes widened and his grip tightened on my hand.

Having just heard his parents talking in the kitchen, which was right next to the den, I kissed him softly on the lips and whispered in his ear, "After they go to bed. I promise. I'll kiss lots of other places."

I watched him gulp one last time and shift in his seat, readjusting himself in the process while trying to maintain his cool.

When he regained his sense of composure, he took his work of art from my hands one last time. Turning it over in his hands, he showed me how the colors gradually swirled and mixed together. Blues morphed into aqua, transformed into lime greens, seeped into warm oranges and finally lightened into the prettiest starburst effect of pale yellows I had ever seen.

"I named it after you, too, you know," he said when he was done showing me the colors.

Reaching into the small box on the couch next to us, he pulled out a small certificate of authenticity. "Reena, my mom's friend, prints these out for everything she makes. So when she asked me what I wanted to call it, I couldn't think of anything other than you."

When I held the piece of paper in my hand, my heart swelled as my eyes danced over the name Starlight Lucy.

"Jimmy." My eyes shone with unshed tears of happiness. "You're just the most thoughtful boyfriend on the planet."

"That's your song, sweetie. You'll always be my Lucy in the sky."

Knowing the emotional onslaught looking at that ornament would bring, I didn't take out that particular box from the garage when Ray and Linda were here. But now, sitting here all alone, the urge to run my thumb over the same spot where Jimmy's thumb once was, draws me to the box I was avoiding earlier in the night.

Setting the box down on the floor, I cross my legs underneath me and cautiously open it. It's right there on the top, always the first ornament to go on the tree and the last to come down. Jimmy's work of art, his Starlight Lucy, somehow looks more beautiful this year than it did last year, or in all the years before.

Holding it lovingly in my hand, I move over to the window and stare up into night sky. There's a sapphire blue undertone to what's normally bleak and pitch black. Dotted with a million points of light, I feel as if Jimmy made this ornament all those years ago with this exact image in his mind.

"I miss you, baby," I whisper to myself, ghosting my finger over Jimmy's thumbprint. "We set up the tree tonight. Ray came over to help. I know it's not nearly as beautiful as it would have been if you had done it, but I hope you like it."

I spend a few more minutes talking to Jimmy through the stars. I tell him about Melanie, about how beautiful she is and how much I know he would love her. I tell him about her most recent doctor's appointment and how much she's grown already. I tell him about how much I miss him and about how much I love him.

That's when the tears start, but then again, maybe they never really stop. Maybe they're just kept at bay by some magical force when the sun is out. But here, in the uneasy solitude of the night, that's when they come out. My tears are nocturnal, fearful of being exposed in the sunlight. They only appear when I seek the comfort of the only man I've ever loved when the black sky spreads out before me.

When my chest hurts from heaving and sobbing and my eyes are nearly closed with puffiness, I stare out into the night. "When does it get easier? What did I ever do to deserve this? Why?" My voice rises in intensity, falling just short of yelling. Of course, there's no answer. There never will be. I guess that's just the way life works.

Now, it's up to me to figure out how to make the best of my new life.

My life without Jimmy.

My life as a single mother.

That last thought helps bolster my strength and calm my tears just enough to finish going through the rest of the box. If I thought the flood of emotion was overwhelming at seeing my Starlight Lucy ornament, I am clearly not ready for what else is waiting for me.

I knew that he kept in touch with Reena, his mother's friend and the woman who helped him make his first present for me. She's helped him at work, creating custom lighting pieces for his high-end clients, but somehow I never pieced together he would do this. But, knowing just how thoughtful and sweet Jimmy was, it all makes sense now.

And I know he made it, not Reena. He wouldn't have had it any other way. He must have made it after he found out we were having a girl. The palest shade of lavender deepens into a saturated, almost royal purple as I twirl the globe by the delicate silver string on top.

What's even more beautiful than the almost tie-dyed movement of colors is the glittery array of sparkles laced through the surface. Pulling the certificate of authenticity out of the box with shaky hands, I read the information through teary eyes.

He named it Opal Mist, and beneath the name are all of the details for a child born in the month of October: astrological sign, birthstone, and other seemingly unimportant pieces of information. But there's nothing at all insignificant about this. It's the only thing Melanie will ever have that came directly from her daddy.

I carefully place the ornament on the tree, right next to mine. "They're beautiful, babe. Thank you," I whisper again, out into the sparkling night.

Over the next few weeks, I'm more than willing to let Linda take the lead on everything holiday related. Food shopping, gift-wrapping, cooking, baking – the woman is my savior. Ray is nothing short of a miracle either. Shoveling snow, fixing a flat tire, he's been more than helpful.

On Christmas Eve, the four of us – Ray, Linda, Melanie, and I spend the night in front of the real tree we decorated together. Even though it's not the same, not even close to what I envisioned my baby's first Christmas being, it still feels like family.

After dinner, we all flop onto the couch. With fully bellies and light hearts, we exchange a few gifts. Even though I told them not to go overboard, they spoil

Melanie. Simply put, I'm in awe of my friends' capacity to love.

After we've opened everything, I get lost in thought, scanning the room that's scattered with torn-apart wrapping paper. "I don't know what we would do without you guys."

Sitting next to me, Linda reaches out for my hand. "There's nowhere we'd rather be."

"There's nowhere I'd rather be either, but I think this might be our one and only Christmas here." I didn't want to say anything about it, especially tonight, but I can't hold it in any longer.

"Why is that?" Linda asks, concern coloring her words.

"I go back to work in a few weeks, but I was looking over all the bills and the mortgage, and everything just the other day, and I just can't afford this place on my own." Even with the life insurance money, I don't know that I'll be able to stay here forever.

"Let me..." I stop Linda midsentence because I know exactly what's going to come out of her mouth.

"That's very sweet of you to want to offer to move in, but you're right. Eventually, I'm going to have to move on somehow. I can't depend on everyone else."

This time, it's Ray who does the interrupting. Clearing his throat, he moves next to me on the couch. "You can always depend on us," he says soothingly.

A sad smile pulls at my lips. "Ray, I know you mean that and you two will always be a part of our lives, but I…"

"You what?" Linda pulls her hand out of mine rather abruptly. "We're here, helping you and you're pushing us away. Let us in, Lucy. Let us help you out."

Her outburst catches me off-guard. She's more than a little hurt and I'm at a complete loss for words. She speaks before I can put anything intelligible together. "We're hurting for you. Lean on us and let us hold you up."

"But what if…" My throat tightens and my eyes burn just at the thought. Resting my elbows on my knees, I drop my face into my hands. "What if I lose you guys, too?"

I had never been a weak person, always fiercely independent and modestly confident, but losing Jimmy changed me – that much is obvious. Yet, it is more than his death that has changed me. Losing him and gaining Melanie all within the same time frame altered me on the most basic level. For the first time in my life, I became afraid. I never planned to share those fears, but watching my best friend cry next to me about how much she wants to help, changes that plan.

Linda grabs me by the shoulders, looking me right in the face. "You're right. You could lose us. I'm no fortuneteller. I don't know what tomorrow will bring – no one does. But I do know this, we are here for you now. We love you and Melanie and we want to help, so tell us how to do that. You want to stay here in this house? Then we'll help you do that. You want to move out and start over? Then we'll help you do that, too, but you have to let us."

Her words cut me to the quick, and in that instant, I realize that I don't *have* to do everything on my own.

Linda pulls me into her arms and we cry together for a few minutes. The "ahem" from Ray pulls us from our teary embrace. "I was going to save this until tomorrow, but I guess now's as good a time as any." Ray stands from the couch and walks over to his jacket hanging on the coat rack by the door.

He extends a shaking hand in which is a small, simple envelope – there's no address or name or anything.

"What's this?" I ask cautiously.

He stuffs his hands in his pockets and shrugs his shoulders. "Just something me and everyone at CBA wanted you and Melanie to have." CBA. Crane Building Associates. Jimmy's company. It's now my turn for my hands to shake.

Opening the envelope, I see a check inside. "Ray, I can't…"

He doesn't let me finish my sentence. "You can and you will." He drops back down to the couch, gently squeezing my knee. "He was my best friend. Let me do this for him. Let me help take care of you the only way I can. I owe him that much."

I nod, unable to say anything. He's right after all. He's only doing what he knows Jimmy would want to be done.

I pull the check from the envelope in utter disbelief of the amount. My hand flies to my mouth, covering the gasp of shock. "Ray...my God...this is..."

"It's enough to pay off the house and stay here forever, if that's what you want. It's also enough to start over somewhere else, if that's what you want."

"I don't know what to say."

"Don't say anything right now. Just know that you can do whatever you'd like." Ray steadies my hands in his.

"Thank you so much for this, Ray."

"It's nothing, really." But it's not *nothing* and he knows it. This piece of paper in my hand means everything. It means being able to raise our daughter in the house we bought together – the house Jimmy had massive plans for renovating and making a home.

"My God! The company. I didn't even think of the company and what it means to you." I know it sounds highly unlikely, but I never thought of what would happen to Crane Building Associates, the architecture / construction company that Jimmy and Ray started together. It was only Ray mentioning it just now that brought it to mind.

"That's also up to you, Luce." He's calm and certain, in control like the Ray I've always known.

"What do you mean?" I'm sure my face is twisted in confusion.

"Jimmy and I owned the company right down the middle. You can continue to be involved in the day-today business if that's what you'd like to do. Or you can leave that to me. But, no matter what, Jimmy's half is your half."

"I…I don't know the first thing about running a business." This is too much too soon. I can't possibly make all of these decisions today, right now.

I think Linda and Ray can feel the panic rising in the room, a palpable vibration of anxiety tightly wound around us.

"It's okay, sweetie. You don't have to decide anything right now, right Ray?" Linda looks over at him for reassurance while I sit in the middle of them, panic-stricken and choked mute with fear.

"Take all the time you need, Luce." Ray squeezes my hand and I exhale a deep breath.

"Okay," is all I can squeak out past the hot lump of emotion in my chest.

Swiping away her own tears, Linda stands before us with renewed purpose. "Cookies. We need cookies."

I can't help but laugh as she practically races into the kitchen, grabbing a platter of gingerbread men. She hands us each a cookie and holds hers in front of her. "To friends," she toasts as she taps all of our cookies together in some kind of ridiculous gingerbread man high-five.

"To friends." Laughter bubbling in my chest. I feel a flicker of light and hope crack open inside of me.

In the months following Christmas, that shimmer of light takes on a life of its own. I use the money Jimmy's co-workers raised for Melanie and me to pay off the house. I can't ever imagine myself living somewhere else. I also take Ray up on the offer to let him buy me out of the company. We work out a payment plan to ensure I have a steady source of income and so that Ray doesn't go bankrupt over the buyout. I'll also have enough money to start a college fund for Melanie.

When Jimmy died, a part me died with him. But when Melanie was born, part of me was reborn too, the part that knew I had to keep on living despite the pain, and that I had to find beauty in the midst of all the ugliness. Jimmy had been my everything, but now my daughter owned the only space left in my heart.

Part Two

~ Found ~

18 Years Later

CHAPTER SEVEN

Evan

"We should go back inside, Joe." My breath swirls up and out into the cold winter air. The chill of the evening has nothing on the cold darkness that's fallen on my younger brother's life.

You would think losing Sara, his first wife, to a suicide brought on by her untreated bi-polar disorder is more than any one person should have to deal with. When Joe found Becca all those years later, I felt like he was finally getting the life he deserved.

Then she got sick.

Then he lost her.

"I can't believe she's gone." He stares blindly into the dusty rose of the setting sun, seemingly to avoid looking at me with his tear-filled eyes.

"I'm so sorry." It's lame and pathetic, but there's nothing else to say.

Katie, his daughter from his first marriage, walks up next to us and loops her arm through her father's. "Hey, Daddy. You okay?" My heart breaks looking at her puffy, red eyes and sad face. Even though Becca was sick for a long time, it's not easier to say goodbye to her.

Joe pats Katie's hand as it rests in the crook of his elbow. "I'm not right now, but I'll be okay, sweetie." Just as we turn to walk inside, a few cars pull into the lot. I recognize them from back at Joe's house. It's Becca's son from her first marriage and his friends.

I arrived at Joe's house late this morning so I didn't get the chance to be introduced to everyone. Katie makes up for that now, though. "Uncle Evan, this is Reid and his girlfriend Maddy." We shake hands and Maddy offers up a sad smile.

"Reid, I'm so sorry. Your mom was a really great woman." See? Lame again, but I'm no good when it comes to loss.

Though, you would think that years of experience would make me an expert in it.

"Thanks." He reaches down and pulls Maddy's hand into his. Joe sees it and I can't help but wonder if he feels some kind of phantom pain in his own hand.

The rest of Reid's friends follow behind him and I hold the door for them to walk in front of me. Just as I'm about to follow them in, another car pulls into the lot. The woman who exits the car is clearly flustered as she pulls her jacket around her body tightly. She shuts the driver's door and I can hear her mumbled curses even though I'm more than a few feet away from her.

"Crap!" She pounds against the doorframe.

I startle her as I walk over to her. "Everything okay?"

With her hands cupped against the window, I follow her gaze to her bag, which is opened on the front seat. Inside, I can clearly see her keys. "Yeah, it'll be okay. I think my daughter has a spare." She angles her head toward the building indicating that one of the girls, who just walked in, must be her daughter. Becca's is the only service here tonight so I know she's not here for anyone else.

"Hold on. I think I can help." I walk over to my truck and open the emergency repair kit in the back. Within seconds, I've got the lock shimmied open and her keys back in her hand.

"Thanks," she says with a little uncertainty.

She buttons her jacket and jams her hands in the pockets as a frigid gust of wind blasts through the mostly empty parking lot.

An awkward moment of silence passes between us with our backs pressed up against the cold metal of her car. "So…" I begin so speak but her words interrupt mine.

"Come here often?"

I choke on my laughter. "I'm sorry, what?"

Her laughter, beautiful and soft, feminine and throaty, competes with mine. "That was bad, huh?"

"Yeah, a little bit." I pinch my fingers together in front of my face.

"Okay, what I *meant* to ask was, do you just hang out in the parking lot waiting for people to lock their keys in their cars and come to their rescue?" An arched eyebrow accompanies her joke.

"Now, that just makes me sound like a creep." I cross my arms over my chest and lean back against the car.

"I'm assuming that you're here for Becca Donovan? She's the only service tonight," I ask, already knowing the answer.

"I am. That means you are too then. How did you know her?" There's genuine concern in her eyes, a sense of mourning on her face. I wonder if she was close with Becca; she seems to be really affected by her passing.

"She was my brother's wife. I'm Evan by the way." I offer her my hand.

"Lucy." The touch of her delicate and cold fingers sends a tingle up my arm. "I'm Melanie's mom. Becca's son, Reid, is dating my daughter's best friend."

She shivers again as another gust of cold air flows around us. I see Katie peek her head out of the door, scanning the parking lot for me. I wave over to her and hold up one finger to let her know I'll be there in one minute.

"I guess we should go." Pushing away from the car, I extend my arm to the side letting her walk past me.

"Sure." We both seem to be avoiding going inside; well, at least I know I am.

As we make our way up the few steps leading to the entrance, Lucy trips, somehow managing to trip *up* the steps. She grabs a hold of my pant leg, throwing me off balance as well.

Sprawled out across three steps leading into my sister-in-law's funeral, Lucy and I lose ourselves in a fit of laughter.

"Are you okay?" I ask when I catch my breath again.

She brushes her hands against her legs, dusting off the grains of sand stuck in her palms. "I'm sorry. Didn't mean to take you down with me."

"Glad I could join you for your trip." She laughs at my stupid joke and we find ourselves just sitting on the steps, neither of us making a move to get up and walk inside.

"I hate these places," I say, staring out into the recently turned black night sky.

"Yeah, they're not my favorite either," she admits, forcing me to twist on the stair and search her face for more information.

Just as she looks like she's about to say something, the door creaks open again and the redhead who scooted past me earlier pops her head outside.

"Mom? What are you doing out here? I was worried you got lost." Melanie holds out her hand to help Lucy up from the steps.

When she stands, Lucy brushes her hands over her ass, dusting away the dirt and smoothing out her pants. I can't help but check out her ass, my eyes immediately drawn to the firm roundness. It's sad that I've just checked out a woman's ass outside of a funeral parlor. Maybe God will strike me down or something, but it's a nice ass.

"Hi, honey. I wasn't lost." She stands and kisses Melanie on the cheek. "I just locked my keys in the car and Evan helped me. Then I tripped up the steps and Evan helped me again. We were just about to come inside." Lucy offers her hand to me as I stand.

Despite the frigidity in the air, when Lucy gently wraps her small fingers around mine a flash of warmth passes between us. Our eyes meet; a look of understanding passes between us. Rather than letting go of my hand when I'm standing, she loops her arm through mine, and even though she says nothing, her face tells me I don't have to go in there alone, if I don't want to. I nod my silent thanks and we walk through the doors.

It ends up being a small service, which means I get to spend most of the evening talking with Lucy. I don't bother asking her about why she doesn't like funerals. Besides, I don't particularly like getting into the specifics of why I hate them.

Old wounds, though scabbed over, open easily and bleed profusely.

"So what do you do, Lucy?" Keep it simple, easy.

"Office work. Exhilarating, right?" She chuckles, dismissing the simplicity of her work. "Actually, I was just recently assigned a project to help with Care for a Cure, a children's cancer center research facility," she adds casually, as if it's no big deal she's doing such wonderful work.

"Wow, that's really impressive."

"What do you do?" She turns in her seat to face me and her knee brushes mine. The same warmth that passed through her hand earlier, now courses through my leg.

"Right now, I'm on medical leave, but I'm a captain in the FDNY." The look of shock that passes across her face is also colored with concern.

"Did you get hurt? When will you return?" Her hand falls on top of mine, comfortably, not awkward at all.

I smile to diffuse her worry and cover her hand with mine. "I hurt my shoulder in a drill, so I should be back soon enough. Nothing to cause any concern," I lie. Laying out the details of my PTSD, paired with my lung cancer recovery to the woman I've just met and will more than likely never see again, just doesn't seem right.

Relief washes over her face as her daughter approaches us. Even though we already met outside, Lucy introduces us. As Lucy and Melanie talk, I study Lucy's face.

Her long brown hair falls past her shoulders in waves. When she casually tosses it over her shoulders, I catch the scent of something sweet. Vanilla, maybe. Her eyes are her most striking feature, by far. Sapphire blue, sparkling with such emotion, they light up her entire face.

Lost in my open perusal of her beauty, I don't even realize that Melanie has stopped talking. She looks directly at me, arches an eyebrow – playfully not suspiciously. "Oh, my God! You were just checking out my mom."

I choke on my tongue, trying to spit out a defense I know will only make me sound guiltier than I already am.

"Um…well, no…. not exactly." Lucy's scrunched up and confused face clearly tells me that's the wrong answer. "Well, I mean…yeah, but not like you think…" Okay so trying to clarify isn't helping either.

Just as quickly as she hung me out to dry, Melanie swoops in for the save. Totally ignoring my comments of stupidity, she directs her words at her mom. "See? I told you, Mom. You still got it."

Now it's Lucy's turn to feel embarrassed. "Okay, I'm going to head out with Maddy and Reid. We'll meet you at home later." Melanie leans in to kiss Lucy's cheek. As she hugs her mom, she winks at me almost as if she's giving me the go-ahead. Sneaky kid. I like her already.

Already? Listen to me. Like there's going to be more.

As Melanie walks away, Lucy says, "Sorry about that. Sometimes her brain to mouth filter is completely turned off."

"It's okay. She was right, you know." I lean in closer to whisper my next words. "I was checking you out."

Her cheeks turn bright red, making her blue eyes pop even more. It takes mere seconds for both of us to get lost in a loud laugh, catching the attention of the few people left in the small room.

The last guests leave and Katie walks over to Lucy and me. Lucy stands and hugs Katie. "If you ever need anything, don't you dare hesitate to call me?" She runs her hands up and down Katie's arms, consoling and comforting. Something in me I thought was long gone, cracks open. Lucy's only known Katie for two days at the most, yet here she is, offering her help in any way she can.

In the few hours I've known her, Lucy has proven to be a kind soul – and a beautiful one at that.

"I guess I should be going." Lucy stands and pulls her jacket on. "Evan," she offers me her hand, "it was really nice to meet you." I pull her hand up to my lips and pop a gentle kiss there, causing the blush that was just in her cheeks a moment ago to return.

As Katie steps away, leaving us alone, the awkwardness descends upon us. "So…" we both say at the same before sharing another laugh.

"Goodnight, Evan. Maybe I'll see you again."

"Yeah, maybe." I can't deny that I'm sad to see her go. There's something about her that makes me want to get to know her more. But, the part of me that shut down long ago, the part that has kept me from ever being able to commit to anyone, screams loudly for me to just walk away and let Lucy live her own life, free of my problems.

January 27, 2013

CHAPTER EIGHT

Lucy

"Well, now what?" I sigh and say those words to myself as I turn into my driveway. There's no one else to speak them to anyway. It's just me now.

It doesn't have to be. A small voice whispers in the back of my mind.

Sure, it's been just me for the last eighteen years, but this feels different, somehow. Raising Melanie on my own was no easy feat and I relied on Ray and Linda a lot initially. But, as I knew they would, our lives took on very different paths.

Work consumed Ray's. He stayed in touch in those first few years, but after he got married, his family came first. I can't hold it against him; that's how it's supposed to be. We stay in touch, but it's not the same.

A broken marriage nearly destroyed Linda's. She got married about two years after Jimmy died, but her husband ended up being an "unfaithful pig" – those are her words, not mine. Personally, I think her words are too kind.

And a calendar full of ballet concerts and school plays filled mine. Being a mom was all I knew how to be, so I embraced it whole-heartedly. PTA volunteer, class mom, soccer coach – I never wanted Melanie to feel like she was missing out because she only had me. Some may say that I overcompensated; I just wanted to make sure my baby girl knew she was loved.

We always came together on important occasions – birthdays, holidays, high school graduation, but during the minutiae of my day-to-day life, I was always alone. Watching Melanie grow from a chatty and playful toddler, into a beautiful and poised young woman has been the most rewarding experience of my life.

If I'm being honest, it's been the only experience of my life.

Sure. I thought about dating again, and the possibility of getting married flitted through my consciousness, however fleetingly. But at the end of the day, no one measured up to my Jimmy. Maybe I never let them, never gave them enough of a chance. That's what Linda would say, after all.

"He's got a good job and a kind heart. What could have possibly gone wrong?" Linda would ask after yet another attempt at setting me up with someone she kinda-sorta knew somehow through her grapevine of friends.

"Nothing went wrong," I would defend lamely.

"Then what is it, Luce?" By the time the fifth date failed, I could tell her patience was wearing thin.

"He wasn't Jimmy, Lin. None of them are. None of them will be. I'm happy enough. Can't we just leave it at that?"

Her response on that particular occasion stung more than a little, and hit all too close to home. "Enough for what?"

I didn't bother answering her; there was no point. I was happy enough to be Melanie's mom, but that's all I knew how to be.

There was Evan, but it's foolish of me to hold on to a few flirtations that happened over a month ago. That's real sad – in the last eighteen years, the only moments that stand out in my dating life are those from a casual conversation at a funeral.

Pathetic, Lucy.

My non-existent love life aside, there were moments of brightness. When Melanie met Maddy back in middle school, I felt, in some strange way, like she was meant to come into our lives. I never wanted Maddy to have to deal with loss, but maybe in some strange way, pain gravitates toward pain. Helping Maddy heal from the death of her parents and watching her grow up, helped heal me in ways I never knew needed healing. When she came to live with us last year, our family felt more complete, somehow.

I loved watching Melanie and Maddy grow up, become sisters. I loved being able to mother another child, to nurture someone else even though she wasn't my own blood.

When they left for college last fall, it was not an easy adjustment. But Linda, my rock and a constant source of support in my life, was right there to help me. Her divorce left her disillusioned with men, so thankfully, after years of trying, she finally stopped setting me up with friends of friends.

We'd spend our weekends shopping or redecorating room after room in one another's house. We'd go to the spa or the salon, learning to pamper ourselves rather than waiting around for someone else to do it for us.

Just as the girls' first semester was coming to a close, and I was getting excited to have them home for a solid month, my world spun upside down once again. But, loss is a funny thing. You get accustomed to it. It lives with you, breathes your air, and thrums in your veins. It never dissipates completely, just fades into the twilight, hanging in the background, waiting for the chance to present itself again.

Maddy's car accident brought me right back to the center of darkness; it brought the ever-present force of loss back into the foreground. When she recovered, I made a simple, but huge, resolution to myself.

I was going to stop existing and start living.

I just didn't know how.

So I did what I knew how to do best. I threw myself into Melanie and Maddy's lives. I supported them through their tragedies in order to avoid healing my own. I talked Melanie down from her ledge of self-doubt and helped Maddy see the error of her ways.

The irony of it all is I helped all of the people I love the most find their own pieces of happiness, yet in the process, neglected to discover my own.

So here I am, lost in thought in the driveway of my now empty home.

I can't help but get a little misty-eyed at that idea. I'm really and truly alone. Feeling my throat constrict with those heavy emotions, I huff out a deep breath.

I will not cry. I will not cry.

That's been my mantra since I dropped Melanie back off at school and then helped Maddy, move out of the house. That's a lot of emotions to deal with in a short span of time, but I'm trying my best to deal with them.

I grab my purse and the bag of Chinese take-out from the passenger seat. As I unlock the door and step over the threshold, the only thing that greets me is the quiet darkness of my empty house.

I know the nest has technically been empty since Melanie went to school last September, but it's different now. It feels more final somehow. During her first semester, she came home a lot and I went to visit her a handful of times, so it didn't feel like we were really apart. Her being away was still so new I don't think I let myself wrap my head around it, at first. I couldn't be more proud of her, but there's a new sense of being really alone now that's hanging over me. My baby girl is all grown up and on her own.

But, I'd be lying if I said that I'd ever be anything other than a mom. I could tell that there was something just *off* about Melanie as I was driving her back to school the other day. My "mom instincts" were on full alert, but my "girl senses" knew better than to push. Because she was in such a funk, leaving her at school on her own was somehow more gut wrenching this semester than it was last semester.

My hand hovers over the phone as my fingers itch to dial Melanie's number. "No. It's okay. She'll be fine. I'm sure it's nothing that a good, long chat with her girlfriends won't fix." Talking myself out of making what seems to be an unnecessary phone call, I laugh at my ridiculousness.

I'm talking to myself. Maybe I should get a cat. Nah, I'd probably adopt more than one and eventually turn into the crazy cat lady. A dog might not be a bad idea, though.

Shaking away the ideas of a pet and me, I get out a plate for my shrimp dumplings. Setting myself up in front of the television, I turn on the news. After a few minutes of hearing about "this" shooting and "that" tragic accident, I turn it off and finish my meal in silence.

When I'm all done, I load my plate in the dishwasher and lean up against the counter. Scanning the empty room, I feel a pang of guilt for every time I ever wished for peace and quiet when Melanie was a child.

I would give anything for a little bit of noise right now.

The silence is deafening. The solitude is depressing.

A bath. I need a bath.

But even that doesn't help. The bubbles are soothing and the aroma of jasmine permeating the room is calming, but there's still the gnawing emptiness that I feel creeping in. I guess in the last few months I've been able to shake it off most of the time. My ability to shake away my loneliness is apparently a superpower that's fading.

"At least I have work tomorrow." Talking to my reflection as I comb through my wet and tangled hair, I sigh sadly. Maybe a good night's sleep will help.

I'm probably just feeling down because Melanie isn't here. It's been virtually just the two of us forever and now the only person who I have ever loved more than life itself is no longer here with me every day.

Feeling more than a little sentimental, I cozy up in bed and dial Melanie's number. I know I shouldn't be bothering her. Hell, I only dropped her off two days ago, but I just need to hear her voice.

Who am I kidding? I just need to hear *a* voice.

It rings and rings, but she never picks up. Sadly, even hearing her voicemail greeting is enough to calm me a little. They might be fitful, but at least I'll be able to get a few hours of sleep tonight.

At least, I hope so.

"Good morning, sunshine." Linda's sarcasm is the last thing I need right now, but apparently that's what she's dishing out at seven a.m. on this fine Monday morning.

Through my yawn, I tell her to "shut it" as I playfully swat her sweatshirt-covered arm. We walk together every morning. "I didn't sleep well last night. I must have overdone it this weekend, that's all." We begin on our usual route of two miles around the neighborhood. It's been a fairly mild winter. So even though upstate New York in January usually isn't the most ideal locale for a Monday morning power-walk, it's been nice enough to actually walk more days than not. The only time we miss our daily walk is when one of us is sick.

When about a quarter of a mile goes by in silence, which is only interspersed by my persistent yawns, Linda nudges me in the side with her elbow. "So what kept you up?"

"I don't know. I guess a little bit of everything." I can see my breath in the early morning air as I say, "It was just so quiet."

Linda slows her pace slightly and looks at me. "Isn't that a good thing? The girls are all on their own now, so you have all the time and space to do whatever you want."

"Yeah, I guess so." Shrugging my shoulders essentially puts an end to the conversation, but it doesn't help me shake the feeling of loneliness that is slowly creeping toward me. Out of the corner of my eye, I catch Linda smirking at me. Her eyes are alight with humor. Something is going on in that pretty little head of hers. "What are you thinking about over there?"

"Oh, nothing," she chirps as we round the corner and head back toward our block.

Now, Linda is not only smirking but she's almost laughing. "Would you just spill it already? What's going on?"

"I just think it's funny. That's all."

"What is? I'm over here telling you it's too quiet and that I'm lonely, and you're laughing at me. Thanks a lot, best friend!" I snap at her. I guess my sleepless night took more of a toll on me than I thought.

"Oh, calm down. I don't think it's funny that you're lonely." Her warm brown eyes sparkle in the early morning sun. "I was laughing because for all these years when I said you needed to find someone, you wouldn't be a mom forever, you thought I was crazy."

I open my mouth to speak, but Linda just shushes me, all pretenses of laughter are gone. Here we go; I'm getting *the lecture.*

"I know you'll always be Melanie's mother, and I also know that you'll always be a huge part of Maddy's life as well, but right now, they don't need you in the same ways they used to. I've been telling you this for years. Now, here you are." Linda stops walking and grabs my shoulders. "I'm not saying this to be mean, but you deserve a slice of happiness for yourself. All those years you claimed you couldn't date because you were too busy with the girls, well, now here's your chance. They're all grown up. Now, it's your turn to figure out what you want. You're only forty-three-years-old. You've got the rest of your life to live and it's going to suck if you choose to live it alone."

I never told her anything about Evan, or the flutters he set off. Thinking about him is pointless anyway. After the funeral, he returned to his life in Manhattan and I retreated to mine in the middle of nowhere.

I feel the tears building. I'm a crier; I can't help it. There's no point in blinking them back when I know they'll spill. "Oh, sweetie. I don't want you to cry. It's just that you're amazing, Lucy. You have devoted your life to being the best mom possible and Melanie is a shining example of how beautiful your love is. You have so much love to give that you practically adopted Maddy after her aunt died. That girl doesn't love you *like* a mom; she loves you because for all intents and purposes, you are the only mom she's ever had."

Mentioning Maddy and her losses only makes me remember mine.

Jimmy.

Yes, time heals all wounds, but the fact remains that he was taken from me all too soon.

"I just can't, Linda. I had my chance. It was just cut short." I swipe at the tears trickling down my cheeks as she puffs out a frustrated sigh.

"Lucy, I loved Jimmy very much and I know you'll never love anyone as much as him, but don't you think you deserve to give it a try. Maybe you'll find someone who you could love differently." She adds a wink to her lamely shrugged shoulder, urging me to give it a chance.

A tiny voice, buried somewhere in the back of my brain whispers, *maybe*.

In a vain attempt to avoid answering that question, I force my feet to start moving. One step in front of the other − that's how I feel like I've lived the last eighteen years of my life. If I can just keep moving forward, then

I don't have to look back and remember how painful yesterday was.

As we arrive in front of my house, Linda stares off into the distance. She looks like she's trying to choose her words carefully. "I'm not trying to tell you to forget Jimmy or to stop loving him, but I want to see you happy. Just think about it okay?"

Knowing she means well helps to soften the harsh reality of her words. I smile through the heaviness I feel. "I know. I'm sorry for getting upset. I'll think about it; I promise."

Linda smiles and waves as she walks away. Calling over her shoulder, she says, "I'll see you at work in a bit." I wave at her as she rounds the corner, and thank my lucky stars I still have her in my life on a daily basis.

Rounding the corner and peering over the top of her office cubicle, I catch a glimpse of Linda's computer screen.

"Oh no you don't." My words startle her, making her nearly fall out of her swivel chair.

Clutching her hand over her heart, she gasps, "Freaking hell, Lucy! You scared the crap out of me."

Completely ignoring her reaction, I move into her workspace, pointing a finger at my picture on her computer screen. "You better not be doing what I think you're doing."

She shrugs her shoulders, holding her hands out to the side. "I don't know what you're talking about." Her feigned ignorance is pretty transparent.

Leaning in to read the address in the web browser, my fears are confirmed. "Am I really *that* pathetic that you need to register me to Date.com?"

When she doesn't answer me immediately, but rather scans me from head to toe, I wonder if she thinks my question was not the rhetorical kind.

"No, I don't think you're pathetic, but I meant what I said this morning. You need to go and be something other than a mom. Now's your chance to do that. I just took a little bit more of a proactive approach by loading all of your information in here." Her snark is amplified by her arched brow. She's in "deal making" mode.

I sit in the extra chair she has in her cube, cross my legs, and lean forward. If she's going to start talking about the non-existent details of my love life at work, I don't need her yelling it to me from outside of her workspace. "I've made a decision," she says matter-of-factly.

"About my life, I'm assuming?" I tip my chin toward the online dating application that's just waiting for her to click "submit".

"Yes, about your life. I think thirty years of friendship has earned me the right to make *some* decisions, don't you?" She pokes me in the arm and laughs.

"Well, then, oh wise one, please tell me what you've decided." She's not a fan of my sarcasm, but she laughs nonetheless.

"All right, here's my deal," she snaps; a 'take it or leave it' tone hangs in the air. "I'm going to put your profile up and you're going to go on the date I choose for you." She crosses her arms over her chest as a satisfied smile curls her lips.

"What?" That doesn't sound like a *deal* at all.

"Oh, that's cute, Luce. You thought I was going to go easy on you?" I hate that she's laughing at me. I hate that she's right. I did think she would take pity on me, but I guess she's going with the 'sink or swim' mentality.

I think she sees the fear in my eyes or maybe she can sense the rapid increase of my heart beating. Whatever it is, she eventually takes pity. "Fine. I'll give you some time. A week or two at the most." I sag in relief at her words. Who knew that the premise of dating again would cause so much anxiety?

"Okay, I can live with that," I lie, hoping I don't seem too transparent.

"No, you can't, but I'm serious. I just want you to be happy." She reaches over and rubs my shoulder compassionately.

"I know, Lin." I love her for her concern. She's been there in the darkest moments and my happiness is always in her mind. But, when she twists in her chair and hits the button to make my online dating profile go live, the only thing that crosses my mind, is tackling her to the ground.

"What did you just do? You just said you would give me a few weeks!" I stare in horror as the words "your submission is complete" flash across the screen.

"I did," she adds smugly. "A few weeks before I respond." If she had a handlebar mustache, she'd be twisting it in her fingers, while laughing manically right now.

I shoot up from my seat and huff, ready to yell something at her. But then, a slew of "what ifs" fly through my brain. I'll never let her know I'm at least a little bit intrigued to see the men who might be interested in me, so I just poke a finger at her from over the ledge of her cubicle and shoot daggers as I stalk away.

January 31, 2013

CHAPTER NINE

Evan

Dropping the last box on the floor in my condo, I take a look at my new place.

Empty.

That's all I can come up with. I'll never admit it to anyone, but the fact that my life can fit neatly inside of a few dozen boxes, is pretty sad. Well, I guess that's what you get for always putting your job first - for never making room for anyone to stay as a permanent fixture.

No sense dwelling on it. My life is what it is. Hearing my brother's footsteps behind me shakes me from my self-pity.

"This is the last one. Truck's all empty." Joe kicks the door closed behind him, piling the box atop the others.

I pull a Bud out of the case I just carried up with me, twist the cap and hand him one. "Thanks, man. I appreciate you helping." He clinks the glass neck against mine and takes a swig.

Stretching his back and twisting his neck to the side, a loud pop fills the air. "Anytime, man. You helped me move Katie back to her dorm last weekend. It's only fair for me to help you, right?" he jokes, flopping down into the only piece of furniture I currently own – a beat up, old recliner.

I chug back half of my beer letting the alcohol help ease away some of the tension in my sore muscles. Leaning back against the chipped and scratched, ugly brown countertop, I cross my legs at the ankles and fold my arms over my chest.

"How you holding up?" I play cool and distant, but inside, I need to know my little brother is okay.

"I'm good." He's deflecting; I can tell. He takes a sip of his drink too quickly, probably biting back his all-too-obvious pain. Finishing his drink in one large gulp, he looks at me with sad eyes.

"I miss her." He moves toward the small kitchen, grabs another beer and unloads the rest into the fridge. "Guess there's not much I can do about that, though." Deflecting, yet again. But I let him do it. I hate when people make me talk about losing someone close. It doesn't make it easier. It hurts like fucking hell. And no amount of words will ever bring them back, so what's the point, really?

That's what made me move up here, knowing he would need someone, even if it isn't me he wants to rely on. I haven't told him about the medical office pushing me through for early retirement; I haven't told anyone. I guess it is some vain attempt at denying it all.

But reality has a funny way of crashing down around you when all you're trying to do is hold it up with your own two hands.

Lucky for us, the cable company was in here earlier today. Joe clicks through a few channels before landing on a hockey game. Sadly, the only other piece of furniture I have is a folding chair that I usually only need for poker games.

Being the older brother, I *could* make Joe get up out of *my* chair, but I don't. There's something about watching your brother, your only best friend, lose his wife that makes you a bit softer, less of a jerk.

When he gets up to get his third beer in less than fifteen minutes, I can tell he's in no mood for talking. I can understand why, so I make the switch to water so I can drive him home later.

Having to bury your wife somehow earns you the right to get shit-faced. His world flipped upside down since Becca died right after Christmas.

For starters, Becca's estranged son came home after not seeing her for years. They made amends just before she died. I know that's something Joe's happy with; he wanted to see Becca lay those grudges to rest before she died.

All that shit – pain and sorrow – honestly, they're too much for me to deal with. No one understands it. I mean there's nothing to understand. Nothing about watching someone you tried to save die anyway, makes any sense.

With this thought in mind, I lean back in my chair and watch the puck glide effortlessly over the ice.

"Katie all settled?" I ask when a commercial interrupts the tied game.

Joe scrubs a hand over his face. "Yeah. I think so. I mean I heard from her the other day, after we moved her in. She seems okay."

There's another shit storm, another perfect example of why getting married was never something that seemed all that tempting to me. Something about a bipolar-turned-junkie, sleeping around on you with other addicts, who hit on your ten-year-old daughter, just doesn't scream "happily ever after" to me.

"That's good. Is she still coming home this weekend for your birthday?" We just helped her get settled into her dorm last weekend, so I'm not sure she's already planning on coming home so soon.

"Not sure. I didn't make a big deal out of it. She just got back so I didn't want to stress her out with my birthday." Mental note: call Katie and get her home so Joe doesn't have to spend his first birthday without Becca completely alone.

Joe and I spend the next hour or so watching the end of the game and I drive him home around nine.

Parking in the spot labeled 2B, I scrub my hand over my face and stare out into the black sky before getting out of my truck.

"Some fucking life," I huff flippantly, before getting out and walking up to the condo where no one is waiting for me.

Since I don't own much, it doesn't take me long to unpack. Not surprisingly, most of the stuff is for the kitchen anyway. Just as I'm crushing up the last box, the phone rings.

"Hey, Katie."

"Hey, Uncle Ev. I got your message last night. Of course, I'm coming home for Dad's birthday. Where else would I be?" Her chipper voice brightens my otherwise dull day.

I shrug my shoulders, even though I know she can't see me. "That's good. I think your dad could use the company."

So could I, too.

"Cool. I have class until eleven this morning, and then I'll come to your place. I got you a house-warming gift."

"You didn't have to, Katie. But that sounds good. I'll see you around three then. We'll go pick up something for dinner and surprise him. Sound okay?"

"Sounds great." Just as I'm about to say goodbye, she stutters over her words, sounding like she's searching for the right thing to say. "Umm… Uncle Evan… I just…"

"What's the matter, Katie? Is everything okay?" As much as I know she wants to be away on her own and experience college and all that, I can't say I don't worry about her. And right now, she sounds like something is really wrong.

"Yeah, I'm okay." I hear her take a deep breath through the line. I can tell something is bothering her. She's always been my little girl, the daughter I never had, and I hate to hear her upset.

"Then what is it?"

"I just wanted to say thank you; that's all," she says quickly, sounding like she's afraid to let her emotions get the best of her.

"For what?"

"Everything. Helping me move in. Moving from the city to be by Dad, taking care of him. For just being you, I guess." Her voice is quiet and soft.

"I'm just doing what's right, Katie." That's all I've ever tried to do and I smile knowing that it's appreciated.

"I know. And I just wanted to say thank you for it. It'll be good for Dad, having you around now."

"I hope so. I'll talk to you later, then."

She says goodbye and hangs up, leaving me feeling a little bit more excited for the weekend than I was before. Honestly, if it wasn't for her coming home and for Joe's birthday, I'd have a whole lot of nothing filling up my agenda.

"So what's on the menu for this evening, Chef?" Katie jokes, looping her arm through mine as we walk into the local Wegmans around four in the afternoon to do some food shopping.

"Well, what's your dad's favorite?" I grab a cart and walk toward the produce section. This place is a far cry from the specialty markets where I used to shop in Manhattan, but I guess I'll have to get used to it.

"How about something fancy? It's his fiftieth birthday, after all." Shit, had I really forgotten that?

"Okay, I've got just the thing then." I toss some vegetables and potatoes in the cart as I mentally run through the list of ingredients I'll need to make Joe's dinner.

A few aisles later, Katie grabs a few cans of soup and tosses them in the cart. "So, do you miss it already?" she asks, taking over control of the cart.

"Huh? Miss what?" I add a few cans of beef stock to make some gravy.

"Work. The firehouse. Do you miss it since you retired?" Walking past the ramen noodles, she loads up and gives me the 'don't start with me' look. I know she's a college kid, but this food sucks. I don't think you can even call it food.

"You know that's crap, right?"

"Yes, I do, but I'm in college and it's cheap. And you're avoiding." She stops the cart in front of an end-cap of chips and dip. "Do you miss it?"

Persistent little bugger. Katie never was one to give up once she put her mind to something. It's nice to see that hasn't changed.

"Yes and no." She rolls her eyes at me, clearly thinking I'm still trying to avoid her question. "What? It's the truth," I defend, shrugging my shoulders. We make our way toward the cereal and I figure I might as well talk. We've got a bunch more aisles to make our way around and the silence will just get uncomfortable.

"I do miss it. I miss the guys. They were like my family, especially since you and your dad lived so far away. Besides, if it wasn't for that job, I wouldn't know how to cook like I do." I nudge her in the arm and she cracks a smile.

"You are a pretty great cook." Walking along the back wall of the supermarket, I stop at the butcher's counter and place my order. When I turn back to Katie, she has a serious look on her face. "What makes you not miss it?"

I want to say, *"I don't miss it because thinking about the brothers we lost, about the lives I couldn't save, about the lung cancer I battled for years because I spent weeks upon weeks digging through buildings that were destroyed by some crazy, evil terrorists. That I don't miss it because of the nightmares that would keep me up at night – that still haunt my sleep some nights – because of the family I could never have because of my commitment to my job."* But instead of all of that, I simply say, "I don't miss it because if I was still there, I couldn't be here, helping you and your dad."

I think she can tell that's not the entire truth, but instead of pushing, she just leans up on her toes and plants a kiss on my cheek just as the butcher brings out my order. He wraps the roast in a bag and I place it in the cart.

"Cake. We need a cake." Katie spins toward the bakery; the smile on her face clearly intent on lightening the mood. And it does just that.

"I'll meet you there. I forgot something a few aisles back." I make my way to get some milk for the scalloped potatoes. They were Mom's specialty and I know Joe will appreciate them. Even though I learned a lot from cooking at the firehouse, my true inspiration came from my mom.

Turning toward the bakery, I see Katie talking with another woman. I recognize her instantly. Her long brown hair falls over her shoulders in soft curls. She must have come here straight from work because she's wearing a slate-grey business skirt that shows off her curves. Her black heels make her legs go on forever – she looks...well, if I were a teenage boy, I would say she looks hot. But I'm anything but a teenage boy, so I'll go with sleek and sophisticated – and hot, too. When Katie sees me approach from over the woman's shoulder, she smiles mischievously and I can already tell what's going through her mind.

"Uncle Evan, you remember..." Katie starts to make introductions, but none are needed.

"Lucy." Her name sounds like silk as it tumbles from my mouth. She turns to face me when she hears my voice.

A warm smile spreads across her face. It's the kind of full smile that reaches her eyes, making the blue color there seem even more vibrant than I remember it being.

"Hi, Evan. It's good to see you again." Her voice is soft and feminine, pretty, just like I remember it.

"You too." Mine is thick, stuck in my throat.

"Katie tells me that you moved up here. Finally had enough of the city life, huh?" she jokes, shifting the weight of her hand-basket to get a better grip. Damn, she must think I'm some kind of liar. I wasn't at the time. I had no idea I'd be living up here a month ago.

"Yeah, something like that."

Katie laughs from behind Lucy. "Don't let him fool you. He's retired now." Katie seems proud of herself for sharing that piece of information for me. She knows I would never offer it up on my own.

Great! Nothing screams 'old man' like "retired".

"Congratulations, Evan. That's great." Her eyes crinkle softly in the corners as kindness permeates her features.

It's not really. I had to because my lungs are shot. If it was up to me, I'd never leave the job. It's the only life I know.

Again, my words from a month ago come back to me, and I can't help but think she must see me as some kind of bullshit artist. When we last spoke, I told her I was on medical leave – that much was true.

"Uncle Evan and I were just getting a few things for Dad's birthday party tonight." Katie drops a chocolate mousse cake into the cart and turns to grab some candles from the rack next to it.

"How's he doing?" Lucy asks me in a confidential tone as Katie walks away from us to grab a container of chocolate chip cookies. That girl has a serious sweet tooth.

"All things considered, he's okay. I'm just glad I could be here to help him out." I shrug my shoulders and nervously rearrange the produce in the top of the shopping cart.

Katie walks up behind Lucy and makes a kissy face. I smirk and laugh on the outside. On the inside, I can't help but wonder what it would feel like to kiss Lucy's full lips.

Those same lips are pulling into a goofy smile right now as Lucy follows my gaze to Katie still making the kissy face behind her back.

"Why don't you come over, Lucy? I know Dad would love to see you and I think Reid and Maddy said they were going to stop by for cake at least." Katie's invitation dangles in the air, like bait waiting to be taken by a fish.

Lucy shifts the weight of her hand basket once again. "Oh, I don't know, Katie. I don't want to intrude."

"Stop. You're not intruding, right, Uncle Evan?" Hell, if I can see through Katie's intentions, I'm pretty sure Lucy can. But, spending more time with Lucy would make for an even better night, so I have to be sure to thank Katie for her antics later.

"Not at all, we'd love to have you join us." I take her basket from her hands and put it in the cart. "We're ready to check out. Did you need anything else?" I look into her basket – a few frozen meals, men's soap – so much for her being single. That tiny bubble of hope – a hope for something more – pops.

"Yeah, I'm all set." All three of us walk to the check out together. Katie and Lucy chat animatedly about Katie's return to school.

Even though she's been there before, Katie gives Lucy the address and phone number to Joe's house. "Oh, and here's another number, just in case." Katie rattles off seven very familiar digits. My ears must be fooling me because I *think* that Katie just gave Lucy *my* cell phone number.

We walk out to the parking lot and Lucy points to the opposite end of the lot. "I'm over there." She reaches into the cart and grabs her two bags. "I'll see you guys later." Smiling, she waves as she walks away.

As Katie and I walk toward my truck, I pull a face at Katie and she looks at me. "What?" she asks, feigning innocence.

"Get in the car." I chuckle as Katie sticks her tongue out at me. As I load the groceries in the back of the truck, I can't help but smile at the turn of events.

A month ago, I was more than happy with the idea that I would be alone. Now, I'm not so sure that alone is where I want to be.

February 1, 2013

CHAPTER TEN
Lucy

"What the hell am I doing?" I kill the ignition on the car and huff at no one in particular. "Calm down. It's just dinner and birthday cake," I coach myself out of the car and up the small walkway to Joe's house. With my hand an inch away from the door, I take a deep breath and try my best to shake away any unease I'm feeling.

Before I can even knock, the door opens.

"Hey, Lucy." My God, his voice, it does things to me.

"Hi, Evan," I choke out as my words get caught in my throat.

"Come in. Let me take your coat." Evan extends his hand to the side, letting me walk past him. The scent of his cologne fills my senses – clean and kind of citrusy, but purely male. As he slides my jacket off my shoulders, his thumbs graze my neck and shoulders – unintentionally I'm sure. But the shivers that race across my skin are there nonetheless.

"Can I get you a drink?" he offers politely, a casual grin pulling at his lips.

"Sure. Let me come in and help you." I follow behind him into the kitchen. I didn't notice at the grocery store earlier, since he was wearing a bulky winter coat, but his broad shoulders are muscled and strong. His biceps fill the sleeves of his navy-blue FDNY t-shirt. And those jeans, well, they should be illegal – snug in all the right places. And call me crazy, but the dish towel casually draped over his shoulder, because he's busy cooking for his brother, makes him look even more delicious than any amount of tight denim ever will.

"Red or white?"

"Huh…what…oh, wine? Red please." He pulls down a glass and opens the bottle with ease before sliding the glass over to me across the island countertop between us.

"Where's Joe and Katie?" Having spent the last few minutes focusing entirely on Evan, I'm just now realizing that the house is empty.

"She took Joe out shopping for his birthday present. They should be back soon." Turning away from me, he squats down to check whatever is in the oven.

I definitely do not check out his tight ass.

"Smells amazing. What are you making?" I take a sip of my wine and twirl the stem between my fingers.

"Just a roast and some potatoes. Nothing too special." He drags the towel off his shoulders and wipes his hands.

"Well, it beats a frozen dinner or take-out."

"Yeah, I saw those in your basket earlier. You don't cook much then, huh?" He pulls out some lettuce, tomatoes and cucumbers for a salad. That I can help with. I grab a knife from the block on the counter, stand next to him and start cutting the tomato.

"Nah. I mean, now that Melanie is back at school, there isn't anyone to cook for."

"You mean it's just you?" There's surprise and a touch of misunderstanding in his voice.

"Yeah, Maddy just moved in with Reid, so who else would there be?" I'm confused by his tone.

"Nothing, forget it." He dismisses, but all I'm left with is the idea that he thought there was someone else in my life.

A touch of tension fills the space between us. Then, I think back to exactly what was in my shopping basket earlier.

"The soap? That's what made you think I'm not alone." His knife stops mid-slice and he turns to me.

"Uh, yeah. I mean unless you secretly like to smell like a man, I can't imagine another reason."

My cheeks turn pink, both at being caught buying men's soap and at his misunderstanding of it. Call me crazy, but he seems a little disappointed at the prospect of me having a man in my life.

"It was my husband's soap." I put my knife down and sprinkle the chopped tomatoes on top of the salad.

"Was?"

Sipping my wine, I take in the mix of emotions on Evan's rugged face. Confusion and concern are mixed with the smallest hint of relief. That last piece of information makes me smile around the rim of my glass.

"Yes, was. Jimmy passed away eighteen years ago. It's been just me ever since."

"Oh." He continues his slicing and chopping, seemingly uncomfortable with what I've told him.

After a few long moments of salad making go by, the oven-timer beeps. Evan slides on some oven mitts and takes the roast out.

"Wow, Evan. That looks amazing. I haven't had a home-cooked meal like this is forever." I hope that my compliments, which are not empty at all, help to ease some of the awkwardness.

After he places the roast on a serving tray and tents it with some foil, he leans back against the counter, extending his legs in front of him and crossing them at the ankles. Taking a healthy swallow of his beer, I watch the muscles of his neck move, more than a little interested. Everything about him is strong and muscled; watching him move to put the beer down on the counter is like watching a work of art in motion. I let my eyes linger on his hands for a moment as they wrap tightly around the neck of his beer bottle. Briefly, I imagine what those rough and calloused fingers would feel like on my skin.

"You said ever since. You mean in all that time you never got remarried or anything like that? That there's really no one right now?" His words have suddenly taken on an accusatory tone.

"Why would I lie? No, I never got remarried." I take another sip of my wine, a little liquid courage before revealing my little secret. "I was getting the soap because I was feeling lonely, okay? It reminds me of him, makes me feel better, so every now and then, I buy his soap." Jerk. I chug back the last large gulp of my wine and with unsteady hands struggle to remove the cork wedged in the top of the opened bottle of wine.

Evan is by my side in an instant. He puts his hand at the small of my back, the heat permeating through the thin fabric of my blouse. "I'm sorry. I didn't mean to be an ass." He uncorks the bottle with ease. "I've been lied to before." He scrubs a hand over his face as his admission falls from his mouth. "And, it was more about me not believing that you've been alone all this time than thinking that you were lying to me about a bar of soap." He pours my wine for me, and when I take it from his hand, our fingers meet for an instant. Mine graze over his, heat passing between us. He shifts his finger from under mine and gently rubs it across mine, which was just on top of his. It's a slight movement, but it's enough to set loose a swarm of butterflies in my belly.

Needing to redirect the conversation, I ask what else is for dinner. I get lost in the smooth yet gruff lull of his voice. The animated way in which he talks about cooking is hypnotizing. It's also pretty sweet of him to want to do all of this for his brother.

When he pulls the bubbling-over-with-cheesy-goodness potatoes out of the oven, my stomach actually grumbles aloud. "You're putting my Lean Cuisine's to shame."

"I can't believe you eat that garbage," he scoffs as he pulls some plates down from the cabinet.

"One," I hold up a finger as I begin my counting off, "like I said, it's just me so all of the extra food would go to waste. Two, I can't cook like this." I tip my chin at the spread he's laid out before us. "And three, I suck at cooking." The last one gets a loud laugh out of him and me too.

"Maybe I could teach you to cook one day." The laughter falls to silence as I consider his offer. Something tells me he would be a wonderful teacher. But something also tells me it would be more than dangerous – in a good way – to be in a room as small as a kitchen with Evan for more than a few minutes.

Just like now.

Linda's words about giving myself a chance at happiness ring loudly in my ear.

"I'd like that," I mutter quickly as I take another sip of wine. "I go shopping every Friday night on my way home from work. We could go next week."

I'm not sure if it's Katie and Joe coming through the front door that makes him answer quickly, but the abrupt "yes" that falls from his lips surprises me.

I feel like a giddy teenager. I have a date. Can you call this a date? Or is it just a nice guy doing a lame old maid a favor?

Joe and Katie's playful bickering disrupts my thoughts. "I'm never letting you drive again."

"I am not a bad driver," Katie defends as Joe gives her the parental death-ray stare. I nearly spit out my wine. I've given Melanie the same look many times.

"Wow, Uncle Ev, this looks amazing." Evan glows at the compliment. His smile reaches his grey eyes as deep laugh lines crinkle in the corners.

He catches me staring and I smile back at him; an exchange of some kind passes between us.

The doorbell rings and Katie lets Maddy and Reid in. Maddy hugs me tightly when she sees me. "We were so happy when Katie called today to tell us you were coming." Maddy wraps her arm around my waist, as if she's missed me in the few days since she's moved out of my home. I've missed her too, but seeing the way Reid watches her every movement, the way his eyes light as she talks, filling me in on her most recent doctor's appointment, I know she's in the right place.

"Reid, you look so grown up. A shirt and tie works nicely for you." I walk over to him and give him a hug and a quick kiss on the cheek.

"Thanks." He loosens the knot at his neck and drapes his suit jacket over the back of a chair. "It's taking some getting used to, but it's not too bad."

Joe grabs a few beers out of the fridge and hands one to Reid. "You think you'll be there long term, son?"

"I'm not sure, Joe. Dylan said there's a possibility the internship could turn into a full-time spot, but I guess I'll just have to wait and see. But even if I don't end up staying there, it's definitely what I want to do with my career." Maddy watches him talk about his job with a bright smile pulling at her lips. He just started working at a counseling center with the Gay-Straight Alliance with Dylan, a long-lost childhood friend with whom he's only been reacquainted.

"That's great, Reid. Really great. Your mom would be real proud." Joe chugs back a few sips of beer and Reid joins in doing the same, both struggling with their raw emotions.

Katie breaks the sadness by delegating tasks. Setting the table, carrying out the food, filling drinks – the girl is in command. Just as I knew it would be, the food is delicious. We all chat and laugh through the meal. Evan occasionally ribs on his brother for turning the big five – oh.

Other than holidays, I can't remember the last time I was surrounded by this many people for meals. It's odd how just the other day I was complaining about having no one around and now, here I am, surrounded by some really amazing people.

We all sing Joe "Happy Birthday" and he opens a few presents. Katie got him some new shirts earlier when they went out, knowing he wouldn't get them unless she *made* him go. Maddy and Reid got him a gift certificate to a local sporting goods store. Evan enrolled him in a Beer of the Month club. When I slide a card over to Joe, Evan gives me an odd look.

"You didn't have to get me anything, Lucy," Joe protests as he takes the card from me.

"It's not much, but it's your birthday, so of course I had to get you something."

"Well, thank you." Joe grins as he pulls out the Over the Hill lottery tickets. It was more about the card and offering him someone to talk to if he ever needed it; the lottery tickets were just an afterthought.

Evan, who is sitting next to me, leans over and whispers in my ear, "That was really thoughtful of you." His hot breath on my ear sets those damn butterflies swirling in my belly again. Blood pounds in my ears and my cheeks heat yet again. Feeling my face flush with heat, I quickly scan around the table, making sure that no one else has seen us. Maddy winks at me and smiles coyly; so much for going unnoticed

After the cake is all done, Maddy and Reid decide to head home and Katie goes out for the night to meet up with some friends. Joe tries to help clean up, but Evan refuses, telling him that it's his birthday and that he should go into the living room and relax. Joe, who looks more than a little drained, takes Evan up on the offer. Flopping down into his recliner, he clicks through the channels and enjoys another beer.

I help clear the rest of the dishes and join Evan in the kitchen. He cooked, so the least I can do is help clean.

It doesn't have anything to do with wanting to spend a little more time with him.

Alone.

Nope, not at all.

"You wash and I'll dry?" I offer as I grab the dishtowel from his shoulder.

"Sure." He smirks at me, but keeps his attention on the mound of dishes before him.

Now that we're alone again, I can ask him something that's been on my mind since he told me about his retirement earlier at the grocery store. "How's your shoulder?"

"What?" He looks over at me, as if the words I've just spoken were in another language.

"Your shoulder. At Becca's funeral, you said you were on leave because of a shoulder injury, and then the next time I see you, you're retired."

"I didn't exactly plan on seeing you again." His words gut me in a way I wasn't expecting. He didn't think he'd see me, so he lied?

"Oh." I let the sound of the water swishing around fill the air, choosing to bite back my hurt.

He hands me the last of the dishes and pulls another towel from the small drawer to his side. After he dries his hands, he leans back against the counter, crossing his arms over his broad chest. There is absolutely nothing about the way Evan looks that would ever indicate that he's retired.

"How old are you, anyway?"

"It had nothing to do with…"

We both speak at the same time, our words running together.

He scrubs his hand over his stubbled jaw and I notice slight traces of grey there. Pulling my eyes up to his hairline, I notice some grey there too – streaking at his temple, but nowhere else, really. He's got the whole 'George Clooney' look going for him. A silver fox as Linda would call it.

"I'm fifty two." He scans my face for some kind of reaction, but the only one he'll find there is surprise.

"That's pretty young to be retired."

"Yeah, it is, but I didn't have a choice." The tension in his words suggests I've touched on a sore topic; one he apparently doesn't want to get into.

When he doesn't say anything right away, I walk over to the small coat room at the back of the kitchen. Gathering my things, I take a deep breath and wish I could rewind the last ten minutes. Me and my big mouth. Just because we flirted a few times tonight doesn't give me the right to dive into his personal life. Though, he did dive into mine. How'd this get so complicated?

When I re-enter the kitchen, Evan is still leaning up against the counter, a tormented look plastered to his face.

"All right, I'm going to go." I make no mention of what's supposed to be our date slash cooking lesson next week. If he wants to do it, then I'll let him be the one to mention it. Just as I'm at the arched entryway of the kitchen, his low voice calls me back into the room.

"It wasn't my shoulder. It was my lungs." I stop in my tracks and turn on my heel.

"What?"

"I was on medical leave for my lungs. I had cancer, and even though it was in remission, I couldn't be on the job full time. The medical office made me take leave while they ran some more tests." His words sound rehearsed, as if he's had them prepared for a long time — maybe since he saw me earlier.

"Cancer? Oh, God, Evan. I had no idea." My hand covers my mouth, as if it will cover my concern.

He sits at the small kitchen table and I sit next to him. My hand immediately falls to his leg, a simple gesture of sympathy that catches him off-guard.

"I never meant to lie to you about it. It's just that I really had no intention of retiring. But when the tests came back, I didn't have a choice." Before his hand falls to cover mine, he rakes it through his hair roughly then across his face. "It was from 9/11," he adds quickly, as if he's trying to erase the memory.

"Evan…" I gasp and my words stick in my throat.

"I wasn't there when it happened, but I was at Ground Zero a lot in the months that followed. All that shit got into my lungs, and now I don't have enough lung capacity, even after all the cancer was gone, to stay on the job. I got the results after Becca's funeral. When I told Joe about it, he joked that I should move up here with him. The idea of being alone no longer had the same appeal as it did when I was younger, so I took him up on the offer and here I am."

We both must have forgotten that my hand is on his leg because we both look at it at the same time. Just as I'm about to pull it away, he takes my hand in his. It's calloused and rough, large and warm. He strokes his thumb over my wrist, a simple gesture that sets my heart beating like crazy.

"When you brought it up, you caught me by surprise. I would have told you next week. I promise." Something about the way he just said the word promise lets me know that he's serious.

"So then, we're still on for our..." I stumble over my words, not knowing what he considers it before settling on "cooking lesson?"

"It's a date. Unless you'd rather eat microwave dinners forever?" He's still holding my hand. My heart's still racing. And when he winks at me, it crashes into my ribs.

We sit there for a few more moments; the silence no longer tense and awkward. "Well, I should get going. It's kind of late."

"I'll walk you out." He lets me walk in front of him, through the living room where Joe is lightly snoring.

Before opening the door and letting the cold February air blast us with its chill, Evan leans up against the frame. "I'm glad you could make it tonight." His words are sincere and honest. They're a far cry from the defensiveness and anger that was there just a few minutes ago when I asked him about his shoulder.

"Thank you for having me. And thank you for sharing your story with me. It was rude of me to bring it up. I really didn't mean to upset you," I ramble.

He shakes his head and chuckles lightly. "Lucy, I laid into you about the soap you buy to remind you of your late husband, yet *you're* apologizing for being rude? Please, if anyone is in the wrong, it's me."

I don't know what to say to that; his honesty disarms me in a way I never knew possible. He looks behind me, out the front window. "It's starting to snow. I should drive you in case the roads get bad."

"I've driven in worse. I'll be fine." Pulling on my jacket and gloves, he still looks uneasy about letting me drive myself home. "Seriously, Evan, I'll be fine."

"Can you at least let me know that you got home okay? Call me? Or text me even?"

"I will. I promise." I secure the last button and wrap my scarf around my neck. "Goodnight, Evan."

"Night, Lucy." His eyes twinkle like the stars in the clear but still-snowing sky. Before I can even realize what he's doing, he leans down and plants an innocent kiss on my cheek.

When I arrive home, my skin is still buzzing where Evan's lips were. I even consider not washing my face before going to bed, wanting to ghost my fingers over the same spot he kissed knowing some essence of his lips is still there. My God, his lips – they are the perfect combination of soft and firm, sweet and rough. I try to convince myself that my heated reaction is because I haven't been kissed in forever, but that's definitely not the case.

Not wanting to make him worry any longer, I text him the second I walk in the door.

His reply is immediate.

OK.

I said immediate, not poetic. Brushing away my irrational thoughts, I take off my jacket and lock the door behind me. Heading up the stairs to my room, my phone buzzes in my hand.

> Sorry. Was getting out of the shower. Glad you made it home okay. Can't wait 'til next week.

My mind is suddenly flooded with images of Evan's muscles dotted with water, a towel secured tightly at his waist. My mouth goes dry at that thought – then my conscience weighs in, telling me I'm crazy to be thinking those things.

Brushing thoughts of a just-showered Evan out of my mind, I type back a quick response before getting ready for bed.

> Me too. Meet you there at 5? What are we making?

> 5 it is. And it's a surprise ;) G'nite, Lucy.

I can't help the dorky smile that spreads across my face thinking about Evan texting me a winky face. Unable to let it go, I joke in my response.

> Did you just winky face me?

> I guess I did. You can blame Katie for that ;)

That bit of information, that he's close enough with his college-aged niece to text her, makes my heart warm to him even more.

> I think it's cute, so I'll thank her rather than blame her. Going to bed now. Nite, Evan.

> Nite. Sweet dreams.

Smiling goofily, I can't resist the bait. I quickly type out,

> Is that more of Katie's influence showing?

Again, his response is immediate and I wonder if he's smiling like a fool at the thought of texting back and forth at ten at night.

Nope, that one was all me. See you Friday.

I fall asleep easily – thoughts of Evan and our upcoming date lulling me away into a vivid dreamland of which I never thought I would ever have the chance to experience.

February 8, 2013

CHAPTER ELEVEN

Evan

Parked outside of Wegman's at ten to five on Friday afternoon, scanning the lot for Lucy's white Corolla, makes me feel more like a stalker than a guy waiting to go food shopping. Shaking away the crazy, I see her pull into the lot and a bubble of excitement fills my chest.

I haven't had a date – if this is even considered that – in forever.

She pulls down my row and catches sight of my truck. She waves as she pulls into the spot next to me. I get out of my truck, wanting to at least be a gentleman and open her door for her. Luckily, the snow that fell last week has all been washed away because I'd hate to see her have to navigate through the slush in those heels.

Okay, I have a thing for legs and it's impossible to miss hers as she steps out of her car. They're sleek and athletic, but fucking sexy as sin. Lost in my gaze, I imagine running my fingertips up her thighs as she curls her calves around my waist.

"Hi," I croak, pushing my erotic musings aside for a bit. I keep it simple – manage not to sound like an idiot. Like last week.

"Hi to you, too." Her smile is just so bright and warm that I can't help but smile back.

The snow may have been washed away, but it's still colder than fuck out here. We walk against the wind into the store. I grab a cart and we fall in step like we've been shopping together many times before.

"So…" Her words are tinged with a bit of awkwardness and unease.

We round the corner of the produce section and I head toward the salad. "So I thought we would start with a salad. You seemed to be able to handle that last week." I nudge her arm with my elbow and the unease is gone.

"Wise ass." She elbows me back and grabs a few items, placing them in the top basket of the cart. "Yes, I can make a salad; usually, I just get the kind in the bag. What else is on the menu?" she asks casually, but it almost sounds like she's a bit nervous.

"I figured we could start out with something simple. Something you could make on your own, if you wanted to." I grab a few more produce items and make my way over to grab pasta.

"How does pasta primavera with chicken francaise sound?" I toss some angel hair in the cart and she looks up at me almost terrified.

"Sounds like it's perfect for me to screw up," she jokes and scrunches her face at me.

"Don't worry. I'm a good teacher. I won't let you mess it up." Her face relaxes a little and we make our way through the rest of the market.

As she fills me in on the project she was just recently assigned at work, she talks animatedly, clearly excited about the prospect of helping kids. Unfortunately, I can't contribute much to the work topic.

"Are you all settled in your new place?" she asks as we approach the checkout.

"Pretty much. Got a few pieces of furniture delivered this week so I'm mostly set now." Another topic that I don't have much to contribute to. Unless me describing my white-walled and bare condo has recently been added to the list of really exciting things to talk about.

She offers to pay, which of course I refuse. "Thank you, Evan," she finally concedes as we walk back out into the lot. She tells me to follow her to her house and I do, committing the directions to memory on the way.

On the short drive to her place, I give myself the mental pep talk that I obviously need. I want tonight to go well. Despite all the talk of dead husbands and lung cancer last week, it seemed to me like we hit it off. That doesn't mean she felt that way and the nervousness with which things started out at the grocery store would suggest that maybe she doesn't feel like things are going well at all.

She pulls into her garage in front of me, the automatic door sliding up a bit unevenly – looks like it could use a few tweaks to make it work more smoothly. But despite that, even from the driveway, I can tell her house is a home. The soft green siding is offset by black shutters, and even in the winter, there are a few small bushes to keep the front garden looking inviting and well maintained.

She walks out of the garage and steps in front of me as we make our way up the front steps. After unlocking the door, she holds it opened for me as I walk past her, my hands filled with the bags of groceries.

"Kitchen's right through there," she directs me and hangs her coat up. The kitchen is small and perhaps a little outdated, but after cooking in restaurant grade firehouse kitchens for the last twenty plus years, even I can admit that I'm a bit spoiled.

"Can I take your jacket? Get you something to drink?"

"Yes and yes. Thanks, Lucy."

I unload the groceries and poke my head into the pantry to pull out some spices and a few staples that I assumed she would have.

"Here you go." She slides a beer over to me.

"Funny. I don't remember these being in the cart." I twist open the cap and take a sip.

"I stopped the other day and picked them up for you. They were what you had a Joe's last week so I hope I got the right kind." She shrugs her shoulders, that nervousness from before returning.

"Thanks, that was…nice of you." I stumble over my words a little, mainly because it's been so long since someone's done something nice for me — even if it's something as simple as remembering what kind of beer I drink.

"I'm going to go change real quick. I'll be right back, okay?" I nod and she pads away from me.

When it's just me in the kitchen, I lean up against the counter and scrub a hand over my face and through my hair. I need to pull this together. It shouldn't be too difficult to make dinner with someone who I've already spent time with and gotten along with. But apparently, it's more difficult than you would think.

Maybe it'll get easier once we start cooking.

When I hear her soft footsteps coming down the stairs and back into the kitchen, I grab a large pot for the pasta and fill it with water.

"Put me to work," she jokes as she rolls up the long sleeve of her light pink thermal t-shirt. A shirt that clings to her body in all the right places. Speaking becomes impossible as I take in how she looks. Her hair is pulled up into a loose ponytail. The few strands that hang freely about her face make it look sexy and not at all sloppy. Even though I'm mourning the loss of being able to look at her legs, the jeans she's changed into leave very little to the imagination in the way of her curves. Everything about her is soft and feminine, pretty and delicate.

"Hello? You in there somewhere?" Snapping her fingers in front of my face, I wonder how long I just zoned out for.

"Sorry, I was just running through the checklist in my head." Sidestepped that one, but the blush on her face suggests that she knows what I was really doing.

I hand her a cutting board and slide over the salad and vegetables. "Prove you can handle this, and I'll promote you." I wink and she elbows me.

"That's low. Insulting me in my own kitchen." There it is – the light, flirtation that was there last week, and even last month. It helps me relax and smile broadly over at her.

We talk about little things – how Melanie and Katie are both adjusting to college life. Lucy's face absolutely glows with pride as she talks about Melanie. It's not difficult to understand why – the girl sounds pretty amazing, even if the description is coming from a slightly biased source.

"Salad's all done. Now what?" Grabbing a small towel, she wipes her hands clean and sets the bowl of salad to the side.

"Not bad." I inspect her work. "Next up is the squash and zucchini for the pasta."

I demonstrate how to cut everything into uniform pieces to make sure everything cooks within the same time frame. When I've got about half of the zucchini done, she looks up at me with rapt attention. "I can totally do that."

I step out of the way and let her take her station at the cutting board. I watch her for a few moments, making sure she's doing okay, before stepping away to get another cutting board out for the chicken.

"Shit!" Her curse makes me smack my head on the underside of the counter.

"What happened?" I rush over to her side and see that she's nicked her finger.

"It's nothing." She tries to shoo me away, but it's definitely not nothing.

"Let me take a look." Taking her small hand in mine, I inspect her sliced thumb. "It doesn't look like it'll need stitches." I grab the dishrag and wrap it on her finger. "Here, keep some pressure on it and I'll get you bandaged up in a second."

She nods quickly and tells me where the bathroom is.

After pulling some first aid supplies out of the bathroom, I come back down stairs and kneel before her as she sits in a kitchen chair. I clean it and get it all wrapped up before looking up at her. Smiling, I tease, "You were *supposed* to chop the veggies, not your fingers."

She quirks an eyebrow at me. "Finger, not fingers. At least give me that much credit."

Looking over at the cutting board, I cringe. "So much for those, huh?" I quickly clean up the mess and scan the cabinet for at least a jar of sauce of something to salvage the pasta part of the dinner. She wasn't kidding when she said she doesn't cook much. I figure I can do something with the chicken to make a sauce, so I start the pasta and get everything out for the chicken.

I slide a plate of flour in front of Lucy and show her how to coat the chicken so I can sauté it.

"*This* I can handle." She laughs.

After she's done with the first one, I lay it in the pan carefully and she looks on in awe as is sizzles in the pan.

"Can I try this one?" She holds a floured cutlet in her hand and she looks so intent on proving that she can do something.

"Sure, just go slow. Don't want to add a burn to the list of injuries for the night."

"Oh, stop it!"

"Did you just roll your eyes at me?"

"Maybe. I could do it again if you missed it."

"Just put the chicken in the pan already." I watch as she carefully does as she's told and we both stare wide-eyed as the bandage that I *thought* was secured to her thumb, effortlessly slides off and into the pan.

Her hand flies to cover her mouth. "Shoot. I'm so sorry, Evan." Trying to fish the Band-Aid out proves to be pointless as it sizzles and pops in the hot oil.

I turn off the burner and set it to the side. "Maybe you *are* better off with microwave dinners," I tease and she's has the good sense to laugh.

"I can't believe I ruined the meal."

"I would offer to make something else, but you really have nothing here. Seriously, Lucy, you need to stock up on some basics."

Why? Because I plan to cook for her more often?

"I can fix it." She stands with renewed energy and I wonder what the hell she has in mind. Really, nothing can be salvaged. It looks like we'll be feasting on salad. *Yum.* And yes, that was sarcasm.

A loud chuckle slips out as I overhear her place an order for pizza delivery. She covers the mouthpiece and asks, "Pepperoni or mushrooms?"

"Both." I laugh again and take the last sip of my beer.

"See? I can do more than microwave." Hands on her hips and everything, she looks adorable – so much so that I have to smile at her.

We've got the kitchen cleaned up just as the pizza arrives. What I had hoped to be a … well, I'm not really sure what I hoped for tonight to be, but I hadn't intended pizza on paper plates while watching TV.

We get situated on the couch and I scan the living room, taking in the cozy hominess that fills the room. "You ever use that?" I tip my chin at a beautiful brick façade fireplace that's in the corner of the room.

"Um, no. Definitely not." She huffs a small laugh.

"You maintain it though, right?" I may be retired, but the firefighter in me will always put safety first. "I mean they need to be cleaned and all that. You need to be safe with it."

"Yes, sir," she jokes and I realize maybe I'm being a little over the top. Just because she's on her own, doesn't mean that she's an invalid. Patting my arm, she smiles up at me. "I get it inspected every year; don't worry. They were just here the other day, actually. I was thinking of getting it closed up, since I never use it."

Now talk about a waste. What I wouldn't give to have something like this in my place. Hell, my condo has nothing in it that screams of "home".

"Oh, I love this movie." She settles on *Forrest Gump* as I grab my second slice.

"So, you already know about my history. What about you? Have you ever been married?" Forrest's proposal to Jenny plays in the background.

"No. I mean, I've had a few relationships here and there, but work always got in the way. Staying single was somehow easier."

"Same here. I mean, when Melanie was a kid, it was much easier to just focus on that part of my life."

"Now?" I hazard a question that takes even me by surprise.

She puts her plate down on the coffee table and swallows back a large sip of water. "Now, I'm not so sure."

Suddenly, my mind races with the possibilities of what her words mean. It's crazy to think how just a few encounters with Lucy have made me re-evaluate my feelings. Obviously, she feels the same way. A calm and peaceful air falls on us as a small smile curls at my lips.

A comfortable silence fills the space as we watch the movie, recalling some memories when certain scenes come up.

Nothing prepares me for Lucy's reaction when Jenny and Forrest get married and she tells him she's sick. I try not to look at her, wanting to avoid making her feel like she's in the spotlight or anything like that. I do notice a few stray tears streaking down her cheeks so I can only imagine what's to come.

As we watch Forrest sitting beside Jenny's grave, reading a letter from their son, Lucy reaches for a napkin. Clutching it to her chest, I can see her breathing rapidly. What were just a few tears earlier is now a steady stream. She doesn't say anything, won't even look at me, but I can't watch her cry like this.

I shift on the small, overstuffed sofa and drape my arm around her. The top of her head fits perfectly into the crook of my shoulder. The scent of her hair takes over my senses; the sound of her softly sniffling through her tears tugs at my heart.

I alternate between squeezing her arm and tracing my fingers up over her shoulder. When she seems to have gathered her emotions, calming down a bit, my instincts take over and I act seemingly without thinking.

Or maybe I am thinking and I'm just afraid of what I'm thinking.

Gently pressing my lips to the top of her soft, brown hair feels like second nature. She tenses momentarily, and I realize I may have just overstepped my boundaries.

"Sorry about that." I straighten in my seat and try to move my arm, but her fingers fall to my forearm. She looks up at me through long lashes with puffy, red eyes from crying.

"Don't be." Her voice is soft, angel-like. "It's nice to be held."

That piece of information prompts me to pull her even closer. "Well, I'm glad I could be of service."

She laughs softly and then takes a deep breath before she shifts to move away from me, which just makes me pull her close once again. "Don't," planting another quick kiss to her head, "it's nice to have someone to hold."

So we stay like that through a sitcom and the beginning of the eleven o'clock news. When I feel her yawn into my chest, I move my arm, stretching it up over my head. She sits up and I stand to clear the plates and box of pizza.

When the coffee table is cleared and Lucy is finished washing most of the dishes, I grab my coat from its hook as she walks me to the front door.

"Sorry again about ruining everything." She folds her arms across her chest and I actively have to remind myself that her eyes are about eight-inches north of where I want to be looking.

I pull my jacket over my shoulders and take a step closer to her. When I hold both of her arms, she tilts her head up to look at me. "Tonight was the best night I've had in a long time. Believe me, you ruined nothing."

When she leans into my hand as I cup her jaw, I'm surprised to say the least. She turns her face up to mine, and it's magnetic – a force, a pull between our lips that can't be stopped.

Not that it seems like either one of us want to.

Slowly, she inches up on her toes. Her sweet breath caresses my lips and her hand cups my jaw in return. Our eyes lock, seeking permission for what we know is inevitable. The pink tip of her tongue darts out to trace her bottom lip. My thumb moves on its own accord and traces delicately over the spot that she just licked.

I move in, a centimeter at most away from her soft, plump lips. Her breathing staggers and I swear my heart feels like it's going to burst through my chest.

The instant our lips touch, it's like we simply melt together. There's no heated rush of a wild first kiss – just a bright passionate glow surrounding us. There's no awkward movements – whose head goes to which side or whose hands go where. There's just heat – a spark that ignites so much feeling deep within my chest that it would be scary if it weren't for the sweet woman softly pressed up against my body, panting with a breathlessness that shakes me to my core.

As her tongue licks the seam of my lips, my need to taste her takes over. Moving my hand from her jaw to the back of her head, I pull her even closer – closer than is humanly possible.

We get lost in each other for more than a few long moments – teasing, tasting, devouring. Placing her palms flat on my chest, she looks up at me with sparkling, bright, blue eyes.

"Wow," she murmurs softly.

Brushing my knuckles down her cheek, I echo her thoughts. "Yeah, that was…wow." I add clumsily as she steps out of my arms, "I guess I should get going."

"Good night, Evan." There's a touch of reluctance as we break away from each other; neither one of us are eager to end the night.

With one foot still in the hallway and one stepped over the threshold of the front door, I pause and gather my thoughts. Turning back to face her, I scrub my hand over my face. I feel like a giddy teenager heading home after my very first date. Given the stats of my recent and entirely non-existent love life, that's not completely untrue.

Determined to change that, and so much more about my life, I step back into the hallway and pull the door closed behind me. Now that we've gotten that first kiss out of the way, I let my lips crash into hers with all of the desire I held in just moments before.

She gasps, shocked by my movements, I'm sure. My arms coil around her small waist and I lift her off the ground a few inches. Her softness pressed into my body is…it's just right. There's absolutely no other way to describe it. Her arms wrap around my neck as her fingers dance across my skin.

All of the tension we seemed to be fighting all night simply melts away and we kiss as if we've been kissing like this our entire lives.

Heavy breathing fills the space between us as I pull away. Our foreheads touch, and almost as if we've rehearsed it, we both say "wow" at the same time.

I pop a softer, much more innocent kiss, to her cheek. "Can I call you sometime this week? Maybe we can get together again?"

It only takes her a few seconds to answer, but in that short span of time, it feels like my heart stops beating. "You better." She lifts an eyebrow and quirks a cute, dimpled smile.

As I pull my seatbelt across my chest and drive away from Lucy's home, that dull ache I've felt in my gut since leaving Manhattan has lessened dramatically. Somehow, over the course of a few hours with Lucy, the life I used to be more than happy with, seems dull in comparison to the fire she's just ignited in my heart.

February 9, 2013

CHAPTER TWELVE
Lucy

As I put away the last of the dishes from the meal I single-handedly screwed up, I realize I'm still grinning like a fool. Evan left over an hour ago and I still haven't been able to wipe the smile from my face.

He kissed me. Like really and truly kissed me. Not out of pity, but because he genuinely wanted to.

Even I have to chuckle at the giddiness of my inner voice. At this rate, I'll never calm down enough for bed. I haven't felt this way about a kiss since…well, since my very first one.

Tracing my finger over my lip, my heart warms remembering kissing Jimmy. "I miss you, baby," I say into the quietness of the empty house. But as much as I miss him, I don't feel any guilt over what just happened with Evan. I know Jimmy would want me to be happy, especially after all of this time.

Except when the cabinet door, which has been loose for a few weeks now, crashes down to the floor as I put away the final plate, I have to laugh. "Maybe you're not so okay with it, huh?" Bracing for the cold that I know is on the other side of the door, I grab the broom out of the garage that's attached at the side of the kitchen.

As I clean up the few screws that skittered across the floor, I get lost thinking about how Jimmy never would have let things like this – a silly broken cabinet – happen. "You always said you wanted to fix this place up. I guess I let that slip." My apology blends into the sound of the bristles scratching across the tiled floor.

Propping the cabinet door up against the wall, I sweep up the few splinters of wood on the floor and put the broom back in the freezing cold garage. The crash through the front door as I walk back into the kitchen causes my heart to pound against my chest. "What the hell?" I say to no one in particular. When I hear people – that's right, people – in my house, I race back into the garage. Closing the door as quietly as possible, I crouch down in a corner, anxiety racing through my veins.

I hear mumbles and things breaking. Reality comes at me full force – I'm being robbed. Holy shit! What the hell am I supposed to do? Panic takes over and whether it's from the freezing air in the garage or the sickening feeling consuming me, my hands start shaking.

Deep breaths. Just take a few deep breaths, Lucy. They don't think anyone's home. They won't even be looking for you. I try to coach myself into a calmness that just isn't happening.

It's pitch black and I can't see a freaking thing, so it takes me a minute to get my bearings. Trying to remember where everything is, I step around the garbage pails and side step the box of chopped wood for the fireplace.

I'm straining so hard to hear what's going on in the house that I can actually feel my pulse beating in my ears, the blood, a loud swooshing sound that drowns out the crashes going on inside. I fumble at the tool counter to my side, but when I nearly knock over the gardening shears, I stop, frozen with fear that I'll make noise.

Eyeing my car, I think about crawling into the back seat and hiding, but then again, I'll make noise. My legs are too paralyzed with fear to do anything anyway.

As I slide down to the floor, I realize my cell phone is still in my back pocket. I call 9-1-1 and tell them what's going on, my heart beating like crazy, my voice barely above a whisper. I tell the operator my name and location, but when she tries to keep me on the line, I have to hang up – too fearful of being heard.

It's the longest five minutes of my life as I hear things being tossed around, my house being ransacked. Right before I hear the sirens approach the house, I actually consider going back into the kitchen to rationalize with them.

One thing stops me – Melanie. She's already lost so much - having to grow up without a father is more than she should ever have had to deal with. The thought of her having to go on without me, keeps me cemented to my spot.

The gravel in the driveway sprays up against the garage door as the cop cars speed in. The guys in my living room scramble as the cops swerve in front of the house. Nerves jittering all over the place, I don't know when to come out. I think whoever was robbing me has been chased outside, but I still don't want to chance it.

As a sliver of yellow light filters into the garage, my breath hitches in my throat. I don't even realize I'm holding my breath until my chest starts buzzing with pain. I can barely focus my attention on whatever movements are happening by the door. The recycling pail is kicked over – glass and metal cover the floor. It's only when I see the ray of a flashlight searching the corners of the garage that I piece together that it must be a police officer. Fear paralyzes me. I don't want to move too quickly, afraid that my sudden movements might put me in the way of an itchy trigger finger.

Deep breaths. Just keep calm and wait for…I'm not really sure what, but I'm too scared to make the first move.

The rakes and brooms roll across the floor as the officer makes his way toward me. He doesn't speak, probably afraid to focus any attention on his exact location. But the garage isn't all that big; there's only one corner left to inspect – the one in which I'm currently crouched.

Hugging my knees closely to my chest, I try to stay as still as possible, but the sobs that creep up on me make me shake even more than I already am.

"Put your hands up!" A loud male voice booms out as the flashlight falls on me.

I listen, but can only lift up one hand as the light blinds me. "I l-live h-here." My teeth chatter; my breath swirls steam into the frigid air. Tears stream down my face and I register somehow that he's lowered his gun.

"Are you okay, ma'am? Were you hurt?" Standing next to me, he holsters his gun and wraps an arm around my shoulder.

"I'm fine. I...I came in here as soon as..." my words trail off and mingle with my sobs.

He speaks into his radio, letting the others know that he's found me and that we're re-entering the house through the side door.

An EMT is waiting for me in the kitchen and she drapes a blanket around me. I try desperately to focus on what's going on around me, but it's just too much. Radio static fills the room as the other officers, who were in a foot race with the people who broke in, let us know that they caught the suspects. Two teenagers looking for quick cash. Everything sounds so clinical, so technical, but I just can't get my emotions in check. What if...what if... those words play on repeat in my head. No matter how much I try and tell myself I'm okay and nothing happened to me, I can't shake the sinking feeling of fear that's swallowing me whole.

"Is there anyone you can call?" The officer who found me in the garage asks as he slides into the chair next to me. Linda is out for the night with her sister. If I call Melanie, she'll just panic and want to race home and I don't want to scare her. I could call Maddy and Reid, but something about that screams pathetic.

One last option chimes in, but could I? What would he say? Would he even care? Something tells me he would, so I dial his number in the hopes that he'll answer his cell even though it's past one in the morning.

On the third ring, he answers, his voice drowsy and raspy with sleep. "Lucy?"

"I-I'm sorry, I didn't mean to…" I know he can hear me crying through the line; there's no disguising it.

"What's wrong, Lucy?" I hear him toss back his sheets.

His voice alone relaxes me. Taking a deep breath, I calm myself enough to give him the basics. "Someone tried to break in. I got stuck in the garage until the police officer found me."

"What the fuck?" His anger takes me by surprise. He doesn't strike me as someone who curses all that often, but I can hear him rushing around in a frenzy, swearing like a sailor. "I'll be right there." And then, the line goes dead.

In the fifteen minutes it takes Evan to get to my house, the officers ask me a slew of questions and have me fill out some papers pressing charges against the suspects. Since I never saw anyone, there's no need for me to identify them. In my exhausted state, I hear vague facts about dusting for prints on my TV and computer. I should have my things back in a few days or maybe a week – depending on how long it takes my insurance company to pay out. I honestly don't care about all that. I just want to feel safe again. I just want the mess cleaned up, the furniture put back in place and my home back to normal.

"Where is she?" Evan's concerned voice calls out from the front entryway. "Lucy?"

I swear I feel him walk into the room, vibrating with anger, radiating concern. He kneels down on the floor next to me. Too afraid of the tears that I know will pour when I look at him, I cradle my face in my hands.

"It's okay. Shhh, you're okay. That's all that matters." His words only make me cry more. In a movement that takes me by surprise, he pulls me from the chair and sits down in my place, pulling me onto his lap.

Gently, he strokes his fingers through my hair and my cries recede. The officer, who has been here the whole time, lets me know that he'll be in touch if he needs anything else. Evan shakes his hand while keeping his other one holding me close to his warm, solid chest.

"I'm just going to walk them out and lock the door behind them. I'll be right back," he whispers soothingly into my ear and eases up from the chair.

"You'll take care of her?" the officer asks as he walks with Evan out of the kitchen.

"Of course," he answers with certainty as he closes and locks the door. The need to be held, to be comforted, overwhelms me and I walk across the kitchen and fall into his arms.

"I was so scared." Coiling my arms around his waist, I press my cheek up against his chest as he continues stroking my hair. His lips press into the top of my head before he leans his cheek in the spot he just kissed.

"I know, I know. I'm here now. It's okay." I'm relieved when he doesn't ask me anything about what happened. I don't want any part of reliving the last hour.

We stand here in the unquiet silence of my small home for a few long moments, me pulling some strength from Evan's comforting touch.

When I step out of his arms, he searches my face for some kind of…I guess just some kind of something to let him know I'm okay. On a huge, deep breath, I release a sigh. "Thank you for coming over."

"Of course." He shoots me a 'don't be crazy' look. "If I didn't leave in the first place…" He runs his hand through his hair, gripping on the ends.

"Stop, Evan. Neither one of us could have known."

Stuffing his hands in his pockets, he puffs out a frustrated breath. "Yeah, but your car was in the garage because mine was in the driveway. They must have seen me leave and thought they could get away with everything. I left you here all alone and they…"

"You can't blame yourself." The idea that he's spent his entire career protecting others is not lost on me. I can't imagine the things he's seen, the scenarios that are playing through his mind.

"But something could've happened to you." His words are filled with so much emotion as he softly caresses my cheek with his knuckles. "I wouldn't be able to forgive myself." Crushing me to his chest again, I get lost in the feel of his arms wrapping tightly around me.

"I'm so tired," mumbling through my yawn, I step out of his arms.

He checks the clock on the microwave. "Yeah, it's almost two thirty. I guess I should go."

"What?" Anxiety laces through me. "No, you can't." I reign in my panic, not wanting to look too needy. "I mean, would you stay, please? I really don't want to be alone."

I expect to see him war with the decision; his earlier words about never having settled down with anyone ringing through my head. So when he agrees almost automatically, I'm more than a little surprised.

"I'll camp out down here." He starts moving some cushions around on the too-small couch.

Touching his arm stops his movements. "No…I… would you…" God, I sound like an idiot. He turns and looks down at me with his stunning, but oh-so-tired, grey eyes. "I don't want to sound too forward, but would you stay with me instead of down here."

Now, he wars with what to say. I can only imagine what he must be thinking; I'm sure this isn't what he signed up for and if I could, I would take it back. The unsettled silence fills the room as he considers my question.

"No, you know what…"

"I'll stay."

Our words run over each other once again, as they have a few times before. Strange how that happens.

Hugging him once more, I nearly cry at how safe I feel knowing I won't be alone tonight. "Thank you. I'm sorry to…"

"Lucy, please. Stop with the 'I'm sorrys.'" He cups my jaw and plants a soft kiss to the corner of my mouth. "There is nowhere I'd rather be right now." After kissing the other corner of my mouth just as sweetly as he kissed the first, he wraps his arm around my shoulder. "Come on, let's get you to bed now." And we walk up the narrow stairs arm in arm.

I step into the adjoining bathroom when we get to my room. After washing my face and brushing my teeth, I stare at myself in the mirror. To say it's weird being in this room with another man is a huge understatement, but it also feels strangely normal.

When I go back out into my room, Evan is slouched over on the edge of the bed, elbows resting on his thighs, cradling his head in his hands – his shoes and socks in a pile on the floor. I guess tonight took a toll on him too.

"Bathroom's all yours. I left you out a new toothbrush too." I smile lamely, trying to ease the tension of the night.

"Thanks. I'll be right out." As he walks past me, I catch the scent of his cologne and immediately feel calmer, more at ease.

I make quick work of changing and climb into bed, sheer and utter exhaustion washing over me the second I hit the pillow. When Evan comes back into the room, I fold back the comforter for him to get under the blankets. Fully clothed, he wiggles under the blankets.

"You don't have to sleep in your jeans, Evan. I don't want you to be uncomfortable."

"Sleeping in bed with a beautiful woman and having to keep my hands to myself is going to be challenging enough."

My cheeks heat and I thank God the only light in the room is the muted glow of the moon as a few clouds pass in the night sky.

I never said he had to keep his hands to himself. Must be his own idea at chivalry or something like that.

I decide to drop it, not wanting to make him feel uneasy – not wanting to make *me* feel uneasy. But as he lies back, he squirms in place. Shifting and moving restlessly, he finally forfeits the fight with his pants. Standing abruptly, he shucks them down and quickly climbs back into bed. "Fine. You were right. Happy now?" he snips with more than a little playfulness in his words.

I stifle the "I told you so" that's dancing on the tip of my tongue and cuddle up next to him instead. Nuzzling into the side of his warm body, I smile against his t-shirt-covered chest. "Yes, very happy."

Resting his cheek atop my head, I feel his smile as well. "Good, then I'm happy too. Now, let's get some rest."

I angle my head up to him as he stares hungrily down at me. He reaches out to me, stroking his hand across my cheek for a moment before pulling my face up to his. His lips dance softly along mine, sensually and teasingly at the same time. He rolls to his side and he runs his rough hand up and down my arm, leaving a million points of dotted flesh in its wake. My nipples stiffen under my shirt and he has to feel their hardened points pressing into his chest.

The growing erection settled against my belly makes me fully aware of how I'm affecting him. I press against him, moaning into our kiss. A whimper flies out when he pulls away. "Did I do something wrong?" I search his face for some kind of answer.

He smiles sexily at me, rubbing his hand up and down my arm again. "No, you definitely didn't do anything wrong. It's just with everything tonight... I don't want this to be tainted by what happened earlier." He pops a sweet, soft kiss to my forehead and squeezes me to his chest, accidentally copping a feel as he does so.

"You just grabbed my boob," I giggle and look up at him. I laugh even harder when he does it again.

"Actually, it was just side-boob," he chuckles and we both let out a deep exhale.

"Come on. Let's get some rest," he whispers against my hair and my eyes suddenly feel as if they're weighed down with lead.

Cocooned in his warmth, encircled in his arms, bathed in his masculine scent, I fall asleep faster than I have in years.

Blinding sunlight fills the room. I roll away from it expecting to find Evan, but he's gone. Reaching next to me, I discover I'm all alone, but the bed is still warm. Curling up around the pillow he used, I can still smell him. Sadness punches me in the gut; he's left already.

I knew last night was just about being there for me after the house was broken into, but I was actually looking forward to waking up beside him. Not one to wallow around in self-pity for too long, I get out of bed and head down stairs to make some coffee and call Linda.

Just as I'm about to pull the coffee container out of the cabinet, I hear something out in the garage. Fear grips at me again. What if one of those guys got away? What if they came back? I hear loud clunks as someone climbs the three steps back into the house. With a heavy cast-iron frying pan in hand and ready to go, I stand beside the garage door.

It falls from my hands and crashes to floor when I see Evan coming back into the kitchen.

"Hey! What's all this about?" He picks the pan up from the floor as I clutch at my chest like the damsel in distress that I so clearly appear to be right now.

Slinking down into a chair, I calm my racing heart and laugh at just how ridiculous the scene must have looked from his point of view.

"You weren't in bed when I woke up, so I thought you left. Then I heard someone in the garage and I couldn't exactly go in there and hide. The pan was there, so I just grabbed it." He laughs and sits next to me.

"Why would I leave you?"

Shrugging my shoulders is probably the lamest response I can come up with, but that's all I've got right now.

"Well, you didn't want to take your pants off last night. And then you stopped when I was kissing you, so I figured you…."

His loud, booming laughter cuts my words off abruptly. "Wait a second," he chuckles, placing his hand on top of mine on the table. "You think that just because I didn't want to get nearly naked with you last night after you could have been attacked that I didn't want to be here in some way?" His quirked eyebrow and small smile reveal just how good looking he really is.

"I…well…I mean…yeah, I thought you felt obligated, like I was a burden, a pain in the ass, a helpless….you can stop me anytime here." I'm rambling and he's letting me.

"And how would that be fun?" Winking at me, he stands and continues making the coffee I had just taken out. I scan the kitchen and into the living room office combo spreading out to the side of it, and I realize he must have gotten up early to clean for me.

Gratitude spreads warmly in my chest. Seeing my home back in order and knowing that he took care of it for me makes me fall for him even more than I already am.

But, falling for him or not, I can't let him off the hook that easily. I lean up against the counter, facing him and crossing my arms. "Okay then, hot-shot. What was all the angsty, head-in-hands brooding about last night?"

After snapping the lid to the coffee container back in place, he slides the container back into the cabinet that

I'm just now realizing is also fixed. "I'm not sure," he says softly, shaking his head. "Maybe it was just being in your room. Mostly it had to do with knowing that you needed me and I failed you. I left you alone and you were almost hurt."

His raw honesty cuts through me.

I slide over and squeeze in between him and the counter. His grey eyes are brewing a heavy storm and all I can think is that I want to get to know this complex man even better. But there's something there that's also telling me not push too much right now. Whatever is bothering him, whatever hero complex he might have, he has to share it on his own terms.

"Thanks for fixing that." I tip my head back to the cabinet. "And for taking care of the rest of the place. It really means a lot to me."

He lets out a sigh of relief and presses a kiss to my forehead, seemingly happy that I dropped the 'almost being hurt' subject. "No problem. I also cleaned up the mess in the garage. I didn't want you to have to deal with it."

The feeling of gratitude that settled in my chest moments ago morphs into something much more, but I push it down, knowing it's just too soon to feel those kinds of things. The coffee pot beeps and he makes himself a cup, completely at ease in my kitchen once again. After he's poured my mug, he looks over at me. "Sugar?"

"What?"

"No, sweetness. I was asking if you want sugar."

"Oh, yes please." My palms get all sweaty as embarrassment heats my chest, neck and face.

"That's a nice shade of red, Lucy," he snickers and drops a spoonful of sugar into my mug. After topping it off with a little bit of half-and-half, he hands me the mug and sits next to me.

There are so many things running through my head, so many things I want to ask him about how he's feeling, what he thought about last night – the date part, not the breaking and entering.

I want to ask him if he felt as at home as I did sleeping in bed with me last night, if he slept more soundly because I was next to him, just like I did because he was there.

Afraid of the answers to those questions, I opt for something much simpler. "So what's on your agenda for today?" Since we didn't fall asleep until the early hours of the morning, we didn't get out of bed until almost eleven.

"I actually have a furniture delivery coming in," he looks down at his watch, "oh shit, in like twenty minutes. I completely forgot." He goes to dump out his coffee, but I stop him and offer a to-go mug. Partly because he shouldn't have to go without coffee after being up so late, but mostly because it might give him a reason to come back here.

Pathetic, right?

I walk him to the door for the second time in about twelve hours, but this goodbye is much more rushed than the one from last night. A quick peck on the cheek and an, "I'll call you later," and he's out the door.

With my back pressed up against the closed and locked door, I try to calm my fluttering heart. The knock from the other side of the door scares the ever-living crap out of me. I take a look through the peephole and laugh when I see Evan on the other side.

"I just wanted to make sure that you locked it behind me." He's leaning his hip up against the frame, looking sexy as hell. "Oh and this too."

His hand dives into my hair at my nape, his large and calloused fingers wrapping gently around my neck, tipping it back just enough to unleash the kiss of all kisses on my lips. When his tongue brushes up against mine, my legs buckle and I groan into his mouth.

His lips, so sensual and soft, feel more than heavenly on mine. His arms, so strong and capable, crush me to his body.

I stretch up on my toes and lace my fingers into his silky hair, the silvery silkiness softer than anything I imagined. "Evan," I mumble breathlessly against his lips. He pulls my lower lip in between his teeth, nipping gently before licking over the same spot.

"Lucy," he whispers as he rains down kisses across my jawline before planting a final, soft, wet kiss to that sweet spot right below my earlobe.

"Don't forget to lock this behind me, sweetness." He swipes his thumb across my bruised-by-his-kiss bottom lip. "I'll call you soon. I promise."

February 13, 2013

CHAPTER THIRTEEN

Evan

I've put off calling Lucy for a day or so, not wanting to appear too eager or excited. But, now, with Valentine's Day tomorrow, I feel like I *have* to call; otherwise, I'll look like a jerk. That's the last thing I want her to think of me. Then again, I don't want her to feel obligated about anything.

This is why I've avoided relationships. Too much confusion. Too much worrying about doing the right thing, about hurting someone's feelings and sacrificing your own.

Yet despite all of those issues, there is something so down to earth about Lucy, so honest and real, that I just have this feeling in my gut that she's different. The way her lips danced across mine, the way her soft body curled into my side, the way her eyes bore her soul – all told me she might just be worth it.

I feel like a young kid trying to pep talk myself into calling a girl I like. But "girl" is not a word I would use to describe Lucy. She is all woman – gorgeous, smart, kind, passionate and hotter than any fire I've ever walked into. Just thinking about her moaning through our kiss has me throbbing painfully behind the zipper of my jeans. When's the last time a woman had that kind of effect on me? When's the last time I let myself feel anything more than a lukewarm "ehh, you're okay" sentiment about a woman? When's the last time I let myself experience as much happiness as I did the night I watched Lucy sleeping in my arms?

Finally gathering more courage than I thought I would ever need, I stop pacing the kitchen and decide to go for it. Just as I'm about to dial her number, my phone skitters across the table, vibrating with an incoming call.

"Hey." It's Lucy. I find myself smiling already and she hasn't even said a word.

"Hi, Ev. How are you?" Her voice sounds uneasy; a touch of nervousness shakes her words.

"Good. I'm good. Have you heard from Officer Harper?"

"Oh, yeah. He called yesterday. I guess I should have let you know." Dishes clank in the background. "It was a few kids who broke in, two sixteen-year-old kids. They were looking for drug money apparently."

"My God, that's crazy. So what else did the police say?"

"Well, since they weren't armed and because there was no intent to harm anyone, and because it was petty – just some extra cash I had hidden at my desk and my laptop, they're just being judged as juvenile delinquents. They'll probably get some kind of house arrest followed by probation or something like that. I'm just glad that it should be over fairly quickly, and that I don't have to do more than sign a few documents." The relief in her voice is palpable.

"That's really great." A longer-than-intended pause makes the line go silent for a moment. "I was just about to call you."

"You were?" Sounding all cute and innocent, her surprise might be the sweetest thing I've heard in a long time.

"Uh, yeah. I'd like to see you this weekend." I figure if I don't ask her, maybe she won't be able to say no.

"Oh." She sounds upset or disappointed, or some shit like that. "Um, well, that's what I was actually calling about." Her words and the tone of her voice do nothing to boost my confidence, so I don't say anything and let her fill the silence that's hanging thickly on the line.

"I have a date Thursday night." What now? Maybe my age is finally catching up to me and I've gone deaf. And maybe I can't count correctly, or I have my days wrong, but Thursday is Valentine's Day. Not that I ever bought much into that particular "holiday", but the idea of some other shmuck taking out my ... well, I'm not really sure what she is, but I know that in some way she's mine.

I can joke about it all I want, but the truth is, she has a date and it's not with me. Why didn't I call her yesterday?

Because you're a scared little shit, that's why — a fifty-two year old commitment-phobe. The ladies should just be lining up for you. Ass.

"Yeah, well then, maybe some other time." I'm certain she can feel the chill in my words, the line freezing in frigidity.

"It's not what you think," she offers as an apology.

A humorless laugh flies out of my mouth. "And what exactly do I think, huh?"

"I didn't seek this out, so don't please don't be upset." With my anger receding slightly, I bite my sarcastic tongue and listen to what she has to say. It's not like she knew how I felt. I would have had to tell her that first.

"You're right. I'm sorry." Can you say tail between my legs?

"No, I'm sorry. I tried to get out of it, but Linda, my best friend, set me up." Now, it's her turn to laugh humorlessly. "She has this idea that I need to be saved from my hellish life of single-hood, so she set me up on a dating website. She only just told me about the date today at work. I called you as soon as I got home. It's just too late to bow out of it gracefully. I hope you understand." Lucy's wobbling and sincere voice makes me forget my pissed-off mood. She's not to blame and I don't want to push her away, so I play it cool, unaffected.

But I don't want to sound like a douche either. "It's okay. I understand." I pause and she sighs, frustration seems to be weighing heavily for both of us. "Maybe we can get together Friday?" I ask, almost pathetically.

Lucy must hear the hurt in my words, the disappointment that I'm completely incapable of concealing. "Definitely," she chirps, enthusiastically – overly so.

Deciding to just let it go, not wanting to add to the guilt she's already expressed, I lie to end the call. "Listen, I've got another call. I'll call you tomorrow. Bye."

Knowing that slamming my cell down on the table like I want to will only break it, forcing me to go get a new one, helps me reign in my frustration. Though I want to curse myself for thinking, like a fool, that Lucy would be waiting around for me, since it was only a few days. Her saying she tried to back out of it, but couldn't, doesn't do anything to heal my wounded ego.

A glimmer of hope flickers in my chest when my phone vibrates again. It's gone instantly when I see my brother's goofy face smiling at me on the incoming call icon.

"Hey, Joe. What's up?" Once I'm in the living room, I flop back on the couch. Since I don't have a job, I spent the day painting in here. It's still not a home, but at least it's starting to shape up.

"Nothing, as usual." Joe's lack of energy isn't surprising, but it's still not something I like to hear.

Needing some cheering up myself, I aim to change both of our moods. "You're in luck then. I was just about to head out and grab some dinner. Wanna join me?"

"Yeah, I guess." Playing disinterested doesn't suit him, but seeing as tomorrow is his first Valentine's Day without his wife – Hallmark holiday or not – I don't push him.

We make plans for me to come pick him up and head to a local sports bar. Beers and burgers sound like the perfect distraction for both of us.

"Here you go, boys." The waitress winks at both of us, sliding our drinks to us and dropping a plate of nachos in the middle of the table.

"Thanks." We both nod and dive into the food. Avoiding conversation until at least half of my beer is gone sounds like a fantastic idea right about now. Joe doesn't look like he's complaining about the quiet either.

"I painted today." I dangle that gem of a conversation starter out there.

"Yeah, what color?"

"Beige."

"Way to live on the edge there, Ev." Joe laughs at me, chewing on the last of an overloaded nacho.

"That's how I roll." Mimicking something that Katie has said frequently enough for me to pick up on it makes Joe nearly spit his beer at me across the table. The mood is lightened and the waitress comes over to bring us our second round of drinks.

"Speaking of living on the edge…" Taking a quick sip of the cold brew, I swallow down my pride and figure I might as well ask Joe for some advice on how to handle the Lucy situation.

Or not. I mean is it really something I need to talk about? Doesn't it break some kind of guy code to talk about women over beers while a game plays in the background?

"Today would be a nice time to finish that sentence." An arched eyebrow accompanies his oh-so-funny statement. Joe and I have always been close. With only two years separating us, I don't ever remember a time that we didn't get along. Sure we were a bunch of goofballs as kids, wrestling around and play fighting with one another whenever we could, but even as teenagers we were best friends. There were times – like when Joe married his first wife and dealt with the fall-out of her mental illness, like when Brody was injured and after 9/11 – that we drifted apart. But there are some bonds that can never be broken – those of brotherhood.

"Seriously, were you going somewhere with that thought, Evan? Old age finally catching up to you?" he jokes again – ass.

"Like you're that far behind."

"So seriously, what's going on? It'd do me good to focus on someone else for a bit." Joe's admission of his own lingering sadness helps me start talking.

"You remember Lucy, right?" He nods and smiles knowingly. "Well, we went out once and I thought it went…well – I mean we had a good time."

"So then what's the issue? Run out of Viagra," he says dryly.

"No, you dick." I throw my wadded up napkin at him and he dodges it. After explaining what happened the night her house was broken into, which Joe listens to attentively, concern working its way across his face, I get to the main crux of the problem. "So when I called her today, she said she was seeing someone else."

"Shit, that sucks. How serious is it?" He leans forward slightly, folding his hands together on the table in front of him.

Toying with the condensation on my beer, I consider her unwillingness to go on the date in the first place. Maybe I'm making a bigger deal out this than need be. Maybe I like her more than I'm willing to admit and that's why her date, which she seems to think is a non-date, bothers me so much.

Lamely shrugging one shoulder, I deflect. "Not sure."

Not sure about how serious I want it to be is more like it.

"Can I get you guys anything else?" The waitress asks as she places our burgers in front of us, smiling cheerfully.

"Nah, we're good. Thanks," Joe responds for us while I get stuck in my own head, too distracted to even acknowledge my meal.

We eat in stilted silence for a few minutes before Joe reaches across the table and swats me upside the head. "Dude, what the hell was that for?" I rub my temple as he drops back into his chair, looking like he's ready to drop some pearl of wisdom on me.

"It's simple. You like her. She likes you. You enjoy each other's company." A rueful smile pulls at his lips on that last part. "Fuck the other date. If you want her, go after her. We both know that too much fucked up shit happens every day. And you understand better than anyone that none of us knows when we get our last day."

I lean back in my chair, thinking about what Joe's just said. He's right. I know he's right, but I've kept my distance from anything, well anyone, that could hurt me – that would hurt too much to lose – for so long that it's become part of who I am.

Yet, the more I think about it, the more I think about Lucy and the possibilities of an *us*, and the more I realize what a waste my life has been. My meal tastes like chewing on sawdust suddenly. Is that how it's always been? Has everything in my life been boring and bland, tasteless and dull, covered in beige, just because I was afraid of loss?

"Cat got your tongue?" Joe chimes in, breaking the silence once again, as he tosses his napkin down on his empty plate.

"Not exactly. I was just thinking about how right you are."

Joe, being the ass-slash-joker that he is, pretends to go into a coughing fit, claiming that he didn't hear me correctly.

"You heard me, jerk. I said 'you were right'. Don't look so shocked. We do come from the same genes, you know. You were bound to inherit some of my intelligence." He laughs, a full-bellied chuckle.

When he calms down enough to get all serious again, he says one last thing that rings in my ears. "Don't let your job be the only thing in your life that you ever love."

The waitress comes over and I move to pay, but Joe beats me to it, citing something about beauty before age or some crap like that.

After dropping Joe back home, I feel a newfound resolve. As much as Joe wants to gloat about it, he is right; I do have to fight.

As my truck lurches forward, shifting the gear into park, a stark realization hits me right in the gut. I'm falling for Lucy, hard and fast – and for the first time in my life, the idea of loving someone doesn't scare me half as much as rushing into a burning building.

The next day, I consider sending flowers to Lucy – but some cheesy flower delivery screams, well, cheesy. I don't want to make her feel worse about her date than she already does, but I want her to know that I'm thinking of her – regardless of the fact that it's Valentine's Day and of the fact that she's going out with someone else tonight. I told her I'd call her, needing to make some kind of plans for Friday night, but a simple phone call just doesn't seem like it'd be enough.

Figuring I'll come up with something if I keep myself occupied, I decide to tackle my bedroom today as far as painting goes. In my days as a firefighter, I did a lot of side jobs on my off days as a painter. There is something so calming about being left alone in a bare room with a can of paint and a brush, knowing you are going to transform it into something beautiful. Having been in many houses over the years, I've seen so many different styles and tastes – most of which I don't care for. I like a simple, clean, modern style.

But as I stand before the hundreds of paint swatches lining the wall of the local Home Depot, I can't pick a single color that isn't boring. For the second time in as many days, Joe is right. My life is the epitome of beige.

Raking a hand through my hair, I actually consider ditching the job, but then I'll actually have *nothing* to do. That thought alone motivates me to just pick a fucking color and get on with it. I grab a few swatches and laugh at myself as I stand there actually considering the differences between "Totally Taupe" and "Supreme Sand." So when the sales clerk walks over to ask if I need any help, I let him give me some advice. As he thumbs through a few catalogues, I find a picture that actually looks like a room I wouldn't mind living in. It's masculine and fresh without being over-the-top manly.

After he mixes up the paint and I get a few small supplies, I feel reinvigorated and motivated – and not just to paint my room. A few ideas popped into my head about our date tomorrow night and about getting in touch with her today. Never having been a hopeless romantic, even I have to say that I'm proud of myself for my little plan. I just need to do one last thing while I'm here and then I'm good to go.

I make a few other stops on the way home, to get what I need for Lucy and for our date tomorrow. Smiling the entire time, I feel like a fool – but for once, I'm a happy fool.

February 14, 2013

CHAPTER FOURTEEN
Lucy

"I had a nice time, Aaron." Twisting in the seat of his Benz, I unbuckle my seat belt as he parks in the driveway behind my car. Ever since the break in, I try to park in the driveway as often as I can, just to make it look like I'm home.

Placing his hand over mine catches me off guard. It's warm, but in a smarmy, sweaty kind of way – not at all comforting, like Evan's. That's pretty much all I've done all night – compare Aaron to Evan. So far, he isn't measuring up.

"I want to see you again," he says determinedly, not even asking. Come to think of it, I don't think Evan actually asked me about wanting to see me this weekend, but there wasn't anything creepy about Evan's request. Aaron is all about the creep factor.

"Oh, I'm not sure. I have plans tomorrow night and then Saturday with my friend."

I'm also changing my phone number and probably moving as well. You know, just in case you're really persistent.

"Cancel them," he demands, no please or anything.

"I can't. Tomorrow night has been set in stone for weeks. It's my daughter and she's away at college so I really can't." I flat out lie and don't feel bad about it at all. At the last minute, I half-heartedly add, "I'll call you if anything changes, okay." He moves his hand from mine, a disappointed look on his face – one that I don't really care about.

Stepping out of his shiny, fancy car – one that he talked about for a full fifteen minutes over dinner tonight – I have to restrain myself from shaking off the creepy-crawly feeling that slithers all over my skin. He pulls out of the driveway before I even reach the front steps, clue number, oh I don't know, twenty-seven, that Aaron is a grade-A asshole.

Linda is so getting an earful on this one. I know exactly what she's going to say too. *He's your age; he has a good job and he's hot. What else do you want, Lucy?*

Linda needs to seriously re-evaluate her standards. Sure, Aaron has money – which he talked about *all night long* – but money apparently does not equal class. There will most definitely *not* be a phone call to him in the near future – or far future for that matter.

As I open the storm door, I'm surprised to see a red gift bag hanging on the knob of my front door. When I get inside, I unload the contents and pull out the card, though I already have an idea of who it's from. It's one of those "blank inside" cards so the only thing printed in there is a note from Evan. I trace my fingers over the bold print.

Lucy,

I JUST WANTED TO DROP OFF A LITTLE SOMETHING FOR YOU TODAY TO LET YOU KNOW THAT I WAS THINKING ABOUT YOU. I'M NOT SURE WHAT TIME YOU'LL BE GETTING IN (I HOPE NOT TOO LATE), BUT YOU CAN CALL ME IF YOU'D LIKE. I'D STILL REALLY LIKE TO SEE YOU TOMORROW NIGHT. IF IT'S OKAY WITH YOU, I'LL PICK YOU UP AT EIGHT?

I KNOW YOU'RE SUPPOSED TO GIVE YOUR GIRL FLOWERS ON VALENTINE'S DAY, BUT YOU'RE SOMETHING DIFFERENT — IN A GOOD WAY. ANYWAY, I CAN'T WAIT TO SEE YOU.

SWEET DREAMS ;) ← YES, ANOTHER WINKY FACE

EVAN XX

Tearing through the paper, I actually laugh aloud as I reveal a box of The Little Mermaid Band-Aids. There's a note taped to the front — "Look inside". Wrapped around the brightly colored bandages, is a weathered index card with faded writing scribbled across its surface. It's a recipe card for chicken francaise — a very old card, splotched with a few stains, sauce that bubbled over as the recipe lay on the counter. Surged with emotion, I pull out my phone and call him immediately.

"Hi." He picks up on the first ring.

"Hey." I drop down into the couch, kick off my shoes and trace the lines of the card in my hand. "I got your gift. It's so...sweet."

"Yeah? I didn't know... I mean, I know we're not...I'm glad you like it. It was my grandmother's."

I could tell it was old, but this is too much. "Are you sure? I mean if it's something *that* special, then you should have it."

"No," he says with finality. "It's *because* it's special that you should have it. Besides, I don't need it. I know how to cook, remember," he jokes, and even though I can't see him, I can imagine the smile lines creasing at the corners of his oh-so-kissable mouth.

That brings me to his other gift, "The Little Mermaid, huh? Why is it that every guy has a thing for Ariel? Is it the bikini?" I prop my feet up on the coffee table and lean back, resting my head right next to where Evan sat last week. I swear I can still smell his cologne on the cushions, but maybe I'm projecting.

When he doesn't say anything, except a few incoherent stutters, laughter seeps out of me, filling the room. "Oh, my God! You do have a thing for her!"

"Actually, I'm pretty sure I have a thing for you."

Stunned into silence, I try to absorb his words. On the one hand, it feels right; I know I am ready to feel these things – they are long overdue, after all. But on the other hand, we've only known each other for a little over a month, in which we've spent so little time together.

But even I can't deny the pull between us – the physical and emotional charge that's flickering life back into my hibernating heart.

The prospect of spending more time with him has never seemed more appealing.

Clearing his throat, he breaks the silence, "So how was the, uh, the date?" It sounds like it took a lot of effort for him to even say the word.

Opting for blunt honesty, I spit out the truth. "It was horrible." I can't see him, but I can imagine there's a satisfied grin plastered to his face.

"I'm sorry."

"No, you're not. You can stop gloating over there in all your smugness." If he were sitting in front of me, I'd be shaking my finger in his face, but I also can't help from snickering.

"You're right. I'm not sorry. I'm glad you had a crappy night. It means I get to give you the night you deserve."

"Say more stuff like that," I half joke, half beg.

"Now, who's being smug, sweetness?"

"So, what actually is the plan for tomorrow?" I deploy the change-the-subject-and-dig-for-more-dirt tactic that I honed while raising Melanie and Maddy.

"Nope, sorry, Lucy. You're just going to have to wait and find out. I'll be there at eight, though."

My heart flutters a bit just thinking about what he's got up his sleeve. I know, from his kiss alone, that a night with Evan could never be anything other than boring. "Okay, eight it is."

"Goodnight, Lucy."

"Goodnight, Evan." Before either of us kills the line, I quickly add, "I'm really happy I had a terrible night too."

"Sooo...." Linda drags out the word, her tone inflecting upward as she slides into the extra chair in my cubicle the next morning.

I ignore her, organizing a few papers for the Children's Cancer research project I'm working on. I'm trying to raise some funds and donations to have a princess-themed ball in conjunction with The Cure-For-Kids Foundation for a seven-year-old girl. It's about a month away and I have a lot of work left to make it the perfect night for Chloe – the guest of honor.

"Really? Nothing?" she prods again, digging for more information.

Clicking on a few screens on my computer, I pull up a spreadsheet with email addresses of potential donors. "Luce, it can't be *that* bad."

I swivel around in my chair so quickly I almost fall on my butt. "Oh, I assure you. It can and it was."

Eyeing me over the rim of her coffee mug, she has the decency to at least appear apologetic. Eventually, she concedes, softening to the fact that she was in the wrong, yet again. "So what happened this time?"

"Um, well, to say it candidly, he was an ass." I cross my legs primly and fold my hands on top of my knee.

She nearly spits out her coffee. "But he was so cute."

I tap my bottom lip, considering what she's just said before changing my answer. "Fine, then he was a cute ass, but an ass nonetheless."

I give her the play-by-play for the night. About Aaron being a corporate investor in some huge name firm, one that he was "shocked" I'd never heard about. He was so materialistic and shallow that I'd be surprised if he had pictures of his cars in his wallet instead of his kids – kids who he had, but repeatedly made a point of stating how they lived with his useless ex-wife.

Knowing nothing about exes, but everything about being a mother, there was just something in the way that he talked about her that made me uneasy. A broken marriage or not, you don't trash talk the mother of your children – unless you're really that classless, which in this case, he was proving himself to be just that.

Ending the story with the real kicker, I tell Linda how Aaron didn't even get out of the car to walk me to my door.

"You're shitting me. You mean even after the whole break-in thing? What a dick!" She finishes the last sip of her coffee and places the mug on my desk, careful not to touch any of the paperwork.

"Unfortunately, no, I'm not shitting you. But I also didn't tell him about the break-in. He really wouldn't let me get more than two words in all night. He actually called Melanie 'what's her name' at one point," I sigh, more than exasperated at even just recounting the events from last night. "So listen…"

She doesn't even let me finish my words before saying, "Well, then let's hope this next guy," she pauses, pulling a folded-up piece of paper out of her pocket, "is much better."

Practically shoving it into my hands, I have to take it from her. I unfold what I now realize is an online dating profile. "I really don't…"

"We talked about this. You deserve to be happy. There are lots of fish in the sea." She waggles her brows suggestively.

There are only three words that are going to put an end to this ridiculousness, but just as I'm about to spit them out, she leans forward and asks, "When's the last time you got laid?"

Not all that shocked by her crass, I play it cool. "I don't know." I pretend to count on my fingers.

"And I don't mean by B.O.B. Anything requiring batteries doesn't count." She stares pointedly at me.

Knowing all too well that I definitely won't be able to lie my way out of this one, I give in. "A long time… too long in fact."

"So then let's get on this." She flicks the backside of the dating profile that I'm holding in my hands.

Nip it in the bud already, Lucy. She is your best friend, after all.

Taking a deep breath, more in preparation for her shock than my revelation, I brace myself and let the words tumble out of my mouth. "I'm seeing someone."

"What!" she shrieks more than enthusiastically.

"Shhh. Calm down," I chide sternly when a few heads pop out of their cubes.

"Tell me, now. I need to know everything. Who? What? When?" Bouncing in her seat, Linda can barely contain her excitement.

With more giddiness than I can contain, I lean forward and tell her everything about Evan. When I told her about the break-in, I left out his role in coming to my rescue, knowing that it would raise more questions than I cared to answer at the time. But now, I spill every last detail.

"I really like him. I mean, I just feel safe with him, comfortable. It's like he's always been there – always been somewhere in my life, but it's just that now, he's here in front of me too."

Her eyes are glassy with happiness. "That's freaking amazing. Why didn't you tell me sooner, though?"

Clasping her hand in mine, I hope she can understand why. "Well, you were just so adamant about me meeting someone and I just didn't know what was going to happen with me and Evan. But after going out with Aaron, I knew that I had to give Evan a chance. I had to let myself feel what I was feeling and see where it would take me."

"So the credit is mine after all, huh?" She arches an eyebrow and grins impishly as I look at her with more than a little confusion.

Without even letting me ask the question she knows I'm about to, she says, "If *I* hadn't set you up with Aaron, *you* never would have realized your feelings for Evan." Pride colors her words, as does a touch of playfulness.

I swat the air in front of us, dismissing her silliness. Yet, I have to admit, she is right at least a little bit. Looking down at my watch, I realize I could use a break and another cup of coffee – and a little more girl talk about my date tonight with Evan wouldn't hurt either.

"Wanna grab some coffee? Maybe give me a few pointers for my date tonight?"

Giddily, she pops up out of her chair and hugs me. "Absolutely! I'm so excited," she squeals with girlish eagerness.

I stifle my laughter while inwardly bubbling over with joy at the prospect of what's to come with Evan.

The rest of the workday passes by in a blur. Focusing on the charity fundraiser helps to distract me from thinking of Evan too much. Chloe really wants a ride to the ball with a real prince and princess and I made calls all day long trying to solicit a donation from a limo company. Sadly though, there aren't many in the area that have any availability for the night. Upstate New York is also fresh out of princes and princesses.

I'm not beat though. I will give this little girl the night she deserves.

So even though I was able to clear my brain of Evan for the day, for every single second of the drive home, he's the only thought in my head.

Where are we going to go? What should I wear? What is he going to expect? What do I expect?

I shower quickly and blow out my hair, letting it fall softly in large curls. Standing in front of my closet, I realize my wardrobe could benefit from a few updates. Even though I texted Evan earlier asking about where we were going, he wouldn't give me any details, saying he wanted it to be a surprise.

Can't go wrong with a little black dress. With soft ruching that gathers at my hip under the sparkly clasp, and a to-the-knee flowy skirt, I feel feminine and sexy. There's no snow on the ground so I go with shiny, patent leather stilettoes. A light touch of make-up, spritz of perfume and I'm ready for my date. Cue the swarm of butterflies.

At ten to eight, I flop back on the couch and stare blankly at nothing in particular. For all of my "I'm never dating again" and "I'm more than happy with being single" talk over the years, I guess I never saw how ridiculous I was being in denying myself the chance to feel this kind of excitement. The rush of not knowing what's going to happen, the pull that draws you into someone you barely know, wanting to learn everything about them that you can, knowing, or at least hoping, they feel the same way about you – this is the stuff I've let myself go without.

Not anymore.

My confident, yet inward, declaration of self-proclaimed happiness coincides perfectly with the gentle knock at the front door. Standing, I smooth out my dress and take a deep breath, hoping for the best, feeling a change coming at me from the other side of that door.

Speech completely eludes me as I open the door and let the vision of Evan holding a bunch of flowers, leaning up against the doorframe sink in. In the few times we've seen each other, there was a casual normalcy to his appearance – jeans and a t-shirt, nothing over the top. Even his attitude was mellow and relaxed. But the man standing before me is transformed somehow.

More masculine.

More dominant.

More in control.

And so unbelievably sexy.

The soft leather of his jacket pulls across his broad chest and bunches in his arms as he extends the beautifully wrapped flowers to me.

"These are for you, sweetness," he rasps in a gruff voice. "You look beautiful." Pulling my shaking hand up to his lips, he kisses my knuckles, setting a fiery vibration there; one of which I likely won't be able to rid myself for the rest of the night.

I take them from him and immediately bring them up to my nose. Inhaling their sweet scent, I honestly can't remember the last time someone bought me flowers. It was more than likely Melanie when she was a little girl, picking bunches of bright yellow dandelions from the yard for me. "They're stunning, Evan. Thank you so much. Come in." As he strides past me, the fragrance of the flowers fades away behind the woodsy clean scent that is uniquely Evan.

"I didn't know what kind you liked," he tips his chin at the flowers, "so I got you one of everything." Standing before me, he lowers his face to mine and gently brushes his lips against my cheek, the roughness of his stubble sending shivers across my skin.

It's only when I lean into his kiss that I realize he's got a picnic basket in his other hand. "It's a little cold and pitch black to be going for a picnic, don't you think?"

"Who says we're going outside?" He grins, amused at my obvious misunderstanding. Reaching down for my hand, he laces our fingers together and pulls me into the living room. He tosses his jacket on the back of the desk chair revealing a pale grey, button-down dress shirt, which pairs nicely with his dark wash jeans. You know the kind that are loose in all the right places, but oh-so tight everywhere else. Then, he pulls a red-and-white checkered blanket out of the basket. Shaking it in the air, he straightens it out as he lays it down on the carpet. I watch, completely mesmerized by his kind thoughtfulness.

Now *this* is a date.

Wordlessly, he walks past me, grabs a few pillows from the couch and tosses them on the floor. "Sit," he commands.

I laugh. "What am I? A dog or something?"

At least he has the good grace to smirk at himself. Shaking his head, he steps in front of me and runs his fingers down my arms. "You are most certainly not a dog. Please sit. I want you to be comfortable." It's difficult to resist him when his eyes twinkle the way they do. Some of the awkward tension that was there the first few times we spent time together has eased; it's almost vanished completely.

As I get myself situated on a cushion, he makes quick work of unpacking the rest of the contents of the basket – a bottle of wine, a loaf of crusty bread, a few hunks of cheese and a bunch of grapes. Of course, he's also packed all the plates, cups and utensils that we'll need as well. He even remembered to bring back my travel coffee mug. I guess my plan was effective, after all. After everything is carefully laid out, he heads out to the garage.

He's back quickly, logs for the fireplace in hand. "I saw these in there last week and I knew that there would be no better way to spend the night with you than in front of a fire, sharing a meal together. I hope that's okay with you?" Cautiousness colors his words, and I melt for him even more, thinking about all of the effort he put in to tonight.

"It's perfect," I assure him.

He makes extremely quick work of starting the fire. Flames dance and twirl in the hearth, making the sparkle in his eyes more pronounced now. After he washes his hands, he comes back into the living room.

He sits next to me and I hand him a glass of wine that I just poured.

He makes us up plates of food and we enjoy the simple peacefulness of eating together. The crackles and pops of the fire add to the romantic ambiance. The wine goes down smoothly – almost too smoothly, as I realize that in less than fifteen minutes, he's already refilling my glass.

"Rough day at work or something?" he jokes as he tops off my glass.

"No. Actually it was terrific." I go on to tell him all about the charity work I've just started and he follows intently, seemingly hanging on my every word.

"How was your day?" I ask when I'm done telling him about princesses and cancer patients.

"Nothing exciting. And definitely nothing as meaningful as your day." When he pops a grape in his mouth, I notice how perfect his lips are – the soft curve of the upper bow and the plump fullness of his lower lip are hypnotic.

He catches me staring, but my desire quickly morphs to concern over the tone of his words.

"What do you mean 'meaningful'?" I fold my legs and lean on my arm, angling toward him.

He takes a sip – or a gulp, depending on your definition – of his wine before he speaks. "I guess you could say I'm not really one for retirement. There's not much to do all day." A lamely shrugged shoulder accompanies his response.

"So what *do* you do with yourself all day? You don't seem like one to sit around and watch TV." I find myself absentmindedly tracing my fingers over his forearm, which is revealed from beneath the cuffed sleeve of his dress shirt.

"No, definitely not a huge TV watcher," he chuckles dismissively. "I usually get up early and run a few miles and work out for a bit." That explains his physique – broad and sculpted, muscular and smoking hot. "After that, I really don't have a set plan." Brushing his hand over his face, he seems uneasy about something.

"And it's killing you to have nothing to do?" It's clearly written on his face, but he nods nonetheless.

"I don't know what I was thinking getting a condo. I mean the place is all finished, except for the painting, which I've managed to knock out in less than a week. Getting a fixer-upper would have been more my style. It definitely would have kept me busy."

"This place could keep you busy," I puff out a sad laugh as I scan the less-than-up-to-date state of the home I've always loved. "It wasn't supposed to be like this, you know. We had so many dreams when we bought this place, but then 'real life' happened and here I am – a lonely forty-three-year-old widow."

As I sip my wine, I feel his fingers lock together with mine. "Tell me about it. The 'real life' part is for shit." His calloused thumbs traces roughly over the inside of my wrist and goose bumps dot my skin.

"Jimmy was an architect so he had so many plans to make this place into something really special. We were only living here for a few months before he died."

He smiles sympathetically at me, not a trace of judgment or jealousy in his face as I talk about Jimmy.

"I could help you with some repairs." He pauses, gauging my reaction. "I already said I don't have much to do during the day, so it's not like I don't have the time."

"Really?" Suddenly the prospect of doing some work around here seems a lot less daunting. When he nods, laughing softly at my happiness over his offer, I bounce in my seat a little. "That would be … I don't know, like a dream come true. I've never known where to start around here and I feel like this house is the one area in my life where I've failed. Jimmy wouldn't have let it get this way." The tone of my last words holds more sadness than excitement.

"I'm sorry." His face is twisted in emotion, true compassion for my loss rings out loud and clear. I can hear the anguish of his losses hanging heavily on his words, but I don't push. I'm ready to open up now, but he might need some more time.

"Thank you. But it happened a long time ago and I'm okay with it now. I'll never be over him; he'll always be a part of me, but I guess recently I decided that I needed something that would make me happy."

"Loss never leaves you, but I'm happy that you are ready to move on." He cups my jaw and the thumb that was just passing over my wrist is now gently stroking my cheek. Leaning into his touch is impossible to resist – a true force of nature. Even though he hasn't verbalized it, the look on his face screams that he's also ready to move on.

His lips brush against mine and the kiss is tender and sweet – healing in every sense of the word. His warm tongue seeks out mine and he tastes like the wine we've been drinking, tinged with more than a little lust. Leaning his weight into me, he softly lowers me to the floor as he wraps a strong arm around my waist.

Propped up on one elbow, he combs his other hand through my hair, relaxing me despite my racing heart. As he lowers his face to mine, I watch him lick his bottom lip and it makes my breath hitch in my throat. The feel of his body pressing me into the floor as his lips seal over mine ignites a spark I thought was long gone. Grabbing onto his upper arm, I pull him closer to me – impossibly so. Our legs tangle together and the roughness of his dark jeans scratches against my legs deliciously.

His tongue licks into every dip and curve of my mouth and lips, like he's trying to taste every last inch of me, seeking out every surface of my warm and willing mouth. When I lace my fingers through his soft hair, his chest rumbles in a sound that's a mixture of pleasure and pain.

"God, Lucy…you're so sweet, so beautiful." He pulls back from me and stares into my eyes for a few long moments, stroking the flushed surface of my cheek as my fingers dance over his arms and chest.

"You're pretty stunning too." I cup his jaw then trace my pointer finger sensually down his neck to the opened collar of his shirt. Pressing my lips against the pulse beating wildly there causes him to growl yet again. His rigid hardness presses into my stomach and I lift my hips to rub against him, needing some kind of friction for the fire he's started in my body.

Lust and passion take over, and before I realize it, I've got the top three buttons of his shirt opened, exposing the light dusting of hair that sweeps across his muscled chest. Planting lush kisses across his collarbone and back up his throat, he thrusts his hips into mine, finally conceding to whatever restraint he thought he needed to keep in place.

Evan glides his hand up my skirt, gripping my upper thigh. His hands are so strong, so deliberate, but also delicate and almost reverential when he touches me. "Your skin is so soft." His rough grip relaxes as his fingers dance across the flesh of my thighs.

I can't manage more than a breathless pant and a whispered, "More."

Thankfully, he doesn't need to be asked more than once. Removing his hand from my thigh – which leaves me bereft and cold in the wake of his touch – he unclasps the snap at the ruching on my dress and pulls the fabric to the side, leaving me completely exposed, save for my black lace bra and panties.

I feel his eyes roam ravenously over my body, before he gazes into mine. "Is this okay?" His seeking permission makes my insides tremble. "I don't want to rush this."

"No…please…now. Please touch me. I want this. Please don't stop." I'm not above begging and I've been waiting for this, this intimacy, this heated passion for far too long.

His fingers ghost over my flat stomach and out to the soft flare of my hip, and then dip into the waistband of my panties. A disappointed gasp comes of out my mouth when he moves his hand. "Shh, not yet. I just want to touch you, feel your skin under my fingers. I want to enjoy you."

He drives me crazy, touching every inch of exposed skin, skimming along the lines of my bra, but never letting my breasts fall free despite the heaviness of their arousal. The confident way of his touch, the sure sound of his words – it all makes me feel like we've been here before, like this isn't new for us, but in so many ways it is.

His lips work their magic following the same pattern his fingers just did. Before kissing the upper swell of my breast, he seeks permission, scanning my face for the slightest nod. The scratch of his stubble reddens my skin. Hot, sweet, wet licks glide along the lace of my bra before his tongue dips under the fabric. Dangerously close to the painfully erect tip, I nearly groan in pleasure, but I bite my lip instead.

His thumb skirts over my chewed-upon lip, pulling it from the grips of my teeth. "Let go, Lucy. Let me just take care of you," he coaxes gently.

With painstaking precision, he works his way down the rest of my body, stomach, hips, and thighs – making an extra stop to run his nose oh-so closely to my panty line. He takes his time to rub and massage my calves and feet, settling back on his haunches to do so.

I lay there, boneless and completely immobile, the sounds coming out of my mouth just short of groaning.

That's when he settles his solid, jean-covered thigh in between mine. The pressure of his hard muscle creates a forceful and delicious pleasure that I haven't felt in longer than I care to admit to. Shamelessly, I grind myself against him – and beg.

"Please, Evan. I need to … please let me…" Never having really developed a sexual openness, I can't say the word, though "come" is on the tip of my tongue.

He stares at me longingly, cupping my cheek and then stroking his knuckles down the long expanse of my neck, before lightly strumming them over my lace-covered nipple. "Tell me what you need. Tell me and I'll give it to you."

"I want *you*. I want you to make me lose control." Arching my hips up and grinding against him again, I stare directly into his storm-grey eyes. "Now," I say, on one last grind.

He mumbles, "Anything for you," against my lips as he kneads my breast. I arch my back and he unclasps my bra with skill. When my breasts fall free, the warm air of the fire bathes over them, puckering the skin there.

"So beautiful," he whispers as he nuzzles a hardened point with his nose before latching onto it. Pulling my nipple deep into his mouth, I cry out in pleasure, as I hold his head in place. While his mouth works its magic, his thumb and forefinger pull and twist the other nipple, building a beautiful ache between my legs.

His hands skim my waist, stopping at the thin string of my panties. Slipping his thumbs into the material, he pulls them down my hips, over my thighs and off me completely. I feel the roughness of his hands the entire time – a softly abrasive touch that brings me close to the edge of my sanity.

"My God, you're gorgeous," he chokes out as he devours me with his eyes.

"And you're wearing too many clothes," I somehow manage to joke through my lusty hunger. His shirt is already most of the way unbuttoned, so he makes quick work of the last few buttons and sheds it. On its own will, my hand immediately goes to his chest; the need to run my fingers across it is overwhelming.

I trace through his chest hair, following the darkening line that falls behind the waistband of his jeans, which hang low on his narrow hips. My hand goes to his side, to that deeply etched V of his abs. "I thought these were fictional. I'd only read about them in books up to this point."

Shyly, he cants his head to the side as I stare unashamedly at his sculpted body. A few ragged scars mar his six-pack abs – the only imperfection on his otherwise perfect body. His hips jerk when he feels my fingers unsnap the clasp of his jeans. "Is the rest of you that perfect?" My words are coy but bolder than I thought they would be.

"I guess you'll just have to find out," he challenges and then wiggles so that his jeans slide down a little lower. He has to stand to take them off all the way, which is perfect for me. Standing completely naked before me, his beauty is mouthwatering. Everything about him is virile and alive, completely masculine and strong. He palms what I assume is a condom before sprawling out next to me.

Laying side by side, curled in each other's arms, we explore one another with our mouths and hands. He toys with my breasts and nipples as my fingers travel dangerously close to his erection.

"Fuck. If you don't touch me soon, I'm going to lose it," he rasps out in a gravelly voice that transforms into a low groan as I wrap my fingers around him. Shoving his full length into my palm, he loses himself to the slow, rhythmic motion. When my thumb passes over the wide crown, spreading the moisture there, he grits out a loud, "Fuck," before his mouth crashes into mine.

His hand falls to my sex, tracing through the swollen flesh. "I need to touch you," he mumbles before his finger plunges inside of me. "God, you're so hot...so wet...so fucking tight."

I think I try to speak, but all I can manage is some mumbled combination of groans and moans. When he adds another finger, massaging and readying me, I can barely contain my pleasure. "You, please. I want you."

He rips the condom opened with his teeth and rolls it over his length, before settling between my spread legs. Sliding his arms under my shoulders, he holds me close to him as he nudges at my entrance. "It's been so long...too long." I angle my hips up and add, "But I want you so much."

"I want you too, baby. No more waiting for either of us," he whispers against my lips as he gently slides into me. It's a beautifully slick and delicious friction, feeling every rock-hard inch of his length slide into me.

Evan swipes away tears I hadn't even realized I'd shed as he props himself up on his elbows at either side of my head. "Are you okay, baby?" he asks when he's completely inside of me.

My palm scrapes against his stubble and my fingers lace into his hair, pulling his lips to mine. "I'm perfect, absolutely perfect," I reassure him before attacking his lips with my own.

He moves with deliberate slowness, pulling all the way out before sinking back in. As his motion picks up in speed and intensity, he grips my thigh and throws my leg up, hitching it over his hip. The change in the angle hits that sweet spot deep inside. I feel so full that I'm sure my eyes are rolling back in my head.

Through my haze of desire, I feel him shift slightly, wetting the pad of his thumb with his luscious tongue. When he presses it against the throbbing tip of my clit, fireworks ignite in my belly. "Evan...oh...I can't..."

His thumb moves in alternating patterns of slow circles and rapid flicks. "Yes you can and I'll take you there. Let go. Let go for me, sweetness."

As if his words ease away the last vestiges of my control, I come wildly and more passionately than I ever have in my life. "Shit, Lucy. I can feel you. I'm not going to last much longer." His neck and shoulders are tense and bulging as he tries to draw out our pleasure.

"You let go too, Evan. Let go with me." On one last, long, hard plunge deep inside, he grinds out his orgasm against my pulsing sex, pushing me over the edge once again.

Completely sated and unable to move at all, I feel him pull out of me and I immediately mourn the loss of his fullness. He ties the condom in a knot before wrapping it in a napkin from dinner.

Spooning up behind me, he drapes a blanket over both of us and nibbles on my shoulder as he pulls a cushion under our heads. Lost in the comfort of one another, the only sound, save the crackling fire, is our calming breaths.

I must have dozed off, because the next thing I realize, Evan is carrying me, wrapped in the blanket, upstairs to my bed. I wake in his arms and he smiles down at me, placing a soft kiss to my temple.

"Go back to sleep," he whispers as he tucks me under the blankets.

I stare completely confused as he turns to walk away. "You're not leaving are you?" Screw sounding needy. I want him to stay the night.

He comes back to me, sitting on the edge of the bed. Pushing my hair back behind my ear, he shakes his head. "Not a chance on Earth I'm not sleeping next to you tonight." Relief washes over me. As his lips press against mine, any lingering concern I had over what happened is gone.

"I just want to lock the door and make sure that the fire is out. I'll be right back up, sweetness." He pulls the blanket up to my chin and kisses my forehead before returning to the living room.

A Cheshire cat-like grin spreads wide across my face when he returns a few minutes later. "Happy to see me, huh?" he smirks as I cuddle up next to him.

"More than you know." I throw my leg over his and pull him closer to me.

"You're going to have to give me until the morning at least." He playfully nudges his body into mine.

"I can live with that." A comfortable silence fills the room as the stars twinkle up in the night sky. "Oh and Evan," I add just as I start to feel myself drift to sleep.

"Yes, love." The term of endearment makes my heart swell – especially considering the ease with which is rolled off his tongue.

"For the record, that was the best date ever." His chest rumbles in laughter beneath my hand.

March 8, 2013

CHAPTER FIFTEEN

Evan

As winter begins to fade, I find myself taking my morning runs outside rather than staring blankly at the wall in front of my treadmill. The hustle and bustle that made Manhattan pulse with a life all its own, the beat I thought would always be a part of my soul, is slowly starting to be replaced with the quiet serenity of nature only seclusion can afford. It's in those hours of solitude, where I find a pace in the pounding of my feet on the pavement, that I've finally been able to clear my head.

Watching the sun glimmer between the mountain peaks in the distance, I find myself noticing beauty in a world I was certain would always be an ugly place. I know that Lucy's played a part in that discovery as well. Even through the deep breaths of my fifth mile, just the thought of Lucy makes me smile.

I've got it bad. Hook line and sinker style, I've fallen for her and it's the most scared I've ever been in my life. In a good way, I think. By no means am I an expert in relationships, but it seems like we're both tiptoeing a line, too afraid to lose control – to really admit what we're feeling.

Or maybe it's just me.

I do know this — the last three weeks that Lucy and I have spent dating or seeing each other — use whatever euphemism you want — have been the happiest three weeks in recent memory. And if things go as I plan, they'll continue that way.

After my run and shower, I brew a pot of coffee and think about what I need to do today — a whole fat lot of nothing. I decide to call Lucy to make sure that we're still on for tonight and her next home improvement project. I surprised her last week by fixing her garage door while she was at work. It was a simple task, requiring no more than an hour or two of my time and less than a hundred bucks, but her complete shock at me taking care of her was more pay-off than I'd ever imagined. In that moment, I promised myself that I would help her fix what she saw as broken in her home — no matter what the future held for us. Talking to her will most certainly brighten my day and having another project to work on will keep me somewhat occupied.

"Hey, love." I hear her sigh into the receiver. "Bad day at the office?" I know she's been struggling to pull off this charity ball for the Cure-For-Kids Foundation and I hate to see her so stressed at the prospect of not being able to make it work.

"Kind of." More exasperation seeps into her words. "I had this special horse and carriage thing all set up for Chloe and her family, but her doctors don't think it's a good idea for her to be in the open air like that, so I had to cancel. But the real kicker is that I can't find a decent alternative with only a week left to plan." The noise of papers crinkling and computer keys being punched sound out in the background. "And, as if that's not bad enough, we're a few thousand dollars short of our goal, which means it might not happen at all. So, I've been crazy all morning trying to get some last minute donations before I need to call the Palmer's and let them know that their baby girl's princess ball might not happen at all."

"Is there anything I can do?" I feel useless listening to her frustration.

"Thanks, but I don't think so. I've got Linda helping me out and a few other people making calls this morning, so hopefully things will turn around." After a slight pause, she pitches her voice lower and whispers, "Though, if you want to repeat last night, that might help ease some of my stress."

A proud grin unfurls across my face. "Yeah, you enjoyed that, huh?"

"I'm pretty sure I already told you how amazing you were. Repeatedly, if I recall correctly."

"You sure did, love." We share a laugh, recalling just what she enjoyed.

"So are we still on for tonight?" Now that I know things are getting crazy at work for her, I'm not so sure that a leisurely stroll through Home Depot is exactly what she had in mind. "Unless you'd rather put it off for a few more weeks."

"We sure as hell are! I've been waiting to update my bathroom for years and you did such an amazing job on the garage door last weekend that I can't possibly turn down your help. Besides, it'll help take my mind off work for a bit."

"Oh, believe me. I've got plenty of things that'll keep your mind off work and none of them have anything to do with vanities and tile grout."

"You're terrible," she jokes as I imagine her smiling face begin to blush. "Oh, I've gotta run. I just got a memo for an impromptu meeting about the fundraiser. I'll talk to you later, okay?"

"Okay, love. Bye."

After hanging up, I begin formulating a few ideas of how I can help her out with her charity ball. I make a quick list of the calls I'll need to make and get to work. There's no way on Earth that this little girl is going to miss out on her princess ball over a silly thing like money. And there's no way in hell I'm just going to stand by and watch Lucy struggle when I can help.

A few hours, and more phone calls than I think I've ever made in my life later, I think I've got mostly everything taken care of. I had to call Katie for a few things, and she was more than thrilled to hear that Lucy and I were seeing each other. After a quick bite to eat, I punch out a text to Lucy and let her know I'm on my way over to her place to pick her up for our Home Depot date – definitely not the most romantic of places, but I think what I arranged for today more than makes up for that.

When I pull into her driveway fifteen minutes later, she rushes out her front door, never giving me the chance to get out and open it for her. She slides into her seat and leans over the center console, kissing me quickly, a huge smile plastered to her face.

"You're never going to believe what happened this afternoon?" she gushes. The frustration that was so clear in her voice earlier, is replaced by a happiness, letting me know that part one of my plan was successful.

Without even letting me get a word out, she blurts excitedly, "We got an anonymous ten thousand dollar donation. It looks like Chloe is going to get her princess ball. My boss was actually in the middle of going over our budget and that's what brought on that meeting – the one I got pulled into when I was on the phone with you. Anyway," she takes a deep breath, so excited she seems to have forgotten to take one since she sat down, "we were just about to admit defeat, when we got a notice that someone had donated the money to Chloe's ball. We spent the rest of the afternoon finalizing everything."

"That's fantastic!" I lean over and kiss her, trying my best at a poker face that will hopefully reveal nothing of my part in the "anonymous" donation.

She pulls my hands together in hers, and looks up at me. "Would you like to come with me? To the ball I mean? I know it might not be your thing, but—"

"I would love to take you," I interrupt her, bringing her tiny hands up to my lips. "You're adorable when you get all excited, you know that?"

She shakes her head and smirks playfully at me as she clicks the seatbelt into place. The ten- minute ride to the store is filled with more details about the ball, about Chloe and her family, about how excited Lucy is to finally feel like things are going to go her way with this project.

She's been so focused on it all that I don't think she's even realized that we're standing in front of the sinks and faucets. "Which one do you like?" I ask, tipping my chin at the displays in front of us.

"Huh? Oh, those?" She looks on, clearly overwhelmed at the sheer volume of choices laid out before her. "Um, I have no clue. This one's pretty." She points at the cheapest one with the lowest customer reviews.

Not wanting her to feel like an idiot, I pick up another one, stepping in front of the price tag as I do so. "How about this one?" She turns it over in her hand. Seemingly satisfied with it, she nods her approval and tosses it in the cart.

Her focus is completely lost as we stroll aimlessly through the aisles, her chatter entirely centered on the excitement of Chloe's fundraiser. After taking another call from Linda, she slides her cell into her pocket and looks over at me as I'm inspecting some tiles for the backsplash. "I'm sorry. I guess I'm being a crappy date, huh?"

I pull her to my side, wrap my arm around her shoulder and pop a quick kiss to the top of her head. "Not at all." When her phone rings for a fourth time, I can't help but chuckle at her. She steps away and takes the call from Linda while I busy myself in picking out some samples. After a few minutes, she's back at my side.

"Do you trust me?"

She seems more than a little taken back by my question. "Of course I do. Why?" she asks skeptically, but her trust is also implicit.

"Because I'm going to go drop you off at Linda's so you two can finalize whatever details you need to work on, and then I'm going to come back here and pick up everything I'll need for tomorrow." She pulls a face at me, arching an 'are you kidding' eyebrow.

"No, really, it's good. I'm fine." Her phone rings again and she concedes when she sees that it's Linda again. I only hear her side of the conversation, but the smile that splits her face as she explains her change of plans to Linda totally disarms me.

"Are you sure? I don't want to leave you hanging."

"I'm positive. You'll just have to owe me." I wink and she swats my arm before planting a sweet kiss on my cheek.

I drive her to Linda's and make her promise to call me the minute she gets home. She promises to repay me, a beautifully mischievous look playing across her face that has me anxious to cash in on her plan.

I arrive at Lucy's bright and early the next morning. So early, in fact, I'm pretty sure I wake her up. The bathroom is small enough and only in need of a few hours of work that I want to get it done in one day for her. Nothing major is being replaced, but all of the fixtures and surfaces are getting an update. I went with a pale blue and cream color scheme – very beach-like, airy and soft. It reminded me of a conversation we had about a week ago about where she'd like to go on vacation. She said somewhere tropical and relaxing. So while we might not be ready to vacation together yet, I'd like to at least give her a place where she can feel calm and unwind after a crazy day at work.

After a few hours of work, the small bathroom is stripped of all that's unnecessary and it's ready to be overhauled. Wanting it to be a surprise, I kicked her out of her own house for the afternoon. Some manual labor, mixed in with a little creativity is just what I needed. Before I even realize it, it's early evening, the sky darkening as the sun descends behind the mountains. Twelve hours flew by and now Lucy has a beautifully updated beachside inspired bathroom to show for it. Not having much input into it, all I can hope is that she likes it.

With one last touch of glossy white paint to the wainscoting and floorboard, I stand, stretching my back. I have to say, it looks fantastic. Packing away the last of my supplies, I hear her come through the front door.

I hear her gasp from behind me as I fold up the final drop cloth. "Oh, my God! Evan, this is gorgeous. It's perfect." She snakes her arm around my waist and squeezes me tightly. "Wow. I can't believe you did this all in one day."

A proud feeling blooms in my chest at her approval. Always feeling like I've let someone down, it's been too long since I felt like I really deserved praise. "I'm so happy you like it. I remember you saying something about how you wanted a beach house, so I thought this would be a nice place for you to relax."

"You remembered that?" she asks, seemingly shocked that I recalled a tiny detail about her. She turns in my arms and looks up at me, a mystified look on her face.

"Of course I remembered. I was just worried that you wouldn't like it."

"No. I don't *like* it. I *love* it." She stretches up on her toes and kisses me quickly before inspecting her new bathroom.

"This work is beautiful." Awe colors her words as she traces her fingers over the just-dried paint on the whitewashed wainscoting. "I had no idea you were so talented."

"I'm not so sure about talented, bored maybe. It's been too long since my hands and my brain were occupied."

Seductively, she slides up next to me again. "I could figure out another way to occupy your hands." She winks and smiles slyly.

"Oh yeah?" I ask, pulling her close to me.

"Absolutely, perhaps that could happen over there." She runs her hands up the back of my t-shirt, her nails lightly raking across my skin as she tips her chin at the soaker tub that was already part of the room. Shivers race across my body, the base of my spine tingling at the simplest touch from her.

I mumble against our pressed-together lips, "I think that can be arranged."

Lucy steps over the tub and touches the new fixtures with a mixture of reverence and gratitude. "I feel like I can't say 'thank you' enough. I've never had something just for me."

"It's just a few updates. If I could have, I would have gutted the whole room and did it the right way for you – changed everything from top to bottom."

"No, it's perfect just the way it is," she says quietly as she turns on the hot water. Steam billows up from the tub as the water fills the basin. Lucy grabs some bottles out of the small linen closet and drops some liquid into the tub. The smell of lavender curls into the air, relaxing and intoxicating at the same time.

I pull my shirt off as she watches, her eyes glued to my chest as she reaches out to brush her finger across my muscles. "Your turn." I trace the hem of her shirt, letting my fingers press against her heated skin. When she doesn't move right away, I lift her shirt over her head and pull her closer to me, my fingers tucked into the waistband of her jeans. Avoiding eye contact, she looks over my shoulder.

Suddenly, confused by her shyness, I cup her cheek and pull her face toward mine. "What's wrong?"

"Oh, um nothing," she tries, but fails to deflect my question.

"You're a terrible liar, love. Tell me what's wrong, please." I pull us both down onto the ledge of the tub and reach behind us, turning the water off.

After a long pause where the silence in the room falls upon us, she finally says, "I'm really happy with you." She leans in close to me, resting her cheek on my shoulder.

A confused chuckle passes my lips. "That's a good thing, sweetness. I am happy with you too. Happier than I ever thought I would be, actually." Kissing the top of her head, I feel her smile against my shoulder. "So if we're both happy, what's with the sad face suddenly?"

She jerks upright. "Oh, it's not sad. Really, it's not. I promise." I tuck her hair behind her ear and kiss her forehead, silently prompting her to continue. "It's just guilt I guess."

She smoothes her fingers over my furrowed brow. "That didn't come out right," she backtracks and takes a deep breath. "Please don't ever think I feel guilty about being with you. It's just so much, so fast. I worry I'm not doing the right thing." Her adorable face is knotted in confusion.

"Would you like to explain that to me from the bath?" I reach behind us and test the water. "Before it gets too cold."

"See, that's just the thing. Here I am, hopping into a bath with a man I barely know, who I've only just started seeing, who I let in my house all day while I was gone, who I called after only knowing him one night because someone broke into my house, who I begged to stay the night…"

"Shh." I press my finger to her running one-hundred-miles-an-hour lips. "Look, I don't know how things are *supposed* to go. But don't say you barely know me when you know me better than anyone else has. I'm no good at letting people in, so I'm sorry if my…" I search my brain for the right word and I just can't find it, "…if my issues cause you to feel unsure about us, I'll try my best to fix them. I will."

"It's not just your issues. I've got a boatload of my own too." We both relax into one another. After a minute or two of just sitting here, considering everything we've both just said, Lucy surprises me by standing and stripping out of her clothes entirely.

Standing naked before me, she's utterly beautiful and ridiculously adorable trying to be modest at the same time. She slinks into the water. Lightly patting the spot in front of her, she asks, "Are you going to join me?"

Not one who has to be asked twice to crawl into a bath with a gorgeously seductive and utterly confusing woman, I undress quickly and slide in with her. Sitting on opposite ends of the tub, I look at her inquisitively, quirking an eyebrow. "Change of heart, love?"

She crinkles her nose, shrugging a shoulder. "Maybe," she says quietly. "Tell me something you've never told anyone."

I see her game now. Get naked, pull me into the bath and then drag my life story out of me. But as usual, I'm not afraid to open up to her. After splashing some hot water on my face, I decide to tell her about Brody. It's not something that I talk about often. His injury is one of my deepest regrets, one for which I feel I'll never be forgiven.

"A kid lost his leg because of me." The shock and pity I expected to see on her face aren't there. All I see is love and concern as she reaches for my hand through the water.

"Tell me about it."

For the first time in my life, I tell someone about the whole thing. After it happened, I *had* to talk to the counselors at the medical office, but even then, I didn't tell them everything. I was nothing more than a hotheaded kid at the time. I thought I would be able to deal with anything the world threw at me. Little did I know, I was so fucking wrong. After giving her the short version of how the accident happened, she glances down at my stomach, the top of my burn scar visible above the water line.

She scoots over to me, water splashing over the lip of the tub and ghosts her finger over the scar. "I wanted to ask about this the other night, but I figured you would tell me when you were ready." I try to focus on her fingers as they dance across my skin, but the feeling never fully returned there. When she gets to my side, she notices the other scar. A six inch, raised and jagged line that sits atop my ribs.

"What's this from?" she asks carefully, tilting her head to the side in concern.

Now that's something I've never talked about with anyone, but here with Lucy I feel like I finally can. "That was from 9/11."

"You don't have to tell me. If it's too much, I understand."

Pulling her close to me, so that her back is pressed to my front, I twine our fingers together, letting them fall in her lap. I kiss the top of her head before taking a deep breath. "I wasn't working that morning. I pulled a mutual with my partner because I had to come upstate to help Joe with Katie. Sara had just been admitted to a mental care facility and I couldn't take medical leave for a few days. He needed me so I called in a favor. It cost Drew his life." Reassuringly, she pulls our hands up to her lips and presses a soft kiss to my knuckles. "I went for a run that morning and just as I was leaving to go to Joe's, the first plane crashed into the first tower. All of the bridges and tunnels were closed so I ran through the Lincoln tunnel and found the closest firehouse. I grabbed some bunker gear and got right to work. By the time I was able to get there, the towers were both gone."

Cupping my hands together, I wet her hair and then squeeze some shampoo into my palm. Working a lather into her silky hair relaxes me enough to tell her the rest. "I spent the first few hours there just trying to find someone I knew, someone who knew Drew and where he could have been. It wasn't until late the next day that I learned he never made it out." I rinse her hair when I can't find the rest of the words I need to finish my story.

"It was the most horrific day of my entire life. People jumped. They plummeted hundreds of stories because we couldn't save them all. And to know that one of those lives were lost as a direct result of something I did…" I choke back my rising emotions. It's not a day I let myself think of often, but it's one that haunts every moment of my existence.

"You have to know it's not your fault. Please tell me you understand that, Evan." Lucy nuzzles into my chest and I hold her close.

Drawing from her calmness, I say, "I know it now, but it took me a long time to figure that out."

After a few minutes, I take a deep breath and finish, "In the days following the attacks, I worked twelve hour shifts at Ground Zero, digging through heaps of twisted steel and crumbled concrete to find him. Another firefighter heard his last radio call, so we had an idea of where to look for him. I was just hoping to be lucky enough to find him, to at least return his body to his family."

Lucy leans into my touch as I work some conditioner through her long hair, combing through it lightly with my fingertips. "I found his helmet first, crushed on one side and bloodstained in the lining. In that instant, I prayed to a God I wasn't sure even existed that he died quickly. We found his body later that day. Pulling him out of the rubble, we draped his body in a flag, not allowing any time to truly mourn our losses. Staying focused on finding more fallen brothers was the only thing that got me out of bed. I gave up on life in those months. There were so many funerals to attend, so much loss and sadness. It was easier to shut down than open up. He had a family, too. Two little girls and a boy on the way. And it was all my fault he died."

Lucy nuzzles into my chest and I hold her close, fighting back my demons. "So that," I tip my chin down to where her finger is still tracing over the scar, "is from the cancer. I had to have a portion of the lower right lobe removed. I was lucky they caught it in time, before it spread."

Lucy moves quickly, sloshing more water over the edge of the tub. She sits on my lap, chest to chest, and wraps her legs around my waist. She doesn't speak for a few long moments. "That's why you spent your life alone." It's a statement, not a question.

Holding her slick body to mine, I nod as she tucks her head under my chin. "Maybe we know each other better than I think. I mean, we've got more in common that I thought." I stare down at her, more than a little confused.

"We're both so afraid to lose again, that we never let anyone in," she clarifies. "It was the same for me after Jimmy died. I lost myself to being Melanie's mom, to doing what was best for her. I dated casually, more because Linda made me, but I never let anyone close. The thought of loving someone the way I loved Jimmy scared the crap out of me. Knowing a new love could be ripped from my life, just like Jimmy, I just couldn't deal with that. So I chose not to, and well, here I am." Gazing into her eyes, I get lost there. Her pain is so much like mine – it's as if we were cleaved from the same stone. Sure, I've had a difficult time getting over my own loses, but Lucy suffered the loss of her husband. She has been truly alone, and my heart hurts for what she's had to go through.

I rinse her hair one last time as she looks up at me. "I think *here*," she wiggles in my lap suggestively, "is a pretty fantastic place to be."

"Oh, love, I couldn't agree more," I groan as I take her mouth in a passionate kiss. Her fingers tangle in my hair as we devour each other. Tongues dance and twine, teeth crash and nibble, and the sparks fly between us. Wrapping her hair around my wrist, I pull her head back and lick the long expanse of her delicate neck. Biting softly at her collarbone forces a moan from her lips. With my other hand, I toy with her breast, pulling lightly on the hardened tip.

When she starts grinding against me, I remember her initial reservations at even getting into the tub. "Easy, love." She stops and looks at me, confusion paired with a touch of rejection.

I pull a wet strand of hair from across her forehead before brushing my knuckles gently down her flushed cheek. "You were worried we were going too fast." Looking down at our legs wrapped around one another in a bathtub is the perfect backdrop of irony for what I'm about to say. "I don't want to do anything you might have reservations about. If you feel like this is too much, too fast, then I can take a step back. We'll keep it casual."

She crinkles her nose as she wiggles her hips against me. "Yeah, something about this," she adds another wiggle, "doesn't feel casual." It takes physical restraint not to push up into her. I wonder if she realizes how fucking sexy she is.

"Get over here." I shake my head and smirk, wrapping my arms around her back. "This is definitely more than casual, but I don't want you to…"

Her soft lips push against mine; her tongue licks across the seam of mine, seeking entrance. "I do want this, but I guess I'm just scared," she admits quietly as she curls her head into the crook of my neck.

I mumble against her hair, "Me too, love. Me too." She pulls back out of my arms and searches my face. "But what if we promise to be scared together. Screw what we're supposed to do, how slow or how fast we're supposed to move, what we're supposed to label things. Let's just be together and enjoy being happy for the first time in a long time." I can only hope that's what she wants, too.

She kisses me seductively and I know she can feel me hardening and pulsing between us despite the cooling water. "That sounds like a perfect plan. Now, will you take me to bed so that I can show you my plan?" Winking playfully, she unfolds herself from my lap and struts out of the tub, all sexy-as-sin. Standing at the edge of her bed, which is visible from the tub, she crooks her finger at me, but says nothing.

Who am I not to listen to that?

I tie a towel around my waist and walk toward her. "You won't be needing this," she rasps as she slips the knot free. Taking the towel in both of her hands, she rubs it across my body, drying me off, before she pushes my shoulders down, forcing me to sit on the edge of the bed. Her plan comes into focus – as does her perfect ass – as she leans down to run the towel up her legs and across, wiping the tiny beads of water lingering there.

She steps in between my legs and pushes me further back on the bed, crawling over me as I scoot toward the headboard. Pressing her body fully against mine, I feel the heat of her arousal on my twitching thigh. I grab her ass, pulling her close to me as our mouths mate with animal-like ferocity. Breaking the seal of our lips, she looks up at me, eyes wide and with so much passion that they're more black than blue.

"I want to kiss you," she pauses a beat before adding, "all over" in a seductive rasp that makes me throb with need. Her tongue glides effortlessly down my neck and across my still-wet collarbone. Placing hot, open-mouth kisses across my chest, she more than surprises me when he licks my nipple. Falling lower, she reverentially moves her lips across my scars, making sure to look up at me before she nuzzles her cheek against them. "Your body is amazing, but these, they just prove what a beautiful soul you have too."

Her words strip me bare. Here I am thinking she's the most gorgeous woman I've ever met inside and out, and now she's telling me that she feels the same about me. Some of the fear from earlier melts away as she places one last kiss to the scar above my lung.

Raking her nails down my thighs, she kneels in between my legs and stares down at me, passion and desire heavy on her face.

With a feather-light touch, she traces the tip of her pointer finger up and down my erection, from root to tip and back again. When she wraps her hand delicately around me, it's an instinct to push up into her palm. "You're so good with your hands," I ground out from behind my clenched jaw.

"Would it be okay if I try my mouth?" Her shyness is completely disarming and utterly beautiful.

"This is me and you. You can do anything you want, love. But don't you dare do anything because you think you *have* to, or because you think I want it." Despite my words, I want to beg her to wrap her hot, wet mouth around me.

"No," she declares with a confidence that negates her shyness from a moment ago. "*I* want this. I just want it to be good for you. It's been so long…" Her words fade away and even though she never finishes her sentence, I know what she wanted to say.

On a deep breath, she leans her face down into my lap, pressing her hot lips to the wide crown. When her tongue glides across the underside of the tip, I fist the sheet, a white-knuckled grip. "Fuck, Lucy," I groan her name as it takes every ounce of restraint to keep from pushing past her lips.

Replacing the finger that was tracing my length, she now uses the tip of her tongue. My spine tingles and a drop of moisture falls onto my stomach. Her mouth is absolutely perfect. Using her hand, she rubs me relentlessly, bringing me right to the edge of my control.

With her hand wrapped around the base of my cock, she takes me into her sweet little mouth, inch by fucking agonizing inch. Her name falls from my lips, a groan of pleasure, and a sigh of utter contentment.

Her hair falls in a veil around my lap and I pull it to the side. Watching my cock slip in and out of her mouth, as her hand works what can't fit, is mesmerizingly erotic. Wide-eyed and breathless, she licks me one last time before climbing up onto my lap. "Was that…"

"I swear to God, if you plan on finishing that sentence with 'okay', I'm going to have you mentally evaluated. You were amazing, love." She grins, completely satisfied with her sexual prowess.

She reaches across me and fumbles in her nightstand. When the drawer glides open, the electric pink vibrator catches my attention. "You know when I said you could do anything to me, I didn't exactly have *that* in mind," I joke as I angle my head to the side and she sees what I've just caught sight of.

Seemingly at a loss for words, she looks away from me. "Hey," I reach up and turn her face back to mine. "You're a woman with needs – needs I hope to fulfill right now." Her lips pull up at the corners as I wiggle beneath her. "Besides, I think it's hotter than fuck," I add as I grip her neck and drag her to my mouth for a hot kiss.

I take the condom from her and roll it down as she looks on hungrily. I can feel the heat pouring off her body, her sweet little pussy just inches from my hand. It's more than I can take not to touch her – so I do. Cupping her, I trace my fingers through her lips, not at all surprised to feel how wet she is. As my thumb swirls around her clit, I feel her thighs shake with need.

As I press against her with my thumb, I sink into her – slowly with more control than I thought I'd have. "Ahhhh, Evan. You're so…you're just so much everything. I can't take it. I want you."

"You've got me, love." I grip her hips and drive into her, reveling in the feel of the soft pulses that surround me. We find our rhythm easily, getting lost to the feel of our bodies sliding together in heated passion. Her nipples run against my chest and the need to pull one into my mouth is overwhelming.

"Sit up a little, love. Take me. Make yourself come." She looks at me – her lips full, her eyes heated, her breathing erratic.

Her hips start gyrating, gliding effortless over me. Cupping and kneading at her heavy breasts, I pull on her nipples, gently at first, then with more force, causing her sex to clamp down on mine. With her back arched, she hovers above me, only my tip resting inside of her heat. When she slams down on me, our hips meeting wildly, she calls out my name – almost as if it's a curse.

"Beautiful, love. You look absolutely beautiful."

"God, Evan. I can't take it much longer."

"Then let go and take me with you."

She falls back to my body and I wrap my arms around her waist. Gripping her ass tight enough to leave a bruise, I guide her as I bury myself deep inside. Our mouths move of their own accord as our tongues match the motion of our sex. Changing the angle slightly, I drive into her hard, hitting that spot that makes her go crazy. "Evan…I'm…oh, Evan…"

She falls beautifully, coming with such passion that it doesn't take me long to follow right behind her. "Lucy…" I call out on one last push into her.

Her head falls to my chest and I lazily stroke her back, which is damp with a slight sheen of sweat. "A little bit less scared now, love?"

I feel her smile against my skin as she mumbles, "Hmmm."

Kissing her hair, I pull her to my side, pull off the condom with the other hand and wrap it in a tissue from the box on the nightstand.

Lucy's breathing evens out as sleep bathes over her. She curls into me and drapes her leg over mine, securing me in place. Her desire to have me next to her makes me the least scared I've ever felt.

March 16, 2013

CHAPTER SIXTEEN

Lucy

I'm up and out of the house by nine in the morning. Linda and I have a lot to take care of at the hotel where Chloe's ball is being held. I've loaded up the car with everything I'll need to get ready later on. Although, it doesn't really matter how I look. The only important thing is that Chloe feels more than special tonight. So being the perfectionist that I am, I want to be at the hotel as early as possible to make sure everything is taken care of. Disappointing a little girl and fifty of her closest princess friends is most definitely not on my to-do list for today.

First on my list of tasks is to pick up Linda. She barrels down her stairs, weighed down with half-a-dozen bags and a huge-ass box of God-knows-what. I pop the trunk and she drops all of the bags in there, but puts the box rather carefully into the back seat. "What's that?" I ask as she slides in and buckles her seat belt.

"That's another gown that someone donated for Chloe. I didn't want it rolling around in the trunk, that's all." Linda quickly starts spouting off a list of things we need to do this morning. When we pull up to the hotel twenty minutes later, I'm an anxious mess.

The grand ballroom is a flurry of activity. Tables are being rolled in and chairs stacked twenty high are lined up against the walls. Waiters and waitresses are busy polishing silverware and pressing table cloths. When the flowers arrive, it feels like things are starting to come together. Chloe's favorite color is purple, so the entire room is decorated in varying shades of lavender and lilac. It reminds me of Melanie and it makes me miss her terribly.

"Hey, can you come outside and help me with something?" Linda asks as we finish draping the royal purple tablecloth on Chloe's table.

"Sure thing."

When we step outside, I'm flabbergasted to see a white stretch limo waiting for us in front of the beautiful water fountain that's sits majestically in front of the hotel entrance.

Eyeing her suspiciously does nothing to make her crack. She just smirks and pulls me to the limo door, which is being held open for us by the driver. "Good afternoon, ladies," he addresses us and tips his hat as we slide past him.

"Can you believe this?" Chloe calls out with more excitement than I have ever heard in my life. Bouncing in her seat, she looks like she can barely contain her emotions. She's dressed in a Cinderella dress-up gown and pretend glass slippers. If it wasn't for the pale-blue kerchief covering her bald head, you would think she was a regular seven-year-old who hasn't been battling stage three acute myelogenous leukemia for the last two years.

"Hey, pretty princess." I open my arms and she slides over to me. The four of us had lunch together the other day to make some decisions about the ball. Chloe kept calling Linda and me her fairy godmothers and I feel utterly blessed to be graced with the task of giving her the perfect day.

"What's it look like inside? Is it purple like I asked? Are there lights and stars all over, too?"

Her mom, Aimee, sits, smiling ear-to-ear, next to her daughter. She doesn't say anything and I can't even begin to imagine how she feels today. As Chloe chatters on and on about how perfect everything will be today, Aimee simply mouths the words "thank you" to Linda and me from behind Chloe.

"It is pretty amazing in there, but I'm not saying a word." I pretend to zip my lips and throw away the key. "You're just going to have to be surprised when we walk in. Which reminds me, where are we going anyway?" Confusion filters into my words as I stare over at Linda.

She shrugs her shoulders, and leans in to whisper, "Just relax and enjoy."

Chloe spends the ten-minute ride to wherever we're going talking non-stop about her favorite princesses, and I'm so engrossed in listening to her that I'm not even paying attention to where we are.

When the limo stops, I peek out of the window and find that we're at the poshest salon in a three-town radius. "Did you do this?" I quietly ask Linda, not wanting to make Aimee or Chloe feel like I'm as clueless as I actually am.

"Not entirely, but I did play a part." Her sly response is accompanied by a knowing smirk. I'll figure out what she's up to at some point, but for now, I guess I'll just have to enjoy a little pampering.

We're greeted with flutes of champagne as we walk into the salon. There's even one for Chloe, too – filled with sparkling grape juice of course, but she's still giddy with happiness at the idea of having a "grown up" drink in her hand.

We're all seated in a row of pedicure chairs, soaking our feet when Chloe holds up two bottles of nail polish. "Which one should I get, Mommy?" She dangles a pale pink and a deep purple in front of Aimee who pretends to consider the options with extreme care.

"Hmm, well, since it's your special day, why don't you get both." She finally decides, but she winks at me over Chloe's head.

"Really? Can I?" Chloe clutches the bottles closely to her chest and bounces in her seat.

"Of course you can, baby girl. You can do whatever you want today." Though she tries to hide it, I hear the wavering of Aimee's voice. I see the conscious effort it takes on her part not to be consumed by the swelling emotion.

Next is make-up and hair. Chloe is ecstatic to pick out her own lipstick and blush. After her make-up is done, Cherise, the hair stylist, spins her around so that she can't see anything, telling Chloe that she'll take good care of her. "But I don't have any hair," Chloe mumbles and the reality of today comes crashing back around us as Chloe's bottom lip quivers with sadness.

Stepping to the side of her station, Cherise pulls out a box and hands it to Chloe. "Here. This was delivered for you this morning."

Cherise steps to the side as Aimee crouches down in front of Chloe. "Go ahead, baby girl. Open it." She swipes a single tear from Chloe's cheek and looks like she's holding back a river of her own.

Chloe squeals with excitement as she yells out the words scrolled across the front of the box, "Locks of Love. Mommy, I have hair now. I'll be beautiful." Aimee pulls Chloe into her arms and loses the battle with her tears. Pressing her lips against Chloe's kerchief-covered head, Aimee mumbles, "Hair or not, baby girl, you will always be the most beautiful princess I know."

Linda and I watch on, holding each other in a tight embrace though our tears. Cherise spins Chloe around so that she'll be surprised when she sees the final look. Aimee steps next to us as we gather our emotions off to the side of Cherise and Chloe.

"Thank you, both, so much. We wanted to get her one for so long, but money has been tight with all of her medical bills. We applied for one a few weeks ago, but we didn't expect to hear anything. I don't even want to think of the strings you pulled, but I can't thank you enough." She wipes at her cheeks with a tissue as she takes a deep breath. "I've felt like a failure as a mother because I couldn't provide her with something as simple as a wig."

"It's the least we could do, Aimee. We're just happy that she likes it," Linda says, pulling Aimee into her arms for a brief moment before Cherise calls over to us that she's all done.

"Ta-da," she chirps, spinning Chloe around in her seat.

Chloe's new hair is done in soft, ringlet curls that frame her tiny, heart-shaped face beautifully. The look is finished with a sparkling tiara, which Chloe claims makes her look even prettier than the real Cinderella.

Chloe stares into the mirror, mesmerized by her transformation. Cherise keeps her occupied as some other stylists work their magic on Linda, Aimee and me. I decide on a soft up-do of a low, perfectly messy bun. It's classically elegant and it will help to dress up my simple black cocktail dress – the one I'm just now remembering is back at the hotel, in the backseat of my car.

Stephan, my stylist, sprays a final layer of hair spray before proclaiming I look *"magnifique"* as he kisses his fingertips to his mouth. Just as I'm about to turn to Linda to ask her if she grabbed our dresses before she tricked me into thinking I needed to help her with something, a UPS deliveryman catches my attention as he walks toward me in my seat.

"Lucy Crane?" he questions as he pulls out the small tablet from his side pocket for me to sign.

"Yes, that's me," I respond dumbly. After I sign, he hands me the rather large box and I'm surprised it's much lighter than I expected.

Linda looks on from the chair beside me, absolutely beside herself with amusement. She pops out of her seat as Cherise walks up to us. "This way, ladies." She slashes her hand to the side and ushers us into the back of the salon.

The room, which seems to be used as a massage area, is transformed into a dressing room, set up with a few dividers. Chloe and Aimee step out from behind theirs as Linda and I enter the room. Chloe twirls in her powder-blue puffy dress, every bit the princess. "What do you think?"

The room erupts into a loud round of applause and Chloe jumps up and down with happiness. When the noise quiets and Chloe calms down, she points to the box in my hands. "What's that, Lucy?"

"I have no idea. Let's take a look." I place the box on the vanity that's been wheeled in just for us to primp in front of.

I cut open the plain box outer box and gasp in shock when I reveal the simply but elegantly wrapped box. I peel back the silver paper; as I lift the box top, my heart lurches into my throat.

"Oh, my God," I gasp, shocked and extremely surprised. "This is gorgeous," I mumble through my hand-covered mouth. I run my fingers over the satin fabric and pull the dress out of the box entirely. It's been packaged with such care that there isn't a wrinkle on it anywhere. Stunning isn't even a word I would use to describe the navy blue gown in my hands. The one-shoulder design is accentuated with a black sequined applique that sits atop the gathered fabric at the hip. The flared, trumpet-style skirt is sophisticated and classy without being over-the-top. When I catch a glimpse of the Monique Lhuillier designer tag, I can't even begin to comprehend the price. This dress puts the one I had originally planned to wear to shame.

Very carefully, Cherise takes the dress from me and hangs it on the frame of the makeshift dressing room divider. When a sheet of the tissue paper cascades to the floor, I notice a card that must have been hidden in there. Evan's familiar handwriting graces the paper.

> LUCY,
>
> NO MATTER WHAT YOU WEAR TONIGHT, YOU'LL BE THE MOST BEAUTIFUL WOMAN THERE. BUT, I WANTED YOU TO HAVE THIS BECAUSE, WELL, BECAUSE I WANTED TO DO IT FOR YOU. KATIE HELPED SO I HOPE EVERYTHING FITS.
>
> I HOPE YOU, LINDA, AIMEE AND CHLOE ARE ENJOYING YOUR PAMPERING.
>
> I CAN'T WAIT TO SEE YOU TONIGHT.
>
> EVAN XX

Clutching the letter to my chest, I have to fight back the few tears of happiness that threaten to fall. Linda looks over my shoulder and whispers, "See? I had *nothing* to do with today, at all."

She moves away from me telling Chloe that she thinks she saw some more champagne up front. Aimee follows along, saying that they'll give me some privacy as I get ready.

The second they're out of the room, I call him immediately.

"Hey, love." His voice is gruff and sexy.

"Hey, yourself." Happiness permeates my soft words.

"You sound happy," he mutters, sounding like he's trying to catch his breath.

"I sure am. I've been whisked away to a posh salon and I just got a gorgeous gown delivered to me. You wouldn't happen to know anything about that, would you?"

He chuckles through the line. "Maybe," he feigns cluelessness, but I can tell he most certainly had something to do with all of this.

I sink down into the chair and call his bluff. "Yeah, well the note signed 'Evan' is more than suspicious, don't you think?"

He laughs and finally concedes, "Fine, I *might* have had a little something to do with it."

I smile at his playfulness. "It's really stunning. I can't thank you enough."

"I know tonight is important to you, so that means it's important to me." I want to respond that I have the most thoughtful boyfriend in the world, but we haven't defined our relationship – though if this doesn't put a stamp on what we are, I'm not sure what will.

Not knowing exactly how to react to my own thoughts, I offer up an oh-so-eloquent, "So…" and let it hang in the air between us. "Then what are you going to do today?" I'm totally digging for more information, hoping that he'll own up to whatever else he's worked out with Linda today.

"I just got in from a run, and then the rest of my afternoon is classified." Getting more out of him is obviously, not going to happen.

"Fine, you win. I'll see you tonight then, yeah?" I flop back into my chair, slightly frustrated that I couldn't get anything out of him, but mainly, I feel overwhelmed by his loving kindness.

"I wouldn't miss tonight for the world. Have a good day, love."

"Bye, Ev."

The box that Linda brought with her does *not* have a dress for Chloe in it. Linda smirks as she hands it to me. "Okay, I admit, I played a *small* part in helping him out today." Pinching together two fingers in front of her face so there's no space between them, she chuckles as she hands me the box.

I open it, shaking my head in disbelief. Inside there are black, sparkly shoes that match the design on the hip of the dress and a small black clutch to match the ensemble. "Did you help him with these?"

"Of course I did. He was really sweet about asking for help too. I think you got yourself a keeper there, girl." Linda smiles broadly before applying a final dab of lip gloss. "You look absolutely beautiful." She links her arm through mine and we walk out into the front of the salon where Aimee and Chloe are waiting for us.

Everything about this day – the dress, the hair and make-up, Evan's sweet surprises – makes me feel like I'm floating on a cloud. The feeling of being taken care of is something I've denied myself for so long, and today I feel more than pampered; I feel loved.

"Wow!" Chloe gasps and runs up to me. With her arms tightly banded around my waist, she looks up at me with stars in her eyes. "This is the most magical day ever!"

"It sure is, baby girl. Now, let's get going. Your party is about to start." Aimee wraps an arm around my shoulders as she whispers one last "Thank you" to me.

We're all dazzled one last time as we step outside. If we thought the limo that picked us up from the hotel was fancy, well, this limo puts it to shame. It's big enough to fit at least ten people. Sleek and sophisticated, this is the exact thing I was looking for when I started searching a few weeks ago. The few local companies had nothing more than the standard – nothing special. But this stretch Bentley is more than I could have ever planned for. I look over to Linda. "Did you?"

She shakes her head and points to the opening back door. My breath hitches in my throat as a very dapper Evan steps out. Dressed in a classic black tuxedo, he looks absolutely delicious. Knowing the lickability of everything that's *under* that tux makes him look even more edible.

I walk up to him and he takes my hand in his, softly kissing my knuckles. "Hi, love." His words falter just a little before he asks, "I hope it's okay that I did this. You're not mad, are you?"

I stroke his stubbled jaw tenderly, loving the scratchy feel of it on my fingertips. "Mad? More like in awe. This is just too much. I don't know what to say."

He presses his lips to my cheek. "Then don't say anything. Let's enjoy the night. You look beautiful by the way." He looks me over from head to toe, wide-eyed and more than a little hungry.

I run my hands down the front of my gown. "Oh, this old thing," I joke and we share a laugh.

Turning back to the Bentley, I see Aimee filling her husband Chad in on all of the details from our afternoon. Chloe absentmindedly twirls her full skirt off to the side of the adults – alone. Evan notices too and walks over to her.

"Hey, Chloe. I brought something extra special for you today." She beams with excitement as he walks over to the limo. He pulls out a simple rose corsage for her and slips it on her wrist.

"Thank you," she bubbles as she inhales the roses. "Daddy, look!" She barrels into Chad and he effortlessly lifts her up into the air. "Isn't my hair pretty?"

"Prettier than anything I've ever seen, baby girl."

She coils her arms around his neck, basking in his compliments. "Can we go now? Please, please, please!"

"Sure, thing, Chloe. Let's get you to your ball." Aimee and Chad slide into the limo behind her and Linda, Evan and I follow. Of course, no one can get a word in on the ride back to the hotel as Chloe fills Chad in on her 'princess day' at the salon. I'm more than happy to just sit next to Evan and enjoy the feel of his fingers tracing lightly over my exposed shoulder.

When we arrive at the hotel, Chloe is thrumming with excitement. The door opens from the outside. Expecting to see the limo driver, I'm more than surprised to see Reid there – tux and all.

"Princess Chloe." He extends his hand to help her from the limo and she looks up at him with awe. "I'm Prince Charming. Are you ready for your ball?" he asks sweetly and all Chloe can manage is an eager nod.

Reid winks at me as he escorts Chloe into the hotel, looking like she's walking on a cloud. "Okay, so Katie helped me with more than the dress." Evan answers my unasked question. "You said Chloe wanted a Prince Charming and she doesn't know Reid, so I thought he wouldn't mind helping. He was actually quite willing, which surprised me."

"It doesn't surprise me one bit." I stretch up on my toes and pop a kiss to Evan's cheek. "I don't think I'll ever be able to thank you for everything you've done today. And not just for me, but for Chloe and her family." My emotion swells when I think about the real meaning behind this event. This will more than likely be Chloe's only ball – no prom, or wedding or anything like that. Her life won't turn out like other little girls' lives, but pushing down the sadness, I choose to focus on the happiness that today will provide for her, Aimee and Chad.

"There's nothing to repay, love. Just having someone to do all of this for is payment enough." Tucking my arm into his, we walk into the magical fairyland of the hotel ballroom where cancer and sadness cease to exist, where the only thing that matters is the happily ever after – at least for the night.

When the limo drops Evan and me back off at my house, it's well past midnight - time for the carriage to turn back into a pumpkin.

"You're really great with kids, Evan. I've never seen anything more adorable than you dancing with Chloe stepping on your feet."

We walk into the living room and I notice that Evan is more than comfortable here – hanging his coat on the rack, sliding his shoes off and lining them up with another pair he's left here. A huge smile spreads across my face knowing he is a part of my life and that he feels like he belongs here.

"I hope she had a good night," he says as we walk up the stairs, the skirt of my dress rustling noisily with each step.

"She was barely awake when Chad carried her out of there. I think it's safe to say she had a fantastic time." Evan steps behind me and unzips my dress once we get into the bedroom. It's odd how quickly he's become such an integral part of my day and night. All of the nerves I felt the other week about us moving too fast have seemingly evaporated into thin air.

Evan packed a bag before the ball and left it in the limo. He's pulling a pair of sweats and a t-shirt out of there as I change into some pajamas. Curling into bed next to him, I feel comfortable – and nowhere near as afraid as I did just a week ago.

He's clicking through the channels, catching the tail end of some late-night talk show. "Do you want kids?" The remote slips out of his hand as the words tumble carelessly out of my mouth.

His face transforms from calm and relaxed, to tense and nervous in a heartbeat. "Um," choking on his words, he mutes the television and awkward silence falls around us.

Fumbling for some kid of recovery, I slide up against the headboard and look over at him. "What I meant was you were so great with the kids tonight. Do you ever wish you had had your own?" He's got the world's greatest poker face on, so I can't tell which question bothered him the most – the one where I asked him if he wants kids, assumingly with me, the woman he's only recently started dating, or the one where I ask him if he's felt incomplete because he didn't have his own children.

His body feels tense next to me, reluctance to answer either of my questions vibrating loudly between us. "Do I want kids?" he repeats my question, sitting up next to me. The inch that he moves away from me does not go unnoticed. "I never really thought about it." He carefully considers his words. "I mean, yeah, when I was younger I guess so, but then the situation with Brody happened and I drowned myself in studying to be promoted. I kept myself busy doing things for everyone else – for Brody, for Joe when Sara was sick – so that I didn't have to think about what I wasn't doing for myself. Then 9/11 happened."

He runs his hands through his hair and across his face, puffing out a frustrated breath. "The thought of Drew's kids having to grow up without him because of something I did made me give up on the whole idea of a family. I didn't deserve it."

His last words hurt my heart. How on Earth could he think he doesn't deserve something as wonderful as a family? The fact that he's remained single for the majority of his life is a testament to his self-sacrifice, though. "Hey," I cup his cheek, pulling his face toward mine. "I don't like making you feel like this." I smooth out the lines crinkled in sadness at the corners of his eyes. "You did deserve it and you still do. If it's something you want, that is." Those words don't help to ease his frustration – me and my stupid mouth. "I didn't mean anything by it. I promise. I was just – curious I guess; that's all."

"Do you want more kids?" he asks with a touch of uncertainty, twisting to face me.

Completely caught off-guard, I don't know what the best answer is here to salvage this conversation. I've honestly never given the idea of more kids any thought. It was just something that wasn't meant to be. Now that Melanie is basically an adult, the idea of starting all over again – especially when I've already devoted the majority of my adult life to raising a child on my own –

isn't really one that I want to entertain. But, on the other hand, how can I even begin to be so selfish when Evan has done nothing but sacrifice his own happiness. Trying my best to dodge the bullet that I feel like either answer will bring, I lamely say, "I never thought about it." The tone of my words, calculated and cool, essentially puts an end to the conversation.

When he yawns and doesn't say anything more, I wonder if I said the wrong thing. What if he does want kids? Would I be willing to do that at my age? Why the hell am I even thinking about this? We haven't even defined what we are yet? Even though I feel like I could love him, I don't know if I do right now – and I'm thinking about babies?

In stagnant silence, we pull the covers up and fall asleep, uneasily, without making love or even holding each other, for that matter. For the first time since I've slept next to Evan, sleep completely eludes me.

CHAPTER SEVENTEEN

Evan

"You think you'll be able to keep up?" I poke Joe in his somewhat-slimmed-down stomach. Stepping out of my truck, I inhale the not-so-sweet stench of garbage that fills the air here on Randall's Island, where the FDNY training headquarters is located.

"Yeah, I'll be fine, you wise-ass," he retorts, but I see a look of nervousness fill his eyes. It's his first half-marathon, and although Joe's been training with me for the last two months, I have my doubts he'll be able to pull through. Thirteen-point-one miles is no joke, even for serious runners.

Today is the day of the Ring in the Spring half-marathon, hosted by the FDNY in conjunction with the Paralympics Committee – a race meant to raise the awareness of the capabilities of paraplegics and amputees. A project that, since 9/11, Brody Callahan has spearheaded with more passion and commitment than I have seen in anyone.

I catch sight of him over at the registration table and he waves us over. "Come on. There's someone I want you to meet." Joe slings his bag over his shoulder and we make our way over to Brody.

"Hey, old man." Brody claps my back and stands proudly before us. He got a prosthetic about a year or so after his accident. At first, we would "run" races together – starting with me wheeling him all the way to the last few years when he's been capable of running more than I am, and at a faster pace too, something that he's never going to let me live down.

"Hey, kid. Good to see you. This is my brother Joe."

"Joe, nice to finally meet you. Evan's talked about you a ton over the years." Brody and Joe shake hands, but Joe looks more than a little surprised to find out that I've spoken about him to my "work family", as he calls them. He's my brother, of course my firefighter brothers would know about him.

"So, you ready to get your ass handed to you today?" Brody mockingly punches my arm as his wife, his obviously pregnant wife, walks up to us.

"Hey, Kara." Her platinum blonde hair is pulled into a ponytail, which their three-year-old daughter, Lola, twists nervously in her fingers. "Hey, little Lola." She hides behind Kara, but I catch the faintest glimpse of a smile.

"I didn't know you guys had another on the way." I glance down at Kara's basketball-shaped belly and reach out to shake Brody's hand.

"Yeah, a boy actually." Brody moves next to Kara as Lola leaps into his arms. Kara snakes an arm around Brody's waist and a contented look settles across both of their faces. "He should be here in late May." Brody's hand falls to Kara's stomach, stroking it lovingly as he kisses her cheek. Lola looks on, laughing and making kissy noises.

The scene before me makes me replay the conversation — or argument, depending on how you look at it — I had with Lucy. It also makes me miss her fiercely. As Brody pulls Joe over to the registration table, Kara takes Lola inside to use the bathroom. I'm stuck there, by myself, reflecting on my own stupidity.

Do I want kids, as in now at fifty-two years old? Hell no!

But when she went on to tell me that I deserve a family of my own, with such a loving and hopeful look in her eyes, my gut churned with nervousness thinking that *she* might still want a family. At nearly a decade younger than me, she's in a much better place than I am where that's concerned. So, who am I to deny her that? She deserves more than I can give her and I'd be a selfish piece of shit to keep her all to myself when she wants much more than just me.

It's that conflict that's kept me away from her for the last two weeks — for the most part, anyway, because of course I'm too weak to stay away entirely. She's noticed it too, but I think she's too afraid to say anything about it, too afraid it may push me away entirely.

To say that I'm a fucked-up mess over all of this is an understatement. I'm also an asshole for blocking her out, but I don't know what to do. I didn't even invite her to the race. Childishly, I've blocked her out so I don't even know how she's feeling.

Luckily, my nerves over the start of the race get the better of me, and I push thoughts of Lucy and our current non-relationship to the back of my mind. In the years I've been running this race with Brody, I've never been anything short of amazed at the other runners. Most are war veterans – though they are missing a limb, or in some cases more than one; they are nothing short of inspirational. It's always emotional running alongside true American heroes, Brody being one himself. After his amputation, he studied with me and we were both promoted through the ranks, him higher than me, of course. He's spent the last eighteen years of his career training other firefighters and doing more than one person's fair share of community service, giving back to the war heroes who have sacrificed more than everything for their country.

About an hour in, at the eight-mile mark, Brody jogs up next to Joe and I, looking carefree and not at all out of breath. Joe and I, on the other hand, are sucking wind, in desperate need to slow down. "Still got you beat, don't I?" Brody smiles and laughs as he pulls in front of us. Waving goodbye from about five people ahead, Brody pumps his arms in the air, signaling his victory over me, the old man.

"How you holding up, Joe?" If the pale green color of his face is any indication, Joe is most certainly not doing well.

"I'm okay," he wheezes. "But don't make me talk."

We jog past a water table and I grab two cups from the volunteer handing out cups. I slow down to a brisk walk, which matches Joe's jog and hand him a cup. "Here, don't kill yourself. As long as we finish, we're good." Clumsily, he takes the water from me and swallows it back in one huge gulp.

After a few minutes of walking, Joe's breathing returns to normal, somewhat. "I guess a half-marathon was overshooting it a bit, huh?" I joke as we fall in step together.

"Like you said, as long as I finish, I'm good with that." He looks around, taking in the gorgeous spring day. People fly past us – some on wheels, some on bionic legs, all with massive strength. "This is pretty amazing, brother."

"Yeah, I know. It's my favorite event of the year."

"You mean it tops princess celebrations?" Playful sarcasm intertwines itself with the sense of real appreciation he has for what I took part in a few weeks ago. But, he must notice me tense as soon as he mutters the words because he soon follows his jib with, "Everything okay with you and Lucy?"

"We're fine," I dismiss, my words bearing the heaviness of lead.

"Like fuck you are. Spill it," he demands.

Going for shock and awe, I blurt out, "She wants kids."

He stops dead in his tracks. "Really? Isn't her daughter Katie's age?" It almost sounds like he's calling her old, without doing so, of course.

"Yeah, so."

"Nothing. It's just that having done it once before, and essentially on my own, since Sara was so sick most of the time, I just don't think it's something that I would willingly sign up for at this age."

"I thought that's how she would feel too, but when she asked me if *I* wanted kids, I was dumbfounded."

"Do you? Want kids, I mean? What did you tell her when she asked?"

"I said I never had any because I didn't deserve a family. She told me that I do and she looked crushed when I said that. I asked her what she thought about having more kids and she said she'd never thought about it. So I assumed…"

"Wait a second," Joe laughs, stopping dead in his tracks once more. "You *assumed?*" he scoffs through his increasing laughter. "I guess that's something I know better than you. You can never, ever, even if your life depends on it, *assume* to know what a woman is feeling. If you want to know what she thinks, you have to ask her point blank. And if you're still not sure what she means, ask her again. Play dumb, if you have to. Ask for her feelings in their simplest terms, because when you love a woman, the last thing you want to do is go and screw things up over something as ridiculous as an assumption."

"I never said I love her."

Joe smacks me upside the head, a sign of brotherly love. "You don't have to, you dipshit. It's plastered all over that ugly mug of yours. A word to the wise, you might want to clue her in on how you feel, too. I bet it'll help out with all this assuming shit you got going on."

Energized by his words of wisdom, Joe begins to jog next to me. Within a minute, he's a few paces ahead. Catching up to him, I think back over that night with Lucy, over my feelings for her. We did leave things quite unsettled and then let it sit there, festering between us like a sore. I've seen her less in these last two weeks than I have since I met her; they've also been the two most miserable weeks of my life. It's not the first time that I let my cowardice, my feelings of not deserving happiness, get in the way of something I want.

And that's the raw reality of it – I want Lucy. I want to share my life with her. I want her more than I've wanted anything.

The realization that I do love her comes quick on the heels of the previous one. Maybe it's because I've never really been in love before that makes it so difficult for me to recognize those feelings now. Or, like Joe said, maybe it is just because I'm a dipshit.

With renewed determination, I run past Joe and on to the finish line. Catching a glimpse of Brody being congratulated in the arms of his wife and daughter makes me realize how much I need to have Lucy in my life.

But first things first – I have to ask her what she wants and not assume what she means.

Joe and I drive back home the next morning, choosing to spend the rest of the race-day and night with Brody and his family. I'm pretty sure Joe knows I need some space to think because he doesn't say much during the few hours it takes us to get back home. I drop Joe off and hold back my laughter as I watch him limp out of the truck and up the stairs of his porch.

By the time I get home, it's well into the evening, and even though it's early enough to call her, I use the excuse that Lucy is probably going to bed early because she has work tomorrow.

Spineless, chicken-shit is what I am.

But really, I'm just afraid that we'll want two different things.

And then there's the real crux of the issue: is this love?

Turning that idea over and over again in my mind, I get nowhere. Joe's right – again. If I want to know what she wants, what she feels, I'm going to have to suck it up, act like a man, and just ask her.

Just not tonight.

After a quick meal and a hot shower, I flop into my bed instantly recognizing the cold emptiness in the space beside me where Lucy should be. In this moment of stark realization, it's no longer fear that fills my thoughts over how easily Lucy and I have come together, over how quickly things have progressed. No, what fills my thoughts, and aches in my chest, is a painful, vacant feeling. Memories from no more than a few weeks ago flash through my brain, as I recall just how unemotional and desolate my life was before Lucy.

It was beige.

But, with her in my life, I have someone to hold, to protect, to laugh with and to love.

With her in my life, I have vivid colors to which I had been blind for so long.

Realizing I love her and growing enough balls to tell her are apparently two different things. After tossing and turning all night Sunday, I slept well past my normal wake up of six on Monday. Having just run a half-marathon over the weekend, I was more than fine with taking a day off. But without that motivation to get out of bed, I officially had nothing to do for the day. Getting things in order for Chloe's dance helped keep me busy, but in the weeks following it, in the time that I'd managed to screw things up with Lucy, I hadn't been able to find anything else to keep me busy.

As the hours of the day whittle away, I get more and more anxious thinking about calling Lucy. We haven't talked since before the race – haven't seen each other in more days than I want to count, so I can only imagine that she's waiting for me to call her. The proverbial ball is in my court, at least according to the relationship rules I've gathered over the years.

But then again, Lucy defies all of those rules. The phone rings and an image of the two of us from the ball flashes on the home screen. I wonder if her ears are ringing as I sit here and thinking about nothing but her smiling face.

"Hi." My voice sounds pathetic.

"Hey, I wasn't sure if you were back yet. I hadn't heard from you." Her words sound wobbly and unsure, because of me – the asshat.

"Yeah, I got in last night. Sorry I didn't call. I was beat." It's not entirely a lie, an omission of truth is more like it. And, I was beat, emotionally exhausted just thinking about everything going on with us.

A mumbled, "Oh" falls dejectedly from her lips. Travelling through the telephone line, it smacks me in the face. Hearing her upset, and completely at a loss for words, is not something I'm happy about and it's something that's entirely in my power to change.

"We need to talk, Lucy. There's so much I want to say, but I don't want to do it over the phone." Huffing out a pent up breath of frustration over my own stupidity, I soften my tone, not wanting to imply that "we need to talk" for the wrong reasons. A bit more carefully, I add, "When can I see you?"

"I have plans with Linda tonight, and then there's a PR event with Chloe's family on Tuesday." She sounds wounded, like she's expecting me to see her to break things off. But there's also a pissed-off air to her voice that makes me feel the weight of my mistake.

"Wednesday then?" Yes, I fully admit to there being more than a little begging loaded into that question, but I need to see her. I need to fix this.

"I'm not sure. Melanie is coming home Friday and I have a lot to do—"

"Lucy, I'm sorry for everything. Please let me see you so that I can explain. Please say that Wednesday works for you. Please stop making excuses and let me try and fix this."

"I'm sorry, too. I just don't know what to say." Her voice takes on that wobbling quality again as if she's trying to bite back her emotions.

"You don't have to say a damn thing. Just hear me out. Please tell me you'll see me. I know I've been an ass for avoiding you, but I need to see you." When she doesn't respond, the only sound filtering through the line is her sighs, I feel like I might be fighting a losing battle. "I miss you," I add softly, hoping that she can hear the same emotion in my voice that she's trying to suppress in her own.

"I miss you too. I'll come over after work then, okay?"

"Absolutely, but I can come to you if you want. Whatever's easier."

"No, I'll come to you." She pauses briefly, and in that moment of silence, I know that so much goes unsaid — from both of us.

"You got it, love. See you then."

The call ends and I feel slightly hopeful we might be able to figure this out.

The next forty-eight hours pass by in a blur. I do a lot of running, hoping that it'll somehow clear my mind. It doesn't. All I keep coming back to is that I love her and she needs to know that, no matter how she feels about me.

When my legs feel like jelly, I distract myself with cleaning the condo; not that there's much to clean, and it just makes me realize how empty this place really is. Sure, Lucy's house needs a lot of updating — the design is stuck somewhere in the early eighties — but, even despite the lack of updates, it's still a home. No amount of fresh paint or new furniture could ever make this place feel like a home.

Sadly, just the sound of her softly knocking at the door makes my place feel warmer already. With my hand shaking above the doorknob, I take a deep steadying breath.

"Hey," I fumble awkwardly at the greeting, not sure if I should kiss her.

"Hi," she says cautiously as she steps into the open floor plan living area. The scent of her sweetness invades my senses as she takes off her coat. She looks for a place to hang it and then just folds it over her arm when she doesn't see one.

"Here, let me take that. I don't have many visitors," I admit lamely as I drape her coat on the back of the sofa.

"It's nice." Lucy scans the room. Not that there's much to see. It's a total bachelor pad. Television on the wall, couches focused on it, a coffee table in between. There's no extra lighting save the harsh fluorescents that are installed in the entire complex. The only real personal touch in the space is the paint, and even that doesn't say much other than "I'm boring and bland" just like my beige-colored walls.

I blurt out a soft laugh at her nicety. "Sure it is, if you like minimalism to a fault."

"It is kind of lackluster," she admits. "Doesn't look like you at all." Maybe that's because when I had to move up here, leave behind the only life I had ever known, I lost everything that made me who I am. I lost all sense of who I was, and then stumbling into Lucy's life helped me find a small piece of who I hope to be.

"Listen, Lucy…I—" Her cold hand falling to my forearm stops my words.

"Can we sit?" She eyes the couch in front of us. "There are some things that I need to say and I don't know if I can do them standing up." Her words punch me in the gut. I've wasted two weeks — in almost complete radio silence — over something so fucking stupid. It's my staying away that's pissing her off, not this non-issue of kids.

I let her step in front of me, placing my hand on the small of her back. I try to ignore the feeling of her tensing under my hand, but I fail horribly. When we sit next to each other, Lucy is more than careful not to touch me, which hurts more than I want to say, because usually there's not much space between us.

Knowing that I have to say something first, I stumble over my words, not sure of what the best starting point is. With Joe's words of advice echoing in my head, I decide on clarity; we need to get right to the heart of the matter.

"I don't want kids." I let those words, said with brutal honesty, settle in before saying anything else.

Sitting silently beside me, she takes in my words, carefully rolling them around in her brain, I'm sure. "Good, neither do I," she responds bluntly, but there's still something there, some emotion simmering below the surface.

"Then what—"

She cuts me off and finishes my sentence at the same time. "Then why am I so upset?" I nod, feeling like a fool being scolded. "It's easy, Evan. I'm upset because we lost out on two weeks because you couldn't just tell me how you felt." Her hands fly between us animatedly as her emotions rise.

"I—I wasn't sure. I—I didn't know," I stammer.

"I get that." She lets her flailing arms settle to her side. "I understand you didn't know how I felt, but you also didn't *ask*." Her deep puff of frustration settles between us. "I don't want kids either. I'll go on the pill," she says decidedly and her words settle the anxiety I've been feeling since this whole misunderstanding began.

She takes a deep breath and holds my stare. "If we're going to keep seeing each other—"

I slice through her words now. "There is no *if*. I want you. I want to be with you. I fucked up because I was scared, but I promise never to shut you out again." I pull her hands up to my lips. Pressing against them with so much tenderness, I mutter, "I'm so sorry…" A tense silence starts to fill the space between us. "Are we okay, Lucy?" I pull her chin in between my fingers, angling her face toward me when she won't look at me.

"Yes and no." Well that answer clarifies *nothing*.

"You're going to have to help me out here, love. Are we okay?"

"No," she answers quietly.

Fuck. I fucked up real good this time.

"But we can be," she adds softly, leaning into my touch. "We can be better than good if you just promise to be open with me. You can't shut me out just because you're unsure of something. That's not fair to me."

"You're right. It's not fair and I was an ass. Say you'll forgive me." She laughs at my last words.

"You're a piece of work. Demanding things from me now, are you?" She angles her head to the side, pointing an accusing, but joking finger in my face. We both let out a chuckle as some of the tension fades away. "When you stopped calling, I got really scared you were leaving me," she admits after the laughter subsides.

"Not if I have anything to do with it, love." She visibly relaxes as I pull her into my arms.

"Now, I just need to know one thing." My stomach twists with a touch of nervousness. "I need to know that even though you don't want kids," looking me directly in the eyes once again to avoid any kind of miscommunication, "which is exactly what I don't want either..." My lips quirk up thinking about how well this beautifully breathtaking woman before me already understands me. "If you want me, if you want to be an *us*, then Melanie has to be part of that equation."

"Of course," I answer her instantly, without any hesitation. I squeeze her tightly, hoping to wring out any doubts she may have. "She was always a part of what I hope to be with you." Combing my fingers through her hair helps her relax against my chest. "I just hope she'll be as open to the idea as we are."

"She has no choice, really. You're a good man and she'll see that we're happy. I'd love for you to meet her, officially if you're up for it. She comes home this Friday and I was thinking about having Maddy and Reid over for dinner."

"Wait. You were going to cook? I don't think your microwave can handle that kind of volume." I raise an eyebrow and she slaps my chest playfully before caressing it tenderly.

"I've been getting better, actually. You've inspired me to try harder. Besides, I wasn't a terrible cook when Melanie was younger." Pride swells in my chest at seeing how willing she is to move beyond her comfort zone.

"What I was going to suggest, before you openly mocked me," now she raises an eyebrow, "was for you to come over. You already know Reid from the ball and I've never met anyone who didn't immediately like Maddy. And you know Linda, too. I think it could be a really great night. What do you think?"

"I think I would like nothing more than to meet the person you love most in the world. I would be honored, love. Under one condition," I add quickly and she just stares me down, not even bothering to ask what the condition is. "You let me cook."

Her lips pressing softly up against mine, through a huge smile, let me know that she is more than happy to agree to my terms.

CHAPTER EIGHTEEN

Lucy

"She's here!" Maddy squeals as Melanie and her roommate pull into the driveway. She jumps out of her chair at the kitchen table and races out the front door.

"You ready for this?" I ask Evan, who's standing next to me as I chop the veggies for the salad - well, supervising me is more like it.

Tossing a dishtowel carelessly over his shoulder after drying his hands, he smiles lazily at me. "About as ready as I'll ever be." He leans down as I stretch up on my toes, kissing me sweetly before the girls make their way back inside.

Maddy already knew about us - not like it had to be a big secret or anything like that. But when Evan called Reid earlier in the month – after many assurances from Katie that he would definitely say yes, to see if he was up for playing Prince Charming for the night, Maddy developed a soft spot in her already mushy heart for Evan.

Linda steps in from the garage, carrying a few groceries from the extra fridge out there, when she sees Melanie walk through the door. She shoves the bags into my hands, totally ignoring me as she barrels toward

Melanie. If there's ever anyone who loves Melanie remotely as much as I do, it would be Linda.

When Linda steps to the side, I catch sight of my baby girl. Thoughts of Chloe and how precarious life can be, and how lucky I am to have her here with me, swim in my head. Wrapping my arms around her, I revel in the feel of my daughter's arms holding me back just as tightly as I'm holding onto her. "Oh, Melly Belly! I missed you, baby." When I try to step back, and hold her at arm's length in front of me, she doesn't let me go, whispering softly into the close space between us, "I missed you too, Mom."

We say the rest of our hellos at the front door with Linda carrying on about how Melanie hasn't been home nearly enough. She introduces us to her new roommate, Peyton, who I can already tell is a little firecracker. I like her instantly. Melanie and I share a knowing look, one of sadness. We've talked a few times in the months since dropping her back off at school. I know that something's been going on, but I haven't pushed. This is her time to shine, her time to figure out who she is.

Funny how we're suddenly leading very parallel lives.

Evan's kept his distance, maintaining the pot of bubbling sauce in the kitchen. I think he stayed inside partly to calm his nerves, but mostly to give Melanie and me some space. Reaching down between us, I pull Melanie's hand into mine just as she catches a glimpse of Evan. Her brows knot together in confusion, trying to place him I'm sure.

We both stand before him as he casually drapes the towel over his shoulder, his eyes twinkling at the both of us. Squeezing Melanie's hand, I take a deep breath and dive right in. "Melanie, I'd like you to meet Evan."

She stares dumbly, still not completely getting the whole picture. He offers her his hand in a cordial greeting and I almost laugh out loud at the formality of it. Keeping in mind that he's trying his damned best to make a great impression, I bite my tongue as he introduces himself. "Hi, Melanie. It's good to see you, again." He grins goofily at her as she looks like she's rolling the word "again" around in her head, hoping that it'll stick.

"Hi, Evan," she questions, still not placing him.

Unable to watch this ship sink any further, I jump in. "Evan is Reid's stepdad's brother. You met him back in December, remember?" It's crazy to think only a few months have passed, and the way in which the recognition slides slowly over her face, I can't help but wonder exactly what's been going on in Melanie's life in the same span of time.

Sliding next to Evan, I snake my arm around his waist, hoping to lessen his unease. Melanie looks on as if the whole thing is happening in slow motion, before blurting out, "Oh, my God!" She flails her arms between us rapidly. "Are you two...?"

Her tone is more than shocked — maybe a little angry if I'm reading her correctly, but I hope I'm wrong. Man, this girl needs to adopt some kind of social filter.

Hooking my thumb into Evan's belt loop, I calm myself, hoping that she's not mad. "Yes, we are, Melanie," I mutter quietly, but sternly at the same time.

Looking up at Evan, I hope to reassure him that everything will be just fine.

Her face splits into a huge smile a moment later and her lack of a social filter rears its ugly head again. "Well, it's about freaking time," she shrieks excitedly, pulling both Evan and me into a warm and loving embrace. There's the girl I know.

Reid walks in just as she's letting go of us, giving Evan and me a moment to debrief, I guess you could say. "That wasn't horrible, right?" I sneak a quick kiss, willing him to be okay.

"She's feisty," he says in a very matter of fact tone, before softening to the Evan I know and love, adding, "just like you." His eyes are a stormy grey, a mixture of tension and easiness.

As Reid walks over to us, greeting me with a warm hug and kiss to the cheek and Evan with a handshake and backslap, I stumble over what I just said in my head.

Wait a hot second, the Evan I know and love! *Do I love him?*

Watching on as he talks animatedly with Reid, catching up on the start of the baseball season, I have an epiphany, one that I was too afraid to allow myself to realize before this very second.

I love him.

Who knows how long I've been staring dreamily over at him because when Reid steps back inside, Evan raises an eyebrow at me.

"What?" he asks self-consciously.

"Oh, nothing. Just taking this all in, that's all." He pulls me up in his strong arms for another stolen kiss before it's time to eat the meal he's cooked for us.

Evan keeps his hand on my thigh through the meal, seductively tracing light circles over my jeans, skittering thrill bumps along my skin. Melanie eyes us from time to time, alternating between smiling warmly at us and raising an eyebrow. I can only imagine the list of questions she's compiling in that pretty little brain of hers. Having only just been able to admit that I love him to myself, I'll have to avoid the rather deep conversation she'll try to drag out of me later.

"So what'd you think about Harvey? You think he'll finally pull the Mets out of this rut?" Reid's been engaged in baseball conversation with Evan since the meal started and I love him to death for making Evan feel at home. Though, I guess it wasn't too long ago that Reid was "the new guy" around here.

"The Mets are gonna need a hope and a prayer to pull them out of what they've dug themselves into the last few years, but yeah, I like Harvey. Kid's got some major talent," Evan spouts off his sports knowledge, losing me and everyone besides Reid in the process.

Rolling her eyes skyward, Melanie pretty much hates all things sport related, but at least she waits for a break in their conversation before chiming in. "This is really great, Mom." Melanie raises a forkful of the baked ziti. "It's good to see you cooking again. I know how much you enjoy it."

Evan shoots me a wry look, his eyes mockingly screaming, "Oh really!"

"I haven't had a home-cooked meal like this in months." She continues, totally blowing up my spot, as she would say.

"Yeah, Momma. You're going to cook for us when this little sucker gets here, right?" Reid rubs Maddy's protruding belly lovingly, before throwing her under the rug. "Because you know this one," he kisses Maddy's temple softly to ward off the sting of his playful dig, "she can't cook to save her life."

"I agree, Melanie," Evan plays along. "This puts any meal *I* could cook to shame," he winks, grinning smugly at me. Leaning down to pop a kiss to my cheek, his hot breath tickles my skin, and I feel the smile pulling at his soft, full lips and they press against the burning hot apple of my cheek. "Can't cook, huh? Nice one, love. You had me fooled." His words are mumbled softly; no one else is able to hear them over the lively chatter of the multiple dinner conversations going on.

Evan and I exchange a broad smile as he gently squeezes my thigh, his hand calming my jitters of being outed by my wonderful daughter. Evan lets Maddy, Melanie, Linda, and me get to know Peyton, pulling Reid into the kitchen to help him with the dishes. He says that it's all about letting the girls chat, but I know he could use some guy time, or maybe he's doing some digging of his own. Who knows? Either way, I appreciate it more than he knows.

While I've always loved every square inch of the place in which I've lived, it hasn't felt like much of a home since Maddy and Melanie left. But now, with everyone I love in the same room, my heart feels like it's bursting at the seams.

So as evening falls, and everyone gets ready to leave, I feel a tinge of sadness as the night comes to an end.

Melanie and Peyton are sitting on the couch, lost in idle chitchat about God-knows-what as I walk Evan to the front door. As he grabs his coat from the rack, he says a bit too loudly, "All right, Lucy, I think I'm going to head home too. I'll let you girls catch up." Melanie hears him over the too-loud noise of the rerun sitcom and stands to say goodbye. He speaks before she can get a word in. "It was really great to see you, Melanie. Hopefully, the three of us can get together before you have to go back."

"I would love to, Evan." Melanie's voice is sincere and happy.

Melanie sinks back into the sofa, returning to her conversation with Peyton, but I catch her stealing glimpses of me saying goodbye to Evan; honestly, I don't care what she sees.

He strokes my cheek with his knuckles, and then tucks a lose strand of hair behind my ear. He kisses me quickly, not wanting to draw too much attention to our moment. "Goodnight, love." His lips dance along my jawline. "Oh, and Friday night, you're cooking for me." His chest vibrates with a hearty laugh as his lips pull into that lopsided grin that, before meeting Evan, I was sure was only fictional.

By the time he leaves, Melanie is not so patiently waiting for me at the kitchen table. She asks, "Can I make you some tea, Mom?" But I know what she really means is, *"sit your butt down and fill me in on every single detail."*

Reaching under the cabinet to get a dishwasher tablet, I laugh at her transparency. "I think I'll pass on the inquisition for tonight, Mel." Since the dishwasher is just about as old as Melanie, any kind of conversation would be pointless anyway. Mission accomplished: score one for Mom.

I guess transparency is genetic, because she sees right through my plan. She loops her arm around my waist and we walk up the stairs together. Squeezing me tightly one last time before heading to her room, she quips, "Fine. You're off the hook for tonight, but tomorrow, I want to know everything."

I can't stifle the snicker of laughter that bubbles past my lips. "You got it. Love you."

"I love you too, Mom."

I walk toward my room, feeling as if a cloud of happiness is buoying my weight. A sense of completeness glows around me, and even though he's not here next to me, the "goodnight, love" text, followed by a winky face lulls me to sleep, just as his strong and secure arms would.

Melanie is practically vibrating with anticipation the next morning. She's just dying to get the scoop on my love life. And it's not that I don't want to share, it's just that talking about romance with my daughter is just…well, it's just a bit weird. I don't in any way want her to ever think that loving someone else diminishes how much I loved — and still, in so many ways, love her father. My willingness to fight, as fiercely as I possibly can, for my newfound happiness, takes over and I give her the dirt for which she's digging.

"He's cute," she smirks as the words fall from her wryly-smiling mouth.

Flashes of Evan's chorded muscles moving smoothly above me, dance in my head. The hot sensuality of everything he does plays back in my mind like some kind of erotic instant replay.

"Who?" I play dumb, trying to cool the heated images of Evan making love to me.

"Evan. Besides, Reid was the only other guy here last night and that would just be weird." Melanie shivers and mocks a gagging noise. The giggles bubble in my chest easily as she reaches out to grasp my hand. "I'm really happy for you, Mom," she adds sincerely.

Giddiness fills my chest as I finally let myself share how I feel about him with Melanie. "He is pretty cute, huh?"

"Well, sure. If you like salt and pepper hair, a chiseled face and a muscular body, I'd say so!" Melanie quirks an eyebrow and smirks at me.

After we recover from our fit of girlish laughter, I fill her in on mine and Evan's rather brief history — leaving out our recent "break" of sorts and conversation about kids.

When Melanie candidly asks about what I see in my future where Evan is concerned, I freeze momentarily. I know how I feel, but I can only hope he feels the same way. And, I know she's an adult and all, but I don't want to let her down if things with Evan don't pan out.

"Oh, I don't know. It just seems like such a fuss to change how things are. He's got his life and I've got mine. That's good enough for me." I'm deflecting and I'm sure she can tell, but when a look of sheer compassion fills her young face, I reach out and grab her hand.

Her eyes roll up skyward as she pulls her hand from mine. "But what if your life and his life came together somehow. Maybe it could be some kind of "our" life, she air quotes, mocking my earlier deflection.

But no matter what I try to conceal from Melanie, I can't lie to myself any longer. I do want that. I want an "our" life. I just have to tell him that.

Melanie and I spend the rest of the morning catching up. Well actually, I spend the rest of the morning telling her all about my life, and she clams up big time the second I ask her about hers. That's okay though. She's always been like that and I know in her own time, she'll open up to me.

When she says she's going to spend the day with Maddy while I go to a few yard sales with Linda, I feel better knowing she'll at least open up to someone.

And speaking of opening up to someone, Linda walks through the front door just minutes after Melanie and Maddy step out of it. She walks right into the kitchen and makes herself a cup of coffee. Sliding into the seat next to me, she gives me the once over as her lips pull up at the corners.

"Last night went well, huh?" she says around the lip of her mug.

"Yeah, definitely did. I talked with Melanie this morning too. She seems really happy about me and Evan."

"It's difficult not to feel happy for the two of you. You're good together. That much is plain to see." She pats my hand lovingly and then pulls a paper out of her purse, outlining our stops for the morning.

It's cheesy as hell, but I can't help but feel like there's love mingled into the warm spring air. I pick up a few things for Evan along the way — some decorative accents that his condo desperately needs.

We grab lunch at the local diner. When we're all done and as we're waiting for our salads, I fold my hands together in front of me, and lean across the table.

"I think I love him." I drop that out there, as I begin nervously fidgeting with the napkin.

"You think?" She tosses her wadded up straw wrapper at me as she laughs not-so-quietly.

"It's that obvious, huh?"

"You wear your heart on your sleeve. Of course, it's obvious. Maybe not to him, though. Have you told him?"

"Not yet. With things being a little stilted with him the last few weeks, and then being nervous over him meeting Melanie, I haven't had the guts to say it. And then of course, I've only just been able to say it to myself. The thought of telling him makes me so anxiety-ridden." I hold my palms out to her. "Look. My freaking hands are sweating right now just thinking about it."

"Eww, gross!" Linda shoves my hands away as the waitress strolls over with our food.

My stomach is doing all sorts of flipping and flopping, so I just poke at the lettuce. "What if he doesn't love me back?"

Linda shrugs her shoulders, and around a mouth full of food, mumbles out, "Well, you'll never know unless you tell him. And," she pokes her fork at me, "you're not getting any younger sweetheart. Better let him know now before you end up with even more cobwebs."

"Oh, like you're some kind of spring chicken!" I kick her shin under the table.

"Ow!" She grabs her leg as she pulls a face at me.

We finish out the meal chatting about everything and nothing. It turns out that after Evan and I became an item, those were her words and not mine, she opened up to the idea of dating again – more seriously, not just the occasional fling. So far, she hasn't had much success, but she's hoping the date she has planned for this weekend will change things up where her love life is concerned.

Me, I'm just happy that my best friend finally decided she's ready to give men another chance.

I'm sure she feels the same way about me.

That Friday night, I make plans with Evan — I just don't tell him. I leave work early and head over to his condo after picking up some things.

After knocking on his door, I wait patiently and just hope that he's not too busy. His truck is in the parking lot, so I know he's here, but after two minutes, he still hasn't answered. I knock again, but still no answer.

I try the knob and it's unlocked, so I crack the door open slightly and peek into his living room. He's not there, but I hear music buzzing through the space. I step inside and pinpoint the loud bass of Pink Floyd pounding out from his bedroom. He's singing along, loudly and horribly off key, but it's genuine and full of life. Hearing the words of "Wish You Were Here" fall from his lips makes them sound even sweeter — the rhythm more sensual, the beat more erotic.

I drop the bags next to my feet, lean up against the doorframe and watch him as he pulls a plank for hardwood flooring out of the box next to him. The floor is bare except for the small area he's completed in the corner. There's a small table saw set up and tools scattered all over the sub flooring. Completely void of furniture and a rug, the sound fills the room harshly, echoing off the walls and bare floor. How he still hasn't heard me, I'm not sure. It probably has something with the sheer volume of the music, but I am thoroughly enjoying the show without him noticing me just yet.

With his shirt off, I see every rippled plane of hard muscle gracing his back. Watching him feed the flooring carefully through the guide on the saw, makes my mouth dry. His biceps flex and pull; his ass looks like a work of art shifting under his threadbare jeans.

They slide down his narrow hips slightly and he just lets them hang there, unknowingly letting me enjoy the show.

When the song comes to an end, and he's done trimming the plank of dark, maplewood flooring, he grabs a bottle of water and chugs down half of it in one large gulp.

"Hi," I mumble, my voice all breathy and filled with lust.

He turns at the waist, swiping his chorded-with-muscle forearm across his mouth. "Hey," his word holds a moment of surprise, before licking his lips seductively. "You look breathtaking, love." He scans my outfit — a tight black skirt that falls in a cute ruffle right above my knees and a pale pink shirt with pearly buttons down the center. I've come to realize he has a thing for legs so I purposefully chose a pair of shiny, black three and a half inch heels to wear today.

Strutting over to me, he reaches into my hair and pulls out the clip that's holding it up in a messy knot. "There, that's better." He kisses my cheek as he inhales the vanilla-scented cloud that my falling hair provides.

Pressing my hands to his chest, I stretch up on my toes a little, pressing my lips right next to his ear. "No. You look…" Words escape me, so I trace the tip of my tongue in a steamy, hot line around the outer shell of his ear. I move my hands from his chest, enjoying the feel of his chest hair under my fingertips, and coil them around his neck as I assault his skin with my lips. A groan of pleasure rumbles in his throat as I lace my fingers into his hair, pulling his neck to the side. Lightly grazing my teeth over his skin, I nip gently. "You are absolutely edible."

His mouth attacks mine, roughly and passionately. The velvety slide of his tongue against mine sets a pulse of desire coursing through my body. A small flicker of pain erupts at the nape of my neck as he grabs a fist full of my hair, holding me in place as his tongue plunges hotly into my willing mouth. The pain vanishes quickly and he licks and nips along my jawline and down the exposed skin of goose bump covered neck. Mumbling against my skin, he asks, "What are you doing here? I thought we were meeting later?" He reaches down and grabs my ass, hitching my leg over his hip.

"You don't seem too upset," I rasp as I grind my hips against his rock-hard erection. His only response is a low groan that I feel vibrating against my chest, pebbling my nipples even more than they already are. In two long strides, he moves us to the wall, sandwiching me between him and it.

"God, you're so fucking hot," he says in between sensuous kisses that leave my skin feeling as if it's been licked by a flame. Holding both of my wrists in one hand above my head, he stares fiercely into my eyes as his other hand works the buttons of my shirt. He pulls it out of the waistband of my skirt and gazes down at my breasts as they threaten to fall out my sheer lace, pink bra.

My nipples press against the thin fabric and his hungry stare makes them harden even more — almost to the point of being painful. "Please, Evan," I beg, but all he does is lick his lips and lean his forehead against mine.

"Please, what?" he challenges before moving his mouth across my neck and collarbone. Arching my back, I shove my breasts into his face, hinting at what I want.

"Real subtle, love," he chides as his fingers dance across my ribcage, coming close to, but never touching me where I want him to. "But if you want something, you're going to have to tell me. I want to hear you."

The moan that flies out of my mouth and reverberates through the empty room is one born out of desire and frustration. We haven't made love in weeks and now he wants to test me, to make me beg. Turned on and beyond annoyed, I arch my back again.

He simply tsks at me as he licks his lips. "I don't want anything between us this time, or ever again." He holds my chin in his hand, angling my head to his. "Now, tell me what you want," he demands, sending shivers of desire racing throughout my overheated body.

"I want your mouth on me," I whisper, arching again. He rewards me with an open-mouth searing kiss to the upper swell of my breast. "More," I cry when his lips are gone. He snickers at me, but releases my captive wrists. After stripping me of my shirt, he tosses it on the floor. Hooking his thumbs into the straps of my bra, he slides them down to the middle of my upper arm.

Lowering his head to my breasts, he nuzzles and licks, but doesn't do anything to quench my needs. "Evan, please, your mouth…on me…now. Please…" The frantic panting of my words must set him loose, because without any warning he's got both of my breasts squeezed together - almost painfully. Alternately pulling each nipple into his mouth through the lace of my bra is probably the hottest thing I've ever seen. Both the sight and the feel of his tongue flicking against my nipples sends a rush white hot need straight to my core.

"Yes...yes...yes..." The words fall out of my mouth in time to the grinding of my hips.

"So sweet, love. You're so fucking sweet." He tears my bra the rest of the way off and kisses his way down my stomach. Rucking the skirt up over my hips, he pushes it up so that it bunches at my waist. He kisses across the span of my hips before placing one hot kiss to the juncture of my thighs, over the satin panties. He kisses again, trying to nudge my legs wider.

Kneeling before me, he looks up at me. His stormy-grey eyes could melt the panties off any red-blooded woman. It's obvious what he wants, but I decide to throw his words back at him. "I want to hear you, Evan," I mock sexily, arching a seductive eyebrow.

The sultry smile that pulls on the corners of his luscious mouth makes my legs tremble. Of course, he notices me shaking, but that doesn't stop his torment. Gliding his hands up my thighs, he hooks his thumbs into thin string holding them in place. Just when I think he's going to pull them down, he simply tugs them to the side.

"You want to hear me, love?" he questions pointlessly, as he runs his tongue along the seam of my wet flesh. "Fine," he adds, before probing his tongue just a little deeper. "I want you to spread your legs as wide as you possibly can." His palms move roughly to my inner thighs, spreading me as per his demand. "And then," he says softly, as he nuzzles against the small tuft of neatly trimmed hair, "I'm going to make you come with my mouth, drinking in every last drop you can give me." I whimper at his words and lace my fingers into his hair. "Does that sound okay?" he teases, placing heated kisses on my inner thighs.

"Evan, yes. I want that. Make me come. Please, make me come." My words push him over the edge of his control.

Holding my lips back with his thumbs, he licks and kisses my heated, wet flesh, before dipping his tongue deep inside. Using just the tip of his tongue, he traces lazy circles over my hardened clit. Lost to the feel of his tongue flicking over the tight ball of nerves, I cry out in pleasure when he plunges two thick fingers into me. Curling them forward, he massages and stretches me until I'm pulsing and clenching around his fingers.

He works his tongue in long, broad strokes from my center back over my clit in a rhythm that has me coming wildly on his lips. "Ahhh... Evan... I'm coming."

Grinding against his mouth, I ride out the last waves of pleasure, before standing and unbuttoning his jeans. Shoving them down his hips, he toes them off and kicks them to the side. His arm slides under my knee as he rests my leg in his elbow.

In between wet, passion-filled kisses, he mutters against my lips, "And now, what I'd like to do," the wide crown of his erection nudges at my pulsing entrance. "I'd like to slide into you, slowly, before making love to you up against this wall."

I don't have time to respond as he inches into me. Stretching and filling me deliciously, I feel like my control is dangling dangerously off the edge of a cliff. When he buries himself all the way, it's a plunge I can't avoid taking. "God, Lucy. You're so fucking hot. You feel...so... you feel like heaven. All wet and silky...fuck..." he growls into my mouth.

He pulls all the way out before driving right back in. Pushing hard up against my hips, he rubs against my clit. Stroke after stroke, he builds my desire before it's too much to take.

"Evan, your hands. Use your hands...rub my clit, please, make me come again. Please, baby." He smirks sexily as me − a searing hotness claiming his face. Having gone so long without sex meant that our first few times were filled with a good bit of shyness and me fumbling to voice my desires. Now, just hearing me say that word "clit" has him all sorts of riled up.

He dips his thumb into my mouth and I lick the pad before he lowers it to our joined bodies. Timing his touch to the rhythm of his thrusts, it only takes mere seconds before my inner walls clamp down around his cock, pulsing and beating with the massive force of my orgasm.

"Fuck...Lucy, I feel that. God... I'm..." He cradles the back of my head before pounding into me with more force than he's ever used before. I claw and scratch at his bare back, needing to feel him even closer to me than he already is.

On one long, hard, last stroke, he calls out my name as his orgasm pours into me. He eases my leg out of his arm and settles my feet to the floor. We're still connected, the last pulses of pleasure vibrating between us. He sweeps the hair that's plastered across my cheek behind my ear and holds my jaw in his hand while tenderly sweeping his thumb over my cheek.

Our ragged breaths fill the small space between us and I lean into his touch. "Evan?"

"Yes, love"

I reach up and stroke my fingers through the day-old stubble gracing his strong jaw. "I love you." I say each word slowly, carefully, letting my mouth embrace the full weight of their meaning.

He takes a deep breath, pulls me close to him, presses his lips softly against mine and then leans his forehead against mine. He inhales a shaky breath, and for a moment, I let my nerves get the best of me. "But you don't," I stammer nervously. "It's okay. It doesn't change how I feel," I concede and swallow my pride. Trying to avert my tearing-up eyes, I tilt my head to the side. He captures my face in both of his hands, and brings his lips to mine, pressing a tender kiss there.

"I've never had anyone say those words to me before. I just needed a minute to take them in." Kissing me again, he smiles against my lips. "I love you too, sweetheart. I think I loved you from that first night we slept next to each other. Holding you, I watched you sleep, and my heart, it just melted for you."

Our tongues twine together slowly. Not wanting to rush the moment, we savor the kiss. I trace my tongue over every centimeter of his lips, memorizing him. "Keep doing that and I'm going to show you I love you all over again." He throbs to life inside of me and I kiss him harder, more deeply.

We move again with less rush, but no less passion. We keep focused on one another the entire time, each push and thrust connects our eyes even more. Our bodies are covered in a light sheen of sweat easing the sensuous glide of our skin. I hitch my leg over his hip and dig my heel into his ass, pulling him closer, deeper.

He kneads at my breast, tugging on my nipple before rolling it between his fingers, sending jolts of pleasure to my already slickened sex. "Ahhh…Ev…."

"Oh, love…I'm gonna…Lucy…" he calls as he pushes deeper as he comes again. "Baby, I love you."

I wrap my arms around his shoulders and nuzzle into his neck, inhaling his masculine scent. "I love you, too."

In all of the years I was alone, I didn't realize *this* was what I missing – a complete and utter feeling of contentment, of belonging, of love.

He carries me into his shower, never letting go of me as he turns on the water. We wash each other, letting our hands slip and slide over our slick skin. When we're done and the water turns cold and our fingers pruned, he wraps me in a fluffy, soft towel and carries me to his bed, which is set up in his small guest room during the minor renovation.

It's early evening, not even quite dinner time yet, but our lovemaking paired with his earlier work, sets his stomach grumbling as we cuddle on the bed. "Can I make you dinner?"

"Yeah, about that?" He rolls to his side, facing me. A small smile plays across his face.

I cover my face, sheepishly trying to hide my blush. "Sorry," I mutter from behind the arm I've just thrown over my face.

He pulls it away, laughing at me. I roll my eyes as he kisses my cheek. "You're just so sexy while you cook. It seemed like a good enough way to get you to go out with me without having to ask you and risk being turned down," I admit.

"Oh, love. I never would have turned you down. But that is pretty damn cute of you, playing me like that."

"It worked though, didn't it?"

"Yeah, it worked. You got me, all right." He reaches down and squeezes me ass. "Now, go cook for me, woman. I'm starving."

We eat dinner in his bed, sitting Indian-style across from each other. Concentrating on the conversation is a hugely difficult task since he's just wearing his boxer briefs. But I would imagine his long t-shirt — and *only* his long t-shirt — I'm wearing is also making it really difficult for him to concentrate as well.

After we eat, he pulls me to his side and we lay in bed. Yawning, I move to get up. "Stay the night. I know my room is a mess, but I don't want you to leave."

"I'd love to. But I have to drive Melanie back to Ithaca tomorrow morning."

I stand and pull my now wrinkled skirt back on. I don't even bother with the underwear; I just bunch them up and toss them in my purse. After snapping my bra, I slide my shirt back into place.

"Can I join you for the ride?" he asks timidly as I'm buttoning my shirt.

I sink back down onto the bed and he pulls my hand into his. "If you'd like to, I'd love the company. Dropping her off and coming home all alone is usually pretty depressing."

"Perfect." He pulls me back to his side and undoes the buttons I've just fastened. "So you'll stay the night and I'll take care of you." He slips his fingers into the lace of my bra, strumming his calloused thumb over my nipple. "And then I'll take care of you again tomorrow morning," he pinches lightly, "before I make sure both of my girls arrive where they need to be safe and sound."

And, just because he asked so nicely, I stay the night as he takes care of me again and again — feeling his love in every single touch, kiss and move of passion.

Part Three

~ Home ~

3 Months Later

CHAPTER NINETEEN

Evan

"Yes, we're home, Melanie." I keep my voice hushed as I duck into the bathroom.

"So?" She drags out the word, excitement lacing through her tone. I can almost imagine her rolling her eyes at my non-response. "Did you ask her yet? Did ya?"

I sit on the edge of the tub that Lucy and I have put to very good use these last few months; I get all hot and bothered just thinking about it. And then I remember that I'm on the phone with her daughter. "No," I huff through the line.

"Chicken," she blurts sarcastically.

"I am *not* a chicken. We just got home and I plan on taking her on vacation tomorrow to…"

"You're going on vacation and you weren't going to tell me?" she gasps, playing it up just to lay the guilt on as thick as she can.

"You know you can't keep a secret worth anything, Melanie!" Having recently blown the surprise on Linda's birthday party that her mother had planned, she knows I'm right.

"Fine, fine. You win. But where are you taking her?" She's digging – just like her mother would and it makes me laugh.

"A beach." That's all I'm giving her.

"Whatever. Just make sure you text me the numbers. I want to make sure I can get in touch with you guys. Make sure you got there safe and sound." I can hear the genuine concern and love in her voice – again, just like her mother, and I thank my lucky stars that when I fell in love with Lucy, Melanie came as part of the package. She's kind and sweet, quirky and funny. I never thought I'd be lucky enough to have a family of my own, and even though it might sound more than a little crazy, I already know that Lucy and Melanie will be my family from here on out.

I promise to text her the numbers. Before hanging up, there's one more thing I need to say. "Melanie, I just wanted to say thank you, again. It means a lot to me to have your blessing."

"Evan, you make my mom happy – happier than she's ever been. Of course I want you two living together. It doesn't make sense not to. I gotta go. The girls and I are going out, but I owe you a huge thank you too. I really look forward to hearing from your friend about Camp Hope. I have a really good feeling about it." I recently set Melanie up with a counselor position at a camp for children with special needs. It makes me feel good – accomplished, proud, even – that I can help her do something.

"You got it. Be safe. You're not driving, are you?"

"Not a chance in hell that I'm letting them in my brand new car! Besides, we're just heading down to the commons for dinner. Thanks again for that too. It's a bit over the top, but I love it."

"I'll text you those numbers and I'll be sure to have your mom call you when we land."

"Oooh, so you're flying, then?" There goes the digging, again.

"Goodnight, Melanie," I dismiss her but I know she can hear the warmth in my words.

"Goodnight, Evan."

After hanging up with Melanie, I make one last phone call to Linda to make sure that everything is set for tomorrow, and then Lucy and I can enjoy a full week of peace and quiet on the sandy beaches of Turks and Caicos.

"This is amazing, Evan." Lucy steps into our beachfront suite ahead of me as I tip the bellhop. "My God. The ocean is right there." She opens the sliding glass doors and the tropical sea air billows into the room. It's the perfect crystal blue backdrop to a romantic escape.

I step behind her, sweep her hair to the side so that it falls over her shoulder and press my lips to her neck. Wrapping my arms around her waist, I pull her to me. "I knew you would love it. I just can't believe you've never been on a real, honest-to-goodness, don't-have-a-care-in-the-world vacation."

"Nope. Being a single mom never really left much time for traveling. That's why I'm a spa-junkie. It's a lot easier to get away for the day than it is for the week."

"Oh, you'll have plenty of spa-time." I kiss the top of her head and she leans back against me, folding her arms on top of mine. "We actually have a couple's massage in," I pull my arm out from under her and check my watch, "about an hour."

Turning to face me, she looks up at me seductively. "You mean we don't have to be anywhere for a whole hour?" She steps out of my arms, and pulls the thin strap of her tank top over her shoulder. "Do you know what we could do in an hour?" After pulling down the other one, she grabs the waistband of my cargo shorts.

"Love, the way you're talking, we'll be able to do things *twice* in the hour."

"Now, you're talking." She winks and licks her lips. I lift her easily and carry her over to the bed where we spend the next fifty-eight minutes showing each other just how excited we are to be on vacation together before we get our massages.

Twice.

A few hours, a few orgasms and an amazing massage later, we're getting ready for a romantic beachside dinner. When Lucy steps out of the bathroom, wearing only a towel loosely tied across her chest, I want to rip it off her and devour her all over again. But giving us until at least after dinner to recover seems more than doable.

I walk over to Lucy just as she bends down to get some clothes out of the drawer. God, her ass - I can't help but pinch it.

"Ow," she whelps and jumps a little. Rubbing over the spot I just pinched, she looks up and gives me the side-eye. "What was that for?" She smirks.

"Because I can." I wink and pull her close to me, squeezing her ass in both hands. "And because this," I squeeze once more, just for added emphasis, "is a fantastic ass and it's all mine."

Her eyes soften in the corners as she lifts up on her toes. Bringing her lips to mine, she kisses me softly, but so intensely. As she strokes her fingers through my hair, she presses her soft, luscious body up against mine. "Have I told you how much I love being yours? Because I'm pretty sure it's my most favorite thing to be in the world."

"Good, get used to it." I pop a quick kiss to her forehead. "Why don't I let you finish getting ready? I've got to go check on some things, so I'll be back in a bit to get you, okay?"

She shoots me a wary look, knowing that something is up my sleeve; however, she concedes. An eye roll of course accompanies her concession. She slaps my ass as I walk past her, claiming it as hers. I just chuckle and walk toward the hotel lobby to make my call.

"Hey, Pete."

"Hey, Evan. How's vacation?"

"Great. We just got here. Look, I just wanted to call and check that all of the supplies arrived. You guys are all set to start tomorrow right?" I'm trying to keep my voice hushed as I scan the lobby for Lucy.

"Yeah, man, we're all set. I got the plans from the builders too. Nothing to worry about." Pete, a good friend of Joe's and mine from way back, owns a construction company. He handles mostly the business end of things now and he lets his son, Derek, take care of the actual labor. He's a good guy and his business has never had a single complaint, but it still makes me nervous to leave something so important up to someone else.

"You're sure you're good? Did you see the..."

"The additions on the posts for solar lights?" He laughs, filling in the end of my sentence. "Yes, we saw those changes. I got this, Evan. And I promise if we have any problems, we'll call."

I ramble on for a few more minutes about specifics that I want to make sure he's certain about before catching sight of Lucy as she strolls toward me. After ending the call, I stare, unabashedly so, at her. She hasn't seen me yet, so I hide behind a wall near the phone bank.

She looks like a goddess. Her hair is swept to the side and tossed casually over her shoulder. The ends fall in curls across the creamy skin of her chest and neck. Her floor-length, teal beach dress makes her pop against the crowd. The confused and slightly lost look that travels across her beautiful face as she searches for me makes her look even more adorably sweet than she already does.

"Hey, there you are." She pads over to me through the somewhat quiet lobby. "What were you up to?" Her question is light, but I can hear the accusation there. She's always digging.

"Absolutely nothing. Now, let's go eat." I drape an arm around her shoulder as we walk toward the restaurant.

After we're seated and our drinks have been served, we gaze out to the setting sun. The orange rays of blazing light sink into the crystal blue water. It's so beautiful and surreal that it almost looks as if the water is swallowing the sun up rather than the other way around. I reach across the small, bistro-style table and cover Lucy's hand with mine. As she turns to face me, her eyes shimmer just as the sunlight bounces off the ripples of the ocean — unshed tears threaten, but I see her forcing them back.

I pull her hand up to my lips. "You okay?" I ask quietly.

A small, sad smile plays at the corners of her mouth as she covers up my hand with her other one. "The last time I saw the sun set like this, on a beach like this," she clarifies, letting her gaze fall back to the deep, blue ocean in front of us. "It was with Jimmy on our honeymoon. It feels like a lifetime ago."

No words are uttered in the next few minutes as the sun disappears, morphing the sky into a purple and red haze. Watching her reflect on whatever it is that she's reflecting on, has me all sorts of tongue-tied.

"I'm sorry. I didn't want you to be sad. It's just that you said you always wanted to go to the beach, somewhere tropical. So I wanted to give that to you. If I would have known…"

"Shh, no, Evan. I'm not sad." Her fingertips tickle the top of my hand, calming my nerves. "Right after Jimmy died, I found myself talking to him as I would watch the sun rise and set every day. It became part of my routine − the only way I could still feel connected to him in some small way."

I bring her hand up to my lips again, letting her know to keep going, to keep opening up. "Seeing this," she tips her chin to the darkening sky, "well, it just makes me feel like he's here, but in a good way. Like he's giving me a blessing or something like that."

"I hope for that, too. I hope he approves of us, hope he thinks I'm taking good care of you and Melanie. I know that he would want you to be happy. You have to believe that." She nods and smiles at me, the brightness in her eyes conveying how truly happy she is.

"Did you talk to him just now?"

She takes a sip of her wine and then puffs out a deep breath. "I did. Is that weird?" Her nose crinkles, awaiting my judgment.

"Not one bit," I assure her. Not wanting to ask what she's said, I take a sip of my drink and lean back as the waiter serves our appetizer of fresh oysters on the half-shell.

"You don't want to know *what* I said?" Her words rattle as do her fingers, tapping out a nervous rhythm on the table.

"I figured you would tell me if you wanted to." Lacing our fingers together, I give her hand a gentle squeeze. "He doesn't have to stop being a part of your life just because I am now. You keep talking to him all you need, love."

"I love you," she chokes out as her emotions get the best of her. Pulling my chair to her side, I tuck her into my arm and rest my cheek on her head.

"I love you, too. So much, it scares me sometimes." I can't voice what's really scaring me, the prospect that waits for us back at her house. Yet, despite that particular uncertainty, I know that my life will forever be altered just by having Lucy in it.

"Were the oysters not good, sir?" The waiter chimes in, breaking our emotion-filled silence.

I look down at the plate he placed in front of us a few minutes ago and realize that we haven't touched a thing. "No, no," I assure him, "they're fine. We were just getting started."

Lucy smiles up at me brightly as I reach forward to grab a shell. She kisses my cheek, before whispering, "We sure as hell *are* just getting started."

"I can't believe we have our own private beach." Lucy's words float lazily over to me from her beach recliner. "I don't ever want to leave this place." We're four days into our week-long vacation, but I completely agree with her sentiments. I've never been so relaxed, so at ease in all my life. And I know it has more to do with being with Lucy than it does with sunbathing.

I roll to my side and lower my sunglasses to the tip of my nose. "We could relocate." I waggle my eyebrows at her and she laughs.

"I might be the only person on Earth crazy enough to say this, but I couldn't do that. I don't think I could ever leave my home."

"I know that, love." And that's exactly why I have Pete working away while we're here. Just thinking about how shocked she'll be when we get back to her house has me all sorts of excited and nervous.

"Join me for a swim?" I stand next to her, holding out my hand. She looks back and forth between my outstretched hand and her Kindle — back and forth, back and forth. Oh, that's it.

In an instant, she's scooped up in my arms, Kindle dropped to the sand as she squeals in surprise. "Hey! You're buying me a new one if that one's broken."

I cup her string bikini covered bottom tightly and nuzzle into her neck. "I'll buy you whatever you want, but you're going swimming with me first."

I ease her down the length of my body until her toes touch the wet sand at the water's edge. The warm ocean water laps gently against our legs as we walk into the calm, barely rippling sheet of blue water before us. It's a picture perfect scene, really.

I look over at Lucy quietly wading in the water. Her sun-kissed shoulders are dotted with droplets of water that catch the light in glimmering sparkles. The pale yellow fabric of her bikini top is deceptively innocent looking. The upper swell of her breasts float above the water as she wades there. Suddenly, swimming is the last thing on my mind.

"See something you like, sweetheart?" She shoots me a wry look and swims into my arms, pressing her softness into my body.

"I see a lot of what I like." She wraps her legs around my hips and wiggles against me.

"Yeah, you do." She nips at my neck, rubbing against the harness straining against my shorts.

Wrapping my hands around her ribcage, my thumbs graze the underside of her breasts. She pushes into my touch as she rubs her hips up against my erection — one that can't even be calmed by the coolness of the water. Her back arches, exposing miles of creamy skin to my lips. She's lost to the gentle rhythm and sway of our hips and I can feel her heat through the thin layers of fabric that separate us. I cup her ass with one hand, pulling her hard against me.

"Ahh," she quietly shrieks as she begins to move just a touch more frantically.

As I hold her in place with one hand, I pull down the cup of her bikini. Her nipples pebble beautifully as a perfectly timed cool breeze mingles in with the sun-warmed air. The scent of her arousal fills my senses as it mixes with the fresh saltiness of the ocean water.

I roll her nipple in my fingers, pulling it, elongating it, getting more and more turned on by her desire. Dipping my head to her breast, I pull the pink tip of it deep into my mouth.

"God, Evan," she calls as her hips roll. I pay the same attention to her other breast and nipple, laving and nipping at it gently.

Her thighs begin to tremble as she loses the battle with her control. She buries her face in my chest, nuzzling into me with a loving tenderness that turns me on just as much as the heated thrusting that's going on below the water.

"Evan. Evan… I'm … oh, God… I'm so close." Her words fall from her lips in rapid, lust-filled pants. I push into her and her legs tremble again. Still holding her tight ass in one hand, I reach in between her legs. Dipping my fingers into her, I drag my fingertip up the seam of her lips and press oh-so softly against her hardened clit, just like she likes it.

That thought — the knowledge that I have a woman who I love and who I know how to please — makes me throb with the need to be driving into her. But right now, the need to feel her come, to feel her lose herself to my touch supersedes all of my desires.

At the same time I pull her nipple back into my mouth, I rub small circles around her clit, pushing her over the edge.

"Evan," she keens — pushing, thrusting, rolling against me as her pussy clenches and pulses around my fingers.

When all that's left is the soft sounds of small waves lapping against our bodies and her calming breaths, I carry her out of the water. We walk straight across the beach, past our lounge chairs and right into our room. As I put her down, her ass perched on the edge of the vanity countertop, her limbs fall to her sides, slack and boneless, sated and calm.

We both take a quick shower, rinsing off the salt from the ocean, getting lost to the feel of slick skin under our fingers. Lying in bed, side by side, Lucy looks up at me, longingly. I run my fingers through her hair and let my knuckles trail down her turned-pink-from-the-sun cheek. Without saying a word, she hooks her leg up and over my hip, pulling me underneath her.

"That's some move, love." My hands rest on her hips as she straddles my groin, the heat from her sex pulsating between us.

"Oh, I've got plenty more where that came from," she murmurs as her tongue traces along the fullness of her bottom lip. "Let me show you what I can do."

She kisses my chest before raking her nails across my skin — the perfect mixture of pleasure with just the right amount of pain. Her hot, wet tongue traces a delicious path down my stomach, making my cock twitch to life yet again.

"Oh, love…" The rest of the words get stuck in my throat as she coats my cock with her tongue. When she pulls the whole length of it into her mouth, my hips thrust up on their own will. I pull her hair to the side and watch the glistening skin of my shaft disappear into her lips over and over again. "Christ, Lucy…you're so perfect."

Her ass bobs in the air behind her as she's crouched on her knees in between my legs, a sight that makes my erection even harder by the second. But she knows how far to take me. Just as I know her body, have come to love it and worship it, she does the same to mine. As she swirls her tongue around the swollen head of my dick, she cups my balls then traces her nails over them gently, setting loose a million tingles that race up my spine. "Fuck," I growl as she releases me from her mouth.

She climbs back up into my lap and I reach for her breasts. Arching her back and pushing them into my palms, I pull her closer to me and suck one hard, pink tip into my mouth. She reaches between us and guides me into her — one silky, hot, wet, slick, fucking heavenly inch at a time. With more patience than I could ever have, Lucy sinks down onto me, slowly — so slowly that I have to grip her hips to restrain from pummeling up into her. I'm sure there will be bruising.

Before she takes me all the way, she lifts up on her knees, stopping only when my head is nestled inside the first inch of her pussy. "Fuck. You're driving me crazy," I mutter hungrily as my head lolls back into the pillows.

"That's the point. I'm going to drive you crazy, until you can't take it anymore. I'm going to ride you until we're both shaking, until we're both breathless." Again and again, she lifts and lowers herself on my dick, playing my body like an instrument of pleasure. Unable to take her slow, torturous pace any longer, I wrap my arms around her waist and sit up with her still on my lap.

"I need you, love. I need more of you. I need all of you, now." I ground out my words as I drive up into her and pull her down onto me with all of my strength.

"Evan….ahhh," she cries out as I pound into her. Needing more leverage, I flip us around so that she's under me. Lucy, propped up on all fours, ass swaying gloriously in front of me, pussy lips swollen and dripping wet with desire — now this is something I'll never get tired of looking at.

She angles her head back to me, staring at me with a sexy-as-fuck look plastered to her sweet face. "Please." She lets the single word fall from her lips as she wiggles her ass in front of me.

I slide into her from behind, pulling her up into me as I loop my arm around her waist. Her groans fill the room, which is glittered with the warm rays of the afternoon sun. I toy with her clit, rubbing small, fast circles over it with the work-roughened pads of my fingers. On each thrust, I angle higher and deeper, hitting that sweet spot that causes her pussy to flutter wildly with her impending orgasm.

I feel her pleasure build, pulse by hot pulse, beat by wild beat. She screams into the pillow as she comes. Careening wildly, she's barely able to hold herself up. I feel her body go limp as the heated rush of passion courses through her veins. "Let go, love. I've got you." I band my arm around her waist once again, holding her in place as I drive into her.

"Fuck...fuck....fuck..." I growl and I thrust into her one last time, my orgasm spilling hotly into her still-fluttering core.

We both crash into the bed, panting as if we'd just run a race. Pressing a soft kiss into her shoulder, I pull us onto our sides. Spooning behind her, we drift to sleep, staring out the sliding glass doors to our own private paradise.

CHAPTER TWENTY

Lucy

"That was the best vacation ever. I'm not sure I'm ready to get back to reality." Evan drops his arm around my shoulders and pulls me to his side as the plane starts its descent to Elmira Regional Airport. It was amazing to get away, but now as the lush green landscape of upstate New York rises up to meet us, I already miss the tropical paradise we left behind.

"I know. I'm not ready either." His shaking knee belies his calm voice

"You don't like flying?" I ask, placing my hand on his bouncing leg. I must have mistaken his anxiety on the flight there as excitement. In my own excitement, I completely forgot about his fear of flying – a part of his post 9/11 PTSD.

My heart breaks a little for him. He's so strong in so many ways, but there's always a hint of his pain simmering right at the surface.

He looks down at my hand, taking a deep breath to calm himself. "Nah, it's not my favorite," he deflects, squeezing me closer to him. I'm sure the evening flight isn't helping ease his anxieties any. As the sun dips below the horizon, my peacefulness sets in, a stark contrast to his unease.

"I told him I'd still carry him in my heart." My words softly tumble from my lips as I look out at the sunset, thinking of our conversation from our first night on vacation.

He pulls me closer, squeezing my shoulder almost to the point of being painful, as he presses his lips softly to my temple. "Of course you will. He'll always be a part of you."

"There's more," I add as I straighten and turn toward him. Covering his hand with mine, I lace our fingers together. "I asked him not to be mad at me about finding you and moving on. I asked him to understand that loving you as much as I do doesn't change how much I once loved him. When he died, I had no sense of closure — no chance to say goodbye. He was just ripped from my life, and then Melanie came along two weeks later, so I *had* to pick up the pieces. I think I've just come to realize that never moving on was part of trying to protect myself. If I stayed in love with Jimmy, then there was no reason to move on. But you..." I look up into his grey eyes as I trace my fingertip along his strong, hard, stubble-covered jawline. "Evan, you woke me up. You brought me back to life and you made my heart work again. You made me realize that it's possible to love again."

Evan shifts in his seat as I try to swallow the lump that's just formed in my throat. "Can I confess something?" His words tremble a little, following the rhythm of his still-bouncing leg. "You might think this is odd, but I said something that night too." He rubs his hand over his face, seemingly uneasy about sharing this piece of information. After puffing out a sigh, he looks back at me. "I don't know if it was Jimmy who I was talking to or just to whoever the hell is in charge up there." He chuckles a little as he points to the ceiling of the airplane, indicating the heavens above us. "I promised that I would take care of you, always. That nothing, not even my own stupidity, would ever get in the way of loving you, of being there for you." His shaking leg stops as he searches my face for some kind of response. Overwhelmed by his words, I can't find any of my own to speak. So I sit there, dumbly staring up at this sweet man who has just made me feel like the most cherished woman to ever grace the Earth.

"I know I'll never be Jimmy," he continues, less nervously than before when I don't say anything. "And I truly do respect the love you had with him, but I need you to know that I love you and there's nothing that's going to ever keep me from doing that. Not even if a part of your heart still belongs to him."

"Oh, Evan. I– I …" I take a deep breath, searching for the right words to convey the feelings that are all sorts of jumbled up. I'm not sure what I'm about to say makes much sense, but I hope he'll feel the sincerity of my words. "He'll always be *in* my heart, Evan, but my heart – it belongs to you now." Cupping my jaw with more tenderness than ever before, he pulls my face up to his and presses his lips against mine.

No more words are necessary. Our kiss says it all for us.

Resting his forehead against mine, his lips pull into a beautifully crooked smile. His eyes warm and he pulls my hand up to briefly brush his lips against our joined fingers. It's a simple gesture filled with so much, I'm not likely to ever forget it.

We hold onto each other through the rest of the landing and all of his tension eases as he combs his fingers lightly through my hair. Before long, we're collecting our suitcases from the baggage carousel and waiting for the car service to pick us up.

It's a quick ride back to my house, and the fifteen minutes passes in a calm silence as the exhaustion of traveling most of the day washes over us.

When the car stops in front of the house, Evan turns to face me. "I have a surprise for you, love. So I need you to just close your eyes and trust me." His words set free a swarm of butterflies in my belly and cause my heart to start racing.

"You just took me on a week-long vacation, now you have *another* surprise? Did I hit the lottery or something?" Attempting a joke through my excitement just makes me all the more anxious to see what else he's got planned for me.

"Yes, another one. Now, close your eyes and follow me." After grabbing our bags from the trunk and carrying them up the front steps, he stops in front of the door — at least that's what I'm assuming is going on.

"Open your eyes, love."

My hand immediately flies to cover my mouth. A shocked gasp escapes my lips as I take in the sight before me. "Oh, my God! Evan! When did you…how did you…this is…" Obviously, eloquence is not on my side. But the newly redone front porch, fully adorned with brand new furniture and bench swing has absolutely stolen all of my words. The warm-colored stain makes the outside space feel like an extension of the inside. It honestly looks like something that belongs in the pages of *Better Homes and Gardens*.

"Do you like it?" he asks nervously.

"I *love* it. It's gorgeous. Did you…" I step toward the new porch light as I notice yet another part of his surprise. "You did! You had the house repainted. It's beautiful." The warm olive green, almost mossy color of the new paint, breathes new life to the home I've always loved. The shiny new black shutters are the perfect finishing touch. "I can't believe you." I wrap my arms around him and hug him as tightly as I can. Near tears, I can't believe the limitlessness of his kindness.

"Come on." He pulls his set of keys out of his back pocket and unlocks the door. "There's more I want you to see."

More? What more could he have possible done. This is already too much. As I walk into the entryway, I don't notice anything different. Scanning the living room, I'm sure he sees the perplexed look on my face. But, as I walk into the kitchen and look out the bay window in the back of the room, I see the sparkling lights of the other part of his surprise.

I hear his footsteps behind me as I practically run to the sliding glass doors. Where there used to be a few falling-apart steps leading out to the more than dilapidated backyard, there now stands a beautifully landscaped oasis that spills out from the newly built deck - a perfect match to the one up front.

The classic pergola is draped with what looks like a million points of light, flickering beautifully against the midnight blue backdrop of the night sky. His eagerness to get a late flight back home suddenly becomes crystal clear. The twinkling lights create a moment that could in no way whatsoever be recreated in the daylight.

He stands behind me, coiling his arms around my waist. Leaning into my neck, he presses his lips there and I feel the smile pulling at his lips. "Why?" Is all I can manage, because for everything he's said to me to prove his love, and everything he's already done to demonstrate it, I just can't wrap my head around why someone would want to do all of this for me.

He turns me in his arms, the light catching in his eyes, making them dance with more glimmers of love than they usually do. "Why?" he repeats my single word with a light mocking tone, softly chuckling at me at the same time. "It's simple really." He steps away from me and hits play on an iPod dock that I didn't originally see.

The twang of Clapton's guitar comes to life over the initial crackling of the speakers. Evan extends his hand to me as a bright smile plays across his face, crinkling the corners of his eyes. "Dance with me, love."

As the lyrics flow out into the quiet setting around us, Clapton sings about how wonderful the night has been. When he gets to the part about tucking his woman into bed, Evan pulls me even closer still and sings the lyrics to me, his lips barely a centimeter from my ear. As the song comes to a close, Evan pulls us both down onto a bench, holding me on his lap.

"I did this because I know how much this house means to you. I know it's not simply a house to you and Melanie, but this is your *home*. This is where your life is and I wanted to make it the most beautiful place you'd ever seen, a place you can be proud of and no longer be reminded of what you weren't capable of doing."

"Evan, that's the sweetest—" before I can even get the words out, he presses a single finger against my lips, shushing me.

"Let me finish; otherwise, I might lose my nerve." His leg starts bouncing beneath me. "The other reason I did this is because you're my home, Lucy. I've never been more content, more alive than when I'm with you and I want to be with you always. I knew you'd never let your home go. So instead of asking you to move in with me, I'm asking you if you'll let me move in with you."

A single tear streaks down my cheek as a smile pulls at my lips. "You did all of this just so you could ask to move in with me." Shock colors my words, my heart bursting at the seams. "There was no need to go through all of this." I throw my hand to the side, gesturing to the new deck.

"No, you're right. There was no *need*, but I wanted to give you something you truly wanted, something you couldn't do for yourself. And now, I'm just asking to share it with you."

"Evan," I hold his face in my trembling hands, "there isn't another person who I'd rather share my life with." His lips crash into mine, his tongue immediately searching out mine in a kiss so passionate I'm thinking about straddling him right here on this bench. The thought of splinters in places you just don't want splinters stops me in my tracks.

"So when did you want to move in?" I ask as we break from the kiss, smirking at him playfully.

"Um, I don't know. I hadn't really thought of it. I was just too nervous that you'd say no, so I never got around to figuring that part out."

"Well, you already have a week's worth of stuff with you. That's a start, right." I'm vibrating with giddy excitement.

"It sure is. I'll start bringing my stuff over this week, if that's okay?"

"It's perfect. Absolutely perfect."

It doesn't take Evan long to move his stuff in, and by the end of the week, it looks like he's been here forever. It feels like that, too. The place feels more complete and more alive than it has in years and I couldn't be happier. I feel like I walk around with a permanent smile on my face all day long.

Which, of course, is what Linda comments on as she rounds the corner to my cubicle. "Mornin' sunshine. Happy Friday," she drawls in the worst southern accent I've ever heard. Handing me a cup of coffee, she sits in the extra chair, asking me all about how things are going with Evan and me. Naturally, I can't help but glow in response.

"Things are really great. He's all moved in — didn't have much to begin with. I even got an ugly recliner out of it."

"Typical man crap, huh?"

"Yeah, I guess. It's odd though. That ugly, old, beat up recliner makes everything feel more complete."

"I'm thrilled for you, Luce. I've never seen you like this and it's made me… well, let's just say I've revaluated my stance on men," she admits sheepishly while I busy myself with some imaginary fist pumps.

"Oh, you don't say." Tapping my nails on my mug, I joke with her — lightly sarcastic words that convey how much I think this change is necessary.

She shoots me a wry shut-the-fuck-up face before sighing audibly, "I know. I know," she concedes. "I guess spending all these years making you try to face your fears, trying to make you find happiness, was really just a way for me to avoid seeing my own. I've been alone for far too long, too afraid to trust anyone again. But, maybe it's time." I offer her a small, compassionate smile, patting her hand.

"So glad you finally figured that out, Lin." Our bubbles of laughter catch the stares of a few people walking by. Honestly, you'd think they'd be used to it by now.

"It was that obvious, huh? Well, anyways, I deleted your online dating stuff — which I never should have done in the first place — and I made my own. So, now I just wait and see how things go, but it's time for me to focus on me — find my own happiness."

"That's fantastic, Linda. I'm proud of you." She stands to go back to her cube before taking one backward glance. "Any chance Evan's got some hot friends?"

That gets another loud laugh out of me. Dismissing her with an eye roll, I get back to my newest project. Half-focused and half-daydreaming, the rest of the workday passes by in the blink of an eye. Knowing that there's someone waiting for me at home makes me all the more anxious to get there. But today, for some odd reason, there's a palpable tension filling the living room when I walk through the front door.

Evan is sitting on the couch, his head cupped in his hands, elbows propped on his thighs. He doesn't even realize I've walked into the room because he startles when I sit next to him. Slowly, he tilts his head up to me, his eyes shining with unshed tears, but he doesn't say anything.

"Ev, sweetie. What's wrong?" I keep my tone calm and even, trying to stay calm myself. He opens his mouth to speak, but no words come out. The tears that were threatening just a second ago fall from his eyes as he pulls me to his chest. "You're scaring me," the words fall shakily from my lips. He holds me at arm's length and wipes the tears away from his face. Before holding both of my hands in his, he sweeps my hair from my face and looks me straight in the eye.

The room spins as he says four simple words that crush my heart. "It's Chloe. She's gone." He pulls me back to his chest where I let the emotion overtake me. As I cry into his shirt, he tries his best to calm me, rubbing my back and cooing into my ear.

Looking up at him with what I'm sure are mascara-streaked and puffy-with-red-from-crying eyes, I swipe at my cheeks and let out a shaky breath. "When? What happened?"

I know parts of the story. Aimee called me a few weeks ago to let me know Chloe had a relapse and needed to undergo more chemo, but of course, they were hopeful. Chloe had already beaten the odds once, so they were hopeful that this would be just one more minor setback on Chloe's road to recovery.

I guess the world just isn't that fair, or kind for that matter.

"Late last night." Evan's words break through my silent and angry thoughts. "They tried calling you at work this afternoon, but you must have left already. I just knew it — when I saw their number on the caller ID — I knew the reason they were calling. I almost didn't pick it up," he laughs a humorless laugh. "Like that would make it less true or something like that." He holds me, trying desperately to comfort me through my tears. "Lucy, I'm so sorry. What can I do?" He kisses my hair and pulls me closer.

"Nothing, sweetie. There's nothing anyone can do." I let him hold me, because in this moment, that's all that can be done. The world isn't a fair place; that's a lesson I learned long ago. It's not as if that knowledge makes Chloe's death any easier to deal with. But Evan's strong arms allow some of the pain to seep out of my body and soul.

The next few days are tear filled and gut wrenching. Evan is by my side the entire time, a pillar of strength and compassion, but I know he's hurting inside too. Watching parents say goodbye to their only child, who they fought so hard to save, changes the way you look at the world, makes you value the people you have in your life.

In the days after Chloe's funeral, I spend a lot of time on the phone with Melanie, who reminds me to find happiness in the things we have to look forward to, Maddy's baby shower, wedding dress shopping and a brand new grandbaby who should be here in just a few weeks.

And she's right, because if there's one thing I've learned in all of my years, no matter how many downs there are in life, there's always one more up to pull you out of what you think will be the worst.

CHAPTER TWENTY ONE

Evan

"I can't believe this is actually happening. This is the best birthday present ever." It's quite possible that Melanie is more excited than I am.

"You realize it's not for you, right?" I laugh as she scans the display case at the antique jewelry shop.

"Yeah, yeah. But it's sparkly and I get to help you pick it out. And it's going to make Mom happier than anything. So it kind of *is* for me." This kid is something else, but I'm so relieved that she's happy. I knew she'd be excited when I asked her to go ring shopping with me, but I had no clue she would be *this* elated.

"Sorry I'm late. I got here as soon as work finished." Maddy comes up behind us, looping her arm through Melanie's.

"I was getting worried you weren't going to make it," Melanie says.

"This?" Maddy sweeps her hand across the counter, as if she's auctioning something off on *The Price is Right*. "I wouldn't miss this for the world. I'm just happy you both wanted me here for it." She smiles up at me and I recall the loud shriek that deafened me when I called her the other day to ask if she'd like to join us.

I can't imagine doing this without Lucy's girls by my side. As important as it is to me, I know it's just as meaningful to them. Her happiness is their happiness, and there's no way I could ever deprive them of that. I did, however, know better than to tell Linda. She'd blab in a heartbeat. So she'll just be joining us for dinner tonight for what she thinks is a birthday celebration for Melanie.

The girls go a little crazy, asking the clerk helping us to pull out pretty much every ring on display. They ooh and ahh over all the diamonds, but nothing is striking me as 'the one'.

"What about this one, Evan?" Melanie holds up a ring for me to check out.

"It's okay, but I don't know. It's just kind of plain, you know?" She turns it over in her hand before sliding it back into the case. Maddy suggests a few, but again, nothing is standing out. I'd like to say that my indecision is due in part to my nerves, but that's definitely not the case. I'm not nervous about this at all. I never thought I would have this opportunity in my life - the chance to love someone else with everything I've got, the chance to spend every single day married to the one person I know I can't do without.

"If nothing here is catching your eye," the sales clerk says. "Maybe you'd like something from this case. These are a bit more detailed - filigree bands, unique settings and lots of different profiles." She pulls out a tray of five rings and it's there. My attention is caught immediately, and in a second flat, I know that the one-and-a-half carat oval cut diamond, centered between two quarter-carat sapphires of the same cut is the ring with which I'll ask Lucy to marry me.

The girls agree, almost in unison, clapping hands and all, that this is definitely *the* ring.

Now, all I have to do is ask.

Lucy knows that everyone is coming over for dinner tonight, but she thinks it's just a belated birthday party for Melanie who couldn't make it home on her actual birthday because of classes. What she doesn't realize is that it was all just a ploy to have the most important people in her life be here to bear witness to me asking her to marry me.

"She's here!" Melanie squeals as Lucy's car rolls into the driveway. When she gets inside, everyone pretends to be busy doing something else - not wanting to make a big deal out of her just arriving home from work. The excitement is so overwhelming I'm surprised Lucy hasn't picked up on it.

After saying hello to Melanie, Maddy and Reid, and kissing baby Braden to pieces, she comes over to me to let me know that she's just going to get changed before dinner. She's oddly quiet, letting me know that something's off.

Standing next to me in the kitchen as I put the finishing touches on the meal, Linda leans over, noticing the cool demeanor of Lucy's greeting. "Work's been crazy lately. Maybe she just had a bad day."

Linda's suggestion does little to make me feel as if her stressful day is truly the culprit of her stilted mood.

Leaving Linda in charge of a few last details, I walk upstairs, passing by Melanie and Maddy as they ogle over the baby while Reid watches on. "Hey," I call into our room, but she's not in there.

I find her sitting on the closed lid of the toilet, holding her head in her hands. I crouch in front of her and pull her hands away from her cheeks only to find tears there. "Hey, love. What's wrong?"

Her intake of breath is shaky and sharp and the pained look that flits across her face scares the shit out of me. When she says, "I found a lump in my breast," I swear the ground just swallows me up.

Shaking my head, as if it will shake away what I just heard, the reality of her words is just not settling in. All I can manage is a quiet and repetitive, "No…no…no."

Then resolve sets in. I've dedicated my life and career to saving strangers; there's no way in hell I won't save the one person who means the most to me. "Talk to me, love. What happened? When did you find it? Have you been to the doctor?"

"I found it last week." Her admission catches me way off guard.

"Last week," I gulp down my shock. "Why didn't you tell me?"

"Oh, Evan." Her voice wobbles. "I didn't want to scare you. I was so scared myself that I just… I don't know. I should have told you, but I just wanted to see what it was first before I worried you."

I pull her hands up to my lips, pressing a gentle kiss there as I stare at her bright blue eyes. "You are *never* a burden," I assure her. "Now, tell me the rest."

Over the next twenty minutes, she fills me in on all of the details. She found it in the shower one day and didn't make a big deal of it at first, trying her best to remain calm until the doctor could see her. It turns out that while I was out with the girls picking out an engagement ring, she was off at the doctor, by herself, finding out that she has to have surgery in the coming weeks to have the lump removed and tested for cancer because the initial biopsy was inconclusive.

Part of me is angrier than fuck that she did all of this without me, out of some misplaced need to protect. But I fight back that part and be the man who I know she needs right now. One who stand by her choices and listen to her concerns.

In the few minutes of silence that follow, I hold onto this woman who I love more than anything else in my life, more afraid than ever that I'll lose her. "It's okay, love. We'll figure it all out. I'm right here by your side and so is everyone else." After a brief pause, I pull away from her and search her face. "Do you want to tell them now, or should I send everyone home, let this digest a little."

"I want to tell them now; they need to know." Her words carry more resolve than they did previously, and I know it's because she wants to appear brave and unafraid, knowing full well that everyone else will feel exactly the opposite. Knowing that she only lets herself be weak and vulnerable when she's in my arms, makes my heart break even more.

"I'll be right next to you." She stands and hugs me tightly, pulling strength from me, I'm sure. We lace our fingers together and walk down the stairs.

Melanie sees us first and her face falls immediately. "Mom? What's wrong?" Her words are merely above a whisper, but they're enough to catch Maddy, Linda and Reid's attention. With all eyes on us, Lucy walks into the living room and asks everyone to sit down.

"Momma, is everything okay?" Maddy asks as she holds Braden tightly to her chest. Lucy leans down and kisses the baby's head before cradling him in her own arms. Smiling down at the bright and innocent face of her grandson, she wipes away a final tear.

When she says, "I might have breast cancer," all of the oxygen is sucked out of the room with everyone's collective and shocked gasp.

"Oh, come here, Melly Belly." Lucy cradles Braden in one arm as she pulls Melanie into a tight hug with the other. Tears spring to her eyes. "It'll all be okay, somehow." Maddy moves next to them and they all wrap their arms around each other, the baby cuddled in between all three of them. Linda curls around Melanie, completing the group hug. I can see Reid vibrate with anger. Having just lost his own mother less than a year ago, I can imagine his pain is still raw, still too new to register the possibility of losing Lucy, the only other woman who has loved him as a mother should.

I stand beside him and clap a hand to his shoulder as we stand behind the huddled-together women. He drops a hand to Maddy's shoulder and I drop one to Lucy's. So much goes unsaid in those few moments when we stand there holding each other. But the overwhelming feeling of family, of love and of determination flows through each and every one of us.

Dinner passes quickly and all too quietly, and just around the time I had hoped to get down on one knee and begin celebrating, everyone else is so emotionally drained that they head home for the night.

"I think I'm going to go take a nice hot bath." Lucy stands from the table where she, Melanie and I are sitting. After putting her mug in the dishwasher, she kisses Melanie's forehead and says goodnight. She pats my shoulder as she walks past me, and even though I want to follow her to make sure she's all right, I know she needs some time to herself.

"Hey, you okay over there?" I ask Melanie after Lucy is up the stairs. If she's anything like her mother, she's obviously an ace at hiding what's really going on in her head.

Shrugging her shoulders lamely, she doesn't say anything at first, but I see the pain in her eyes. "Come here, Melanie. It'll be okay." I slide my chair next to hers and pull her into a hug, draping my arm over her shoulders. Her outburst of emotion blasts into me full force and she lets go of everything she must have been holding back.

Through the anguished sounds of her sobbing, she mumbles against my shoulder, "I'm so afraid to lose her. I can't even think about it…" Her words are swallowed by her fears.

"Shh, I know. I can't lose her either, and we're not going to. She's the strongest woman I've ever known. We'll all pull through this together as a family." I let her cry and cry as I bite back my own tears.

After she calms down, wipes the tears away and takes a few deep, unsteady breaths, she looks over to me with such a lost look. "Are you still going to ask her to marry you?" she asks through her quieting sobs.

"Of course I am," the resolute words instantly fall from my lips without a second thought. "No matter what happens, I want to marry her. Asking her tonight just wasn't in the cards, but I promise you, I will ask her."

"She doesn't deserve this, you know?" She searches the ceiling as if some kind of divine intervention will just be dangling there. I reach for her hand and squeeze it gently.

"No, Melanie, she most certainly doesn't. But she's got us to take care of her and that's exactly what we'll do. Speaking of," I tip my head toward the stairs as I get up from the table, "I'm going to go check on her now. Make sure she's okay."

Melanie nods and smiles weakly at me as I leave the room, lost to her own private thoughts about how to best deal with this bombshell.

By the time I get to our room, Lucy's already out of the tub, sitting on the edge of the bed in one of my T-shirts and her pink fluffy robe. Her face looks exhausted, her eyes puffy from all the crying. She curls into my arms before my ass even hits the mattress.

"I'm so scared. I just…I mean…what if, what if …'" she chokes out past her tears.

"Shh…shh." I try to calm her but she rips herself out of my arms.

Standing in front of me, her fists balled tightly at her sides, she's vibrating with anger. "Why is life so fucking unfair, huh?" She throws her arms up in the air, flippantly huffing her frustrations to the ceiling. "Who the fuck decides how much pain one person gets in their lifetime?" She starts pacing the room frantically. Her sudden rage takes me by surprise, so much so I just don't know what to do right away. So I just listen and let her get everything out.

"What have I ever done wrong? What did I ever do to deserve this on top of everything else? Or Chloe for that matter. What on Earth did that poor, sweet girl ever do wrong? Hell, she didn't even get to live long enough to do anything wrong!" Her voice is near screaming, and in between her bursts of anger, I hear Melanie jogging up the stairs.

"And Jimmy," she grabs his bottle of cologne from the dresser where she still keeps it, even after all these years. "Why is it fair that he was taken from me…from Melanie…why?" Her voice cracks with the yell as she hurls the bottle clear across the room. Melanie cracks the door open slightly, just as the bottle collides with the wall, smashing into hundreds of tiny shards. We both watch on, not exactly sure how to handle Lucy's breakdown. Though completely understanding of it, neither of us knows how to react to it.

When the silence becomes too much, Lucy collapses to the floor. Shaking, sobbing and heaving through her pain, I kneel before her and wrap my arms around her. All too willingly, she curls her arms around me and continues crying. "I–I'm…s–so s-orry…" Her words are broken up by shorts gasps of breath as her sobs get stuck in her throat. Melanie falls to the floor with us and wraps her arms around Lucy from behind. "It's okay, Mom. Everything's going to be okay. And even if it's not, we've got each other to figure out how to make it be okay in the end."

Lucy chuffs out a small laugh against my t-shirt. "How'd you get to be so smart?" Lucy shifts so she's sitting cross-legged in between Melanie and me. We exchange a brief look, before Melanie says, "I guess it's just one of those things I picked up from you over the years. I love you, Mom, and we are going to beat this. All of us. Together. As a family, right, Evan?"

"Without a doubt." I've never said anything with more conviction. I know in the deepest recesses of what I thought was a broken heart, I will never be anything but a part of this family.

"God, look what I did. I'm sorry. I should clean…" She moves to stand up, but I beat her to it.

"I'll get it." I cover her shaking hands with mine.

Lucy walks Melanie to her room while I clean up the mess. Just as I'm done vacuuming up the last shard of glass from the rug, Lucy comes back into the room.

"I shouldn't have done that."

I walk over to her and we sink into the large armchair in the corner of the room. "It's okay to be angry. You don't have to be so....so.... so 'Lucy' all the time."

She quirks an eyebrow at me, wordlessly asking me to explain what it means exactly to be "Lucy".

"I mean that you're always so calm and in control, so strong and determined. It's okay to be upset and weak, to need someone else to be strong for you." I press my lips against her silky hair. "I'm here to be that strength for you. Just let me."

With her arms wrapped so tightly around me, it actually becomes difficult to breathe. Against the thin cotton of my shirt, she mumbles, "but what if this is all the time we get?"

I peel her away from my body, holding her shoulder in a firm grasp. "Listen to me, Lucy. There is no way in *hell* that this is all the time you get, that *we* get. We are going to beat this thing and we don't even know what we're up against here. It could still be nothing." I pull her back to my chest and rock her back and forth, repeating my last words over and over in my head, a silent prayer offered up to a God I stopped believing in long ago.

The next morning, I wake up before Lucy. Well, it's not really waking up if you didn't sleep at all. She's still curled in a ball at my side, so I carefully slide my arm out from underneath her, kissing the top of her head lightly as I get out of bed.

Melanie's still asleep and the house is peaceful and quiet. It's just me and my own thoughts — the ones I've been struggling with all night. As the sun rises up through the amber-colored horizon, my anger battles with my sadness. Fists clenched at my sides, I feel like I could punch a hole through the fucking wall.

"Why Lucy?" I mumble through gritted teeth to no one in particular. Leaning up against the frame of the bay window, I try my best to gather my thoughts, to reign in my anger, but I'm still left with the soul-crushing fear that I'm going to lose her.

"Please, please don't take her from me," I whisper to the heavens, hopeful that *someone* is listening to me. Lucy finds solace in speaking to the rising sun, using those quiet moments before her day begins to greet Jimmy. I can see the draw, the desire to find answers in these moments of quiet.

"I promise to take care of her; just please give me the chance. Don't take her away from me before I can save her." My throat constricts as the tears I kept at bay all night well up in my eyes. "I love her and I know you loved her too." My words float up to Jimmy, hoping that he'll hear them. "Please let her stay here with us. Melanie needs her. I need her…" The rest of my words evaporate into thin air as I feel arms wrap around me from behind.

With her cheek pressed flat up against my back, I pull her arms tightly around my waist, lacing our fingers together. "You're not going to lose me. I promise, Evan." Lucy's voice is raspy and heavy with sleep.

I turn around to face her. Tears fall in tracks down her cheeks. Her eyes are bloodshot and her shoulders sag with the heaviness of last night's revelations. "Come here. I don't want to see you crying." I pull her to my chest, lightly combing my hands through her hair. Then a wisp of a thought flits through my mind. What if I do lose her? What if this is the beginning of the end? Will this be one of the last times I'll feel her soft body pressed against mine in need of comfort and protection?

I squeeze her tighter and inhale the sweet scent of her hair. That's when my tears fall. "I can't lose you, Lucy. I only just found you." The thought of losing her – it's just one I can't face. It's more frightening than any fire I've ever battled. Even just the threat of it feels as if I'm falling into a chasm of nothingness.

We hold each other for what feels like forever as the sun rises in the sky behind us. When our tears stop and she pulls away from me, she faces the sun, offering up her silent good morning to Jimmy I'm sure.

"I asked him to help us get through this." My admission of offering a prayer up to Jimmy catches her off guard.

"You did?" Her reaction is one of muted shock.

"I did. I stayed awake all night praying for the strength to get through this…whatever *this* might turn out to be. Then I saw the sun and figured an extra word or two to Jimmy wouldn't hurt either."

Her face softens as a warm smile spreads across it. "That's…Evan, it's so…" she chokes on her words a little. After opening and closing her mouth a few more times, still unable to utter any words, she finally settles on, "I love you more than I thought possible."

"And I love you the same." I press my lips to hers, a silent vow to do everything in my power to get through this together. "Now, let's sit and have some breakfast. You can tell me more about what the doctor said."

The weeks that follow are filled with doctor's appointments, second opinions, medical jargon and a few more biopsies, but the answer still remains unclear. Lucy definitely needs surgery to remove the lump and then there will be more waiting as we hope and pray that it's not cancer.

"It's been three hours. You think they'd have some kind of news by now." Melanie is frantically pacing the waiting room with me. Maddy and Reid are with us too; the baby is with one of Maddy's friends from work. Linda and Joe are also here. If good news could be brought on by the amount of love felt for someone, well, then Lucy would be the healthiest woman on the planet.

"Anyone want some coffee?" Linda has been trying her best to keep everyone calm, and she's been such a support for both Lucy and me in the past few weeks. The girls and Reid join her in a short break from the non-stop worry that fills our time here, leaving just Joe and I in the small space.

I sit next to Joe, stretching my tired legs out in front of me, folding my hands behind my head. "It shouldn't be much longer, Evan."

"That's what I'm worried about." My admission confuses the fuck out of him and he does a shitty job of hiding that confusion, so I clarify it for him before he even asks about it. "I'm not worried about the surgery, exactly. It's what comes after the surgery that scares the shit out of me. What if it is cancer? What if she gets really sick?" After a long pause, I add, "What if I lose her?" I can't say the words *"What if she dies?"* because that's just too frightening to even think about.

"I know what you mean. When Becca got sick, I was plagued by the 'what ifs'. But you can't pay them too much attention. The 'what ifs' drain you of all the energy you need, to face down what *is*."

Worry still courses through my veins so I stand and walk over to the wall of windows that provide a clear view of the lake out in the distance. I've served up lots of prayers in the last few weeks, spent many moments hoping that Jimmy is actually out there listening to Lucy when she talks to him - hoping he'll put in a good word for her.

Please let her be okay, Jimmy. Please let me keep loving her.

Naturally, the doctor takes this moment to walk out into the waiting room. Her return is perfectly timed, as Linda, Melanie, Maddy and Reid return just as she's about to approach Joe and me.

She pulls over an extra chair and faces us all. "The surgery was a success. We were able to get the entire lump, and from the preliminary tests we ran in the OR, it looks like it was benign."

The weight of the last few weeks releases itself from my shoulders and flies away like a helium balloon set loose into the sky. Dr. Foster says a few more things and I try my best to focus through my relief.

"Obviously, we're not out of the woods entirely, but things are looking good."

"Can we see her?" Melanie is bouncing in her chair. I know she won't truly believe Lucy is okay until Melanie can hold her in her arms.

"Sure, as soon as we bring her out of the recovery room, you can see her."

About a half an hour after Dr. Foster first let us know that Lucy was okay, she brings us back into Lucy's room, where she's resting comfortably.

"Hey," she croaks out in a raspy and overly tired voice. A weak smile pulls at her lips and she tries to open her eyes enough to register who's there to visit her. But, the anesthesia is making her groggy, so for our quick fifteen-minute visit, we mostly just watch her drift in and out of sleep.

When Dr. Foster returns, she lets us know that visiting hours will be over shortly and I can see the look of sadness pass across Melanie's face knowing she won't be able to see her mom until at least tomorrow morning.

Linda sees it too. "Don't worry, Melanie. We'll be back first thing in the morning. Come on, let's go grab some dinner and rest up before we spend the whole day here tomorrow." Everyone else decides to join in, agreeing that it's been way too long of a day to go without a meal and some sleep. Just as we're about to walk out of the room, Lucy wakes once again.

"Leaving so soon," she jokes through the haze of her drowsiness. The doctor, who is standing at the foot of the bed finishing up the last of whatever paper work she needs to do, stifles a small chuckle. She also catches the worried look on Melanie's face, softening to it quickly.

"Okay, they can stay a little longer, but just two." She holds up two fingers for added emphasis.

Melanie and I say goodnight to everyone else, and pull up a chair on either side of Lucy's bed. Before long, Melanie is passed out in her seat. I drape a blanket over her and she pulls it up over her shoulder. My moving around the room must wake Lucy, because when I get back to my seat, her eyes flutter open.

I reach under her blanket and find her hand. Careful of the I.V., I pull it out from under the covers and bring it up to my lips. "Hey, love." I tuck her hair behind her ear and she turns her head toward me.

"Hi, yourself," her words filter softly through a weak, but bright-as-ever smile. "Can I have some water? I'm so thirsty," she rasps.

I reach to the small side table that the nurse set up for us earlier. "Not yet, but they said if you wanted you could have a few ice chips." She nods and opens her mouth for me to feed her some.

As she lets the ice melt in her mouth, we sit and stare at each other for a few moments. I stroke my knuckles across her cheek, more thankful than I've ever been to feel her skin beneath my hands.

I offer her more, but she declines. "Did the doctor say anything? Was it cancerous?" I can already hear the rising anxiety in her words and I try my best to calm her.

"Dr. Foster said they were able to get the entire lump and that the initial tests suggest that it's not cancer."

A tear slips out of the corner of her eye as she pulls our hands up to her dry lips. "Don't cry, Lucy." I wipe away her tears with the pad of my thumb. "Shh, it's going to be okay."

"I know it is. I can feel it." She kisses our joined hands again before giving herself over to sleep.

Around midnight, the nurses finally kick Melanie and me out. Lucy isn't doing much other than sleeping anyway. We promise to be back bright and early the next morning, even though we know she can't hear us.

After two days in the hospital, Lucy and I are packing up the last of her things, getting ready to be discharged. We were hopeful that the test results would come back while she was still here, but since we're just about ready to leave, it doesn't look like we'll be that lucky.

With her small duffle bag in one hand, and a bunch of flowers in my other one, we're all set to go. Just as we're about to walk out the door, Dr. Foster walks in.

"Oh good, you're still here. I just got the lab reports back. I guess when you have a friend who owes you a favor in pathology, things move more quickly." The light tone of her words makes us think she has good news to share, but we're both still too afraid to admit the opposite might be true.

She pulls a chair over as Lucy and I sit on the edge of the bed. Lucy is holding my hand so tightly that her knuckles are turning white with tension. As Dr. Foster flips through a few papers, our anxieties rise. My knee starts bouncing and my mind races with all of the possible words that could come out of the doctor's mouth.

"Just as I thought." Dr. Foster closes the lap reports with a bright and reassuring smile plastered to her face. "All tests indicate that the tumor was, in fact, benign which means that you won't need any chemo or further treatments." Unable to hold back my elation, I pull Lucy into my arms.

"Now, you'll have to come back into the office for a few routine check-ups, but I suspect that there's nothing to worry about." Dr. Foster gives us a few more instructions on how to care for the incision and when to see her to have the stiches removed. She stands and shakes our hands, reminding us to call her if we need anything at all.

When it's just the two of us in the room, we both look at each other like it's the first time we're seeing each other. I pull her back into my arms, careful not to touch the tender spot where her stiches are.

"You ready to head home now, love?" My lips are pressed against the top of her head and her face is buried into my chest. "I have a feeling you've got more than a few people waiting for you."

She laughs in my arms. It's a soft sound, but one filled with so much relief that I can't do anything but hold her even tighter. The sun shines brightly in our eyes as we step out of the hospital and I silently thank Jimmy for helping her through this, for listening to our joined prayers and for letting me love her for the rest of my life.

December 31, 2013

EPILOGUE
Lucy

"You okay over there?" I slide next to Evan on the couch as we cozy up for the final half hour of the New Year's Eve special that's on television. His leg has been bouncing around like crazy; it's almost as if we're on a plane instead of in our living room.

"Yeah, I'm okay. Sorry about that." He looks down at my hand on his knee and smiles at me lamely.

I lean my head on his shoulder and inhale his clean scent. "What are you looking forward to most in the new year?" It sounds like a dorky question, but since we had our final follow up appointment with Dr. Foster today and I'm officially in the clear, I'm all about looking to the future.

The bouncing stops as he contemplates my question. He pulls me into his side and kisses the top of my head. "I think I'm most excited about spending it with you. Even, right now, just being here, curled up on the couch watching the ball drop – this is what I've been looking forward to my whole life."

"Being with you is definitely on my list of things to look forward to." I poke him in the ribs, as he laughs at my silliness. We've been less active since my surgery six weeks ago. The doctor said there was no reason not to have sex, but between the lingering soreness of my breast and our persistent worrying, we haven't really been up to the challenge. But having gotten the best news in the world today does wonders for both of our sex drives.

He scoops me up in his arms and drops me on his lap. "Why wait for the new year?" His words take on a sexy tone suddenly. The raspy throatiness of his words washes across my skin. Only Evan has the power to arouse me with a simple question.

He pulls my face into his, crashing his lips into mine. His tongue sweeps against the seam of my lips and I open to him immediately. Our tongues thrash together, stoking the flames of our instantaneous desire. His hands slide under my top and unclasp my bra. In a heated rush, he removes both of them and tosses them on the floor. With the softest touch, he skims just his fingertips over my breasts before holding them in his hands. There's a newfound reverence to his touch as if he's actually worshipping my body. As he leans his head to kiss my small scar, I entwine my fingers into his silver-streaked hair.

As he licks and kisses my nipples, he stands and carries us over to the floor in front of the fireplace — back to the place where it all began.

Wordlessly, we relieve each other of the rest of our clothing, warmed only by the flickering flames behind us. With his mouth still firmly sealed over mine, he lowers us to the floor where his kisses rain down all over my body, bringing my desire to life like a warm spring shower rejuvenates everything it touches.

As he toys with the hardened tips of my breasts, sparks of lust zing across my body - they all settle in between my legs. I feel his cock pulsing against my stomach and I know he's holding back on his own pleasure just to bring me my own first.

His tongue trails down my body, dipping into my belly button, before going lower still. His finger trace through my sex before plunging deep inside. "You're always so wet for me, love." He works me like a magician does his favorite trick. Hitting the perfect spot at the perfect time, the motion of his thumb is flawlessly in sync with the swirling of his fingers inside.

"Evan!" I bellow his name and I drive my body down onto his hand, needing to feel more of him. That's just what he gives me. His mouth replaces his thumb and he draws the tightly wound bundle of nerves in between his lips. The rapid lashing of his tongue against my clit drives me wild - it tightens my nipples and makes my inner walls clench with the need to come like I've never felt before.

When he looks up at me, his mouth still tightly latched over my pulsating clit, I lose it. Desire tightens everything in my body, from my toes all the way up to my teeth as they clamp down on my lip. "I'm coming, Evan. God, I'm coming."

As my orgasm barrels through me, he quickly settles in between my legs and buries himself into my still-fluttering sex. "I needed to be inside of you. I needed to feel you pull me deep into you − to be right here with you." He pushes over and over again as he lowers to his elbows, resting them on either side of my head.

"I need you, too."

Our eyes never break away from one another, and even though we speak no words, we communicate a lifetime's worth of love in that passionate gaze. Our kiss, while so familiar, is brand new at the same time. His thrusts, driving deeper and harder by the second, never allow the waves of my orgasm to recede. As one crashes into the next, he slides his arms under my shoulders and holds me to his chest. My legs wrap around his hips and then climb higher still, allowing him to bury himself deeper and deeper still.

"Lucy!" he calls out, spilling his orgasm into me, his hips still thrusting rhythmically.

Afterward, we lie in front of the fire, a blanket draped over us as he's spooned up behind me, gently stroking my hair. From the other side of the room, we hear the faint cheers of the crowd on the television as they count down to one.

"Happy New Year, love," he whispers in my ear as the crowd on TV erupts into a loud roar of celebration. After pressing a soft kiss to the shell of my ear, I roll over to face him. Just as I snuggle into his warm chest, he reaches behind his head to grab something.

He places a small, red velvet ring box in between us and my heart beats a wild tempo in my chest. "Oh, my God." My excitement rises as we both move, now sitting Indian-style facing one another.

He takes my hand in his as a sincere, yet lopsided and sexy grin pulls at the corners of his mouth. "Lucy, I love you, and there's nothing in the world that would make me happier than being with you for the rest of our lives." He picks up the small box and cracks it open before presenting it to me in the palm of his hand. "I've had this picked out for a long time now and I've wanted to ask you so many times, but you deserved to have me ask you today when you knew for certain that you had the rest of your life to give to me."

Tears of happiness – no, scratch that – of complete and utter contentment fall from my eyes as he pulls the beautiful ring out of the box. Before fitting it on my finger, he stares up into my eyes. "Lucy, be my wife, please. Will you marry me?"

"Yes, yes, yes," I repeat as he slides the ring on my finger. I wrap my arms around his neck with enough might to strangle him if I really wanted to. Holding my hand out behind us, I stare in awe at the ring he picked out for me. He must mistake my silence for dissatisfaction, because as he pulls away from me, he makes the most ridiculous offer I've ever heard of.

"If you don't like it, we can exchange it. I brought the girls with me…"

I use my lips to silence him. "You silly man you. Exchange it? Never in a million years. And that you thought enough to include Melanie *and* Maddy, means more to me than you'll ever know. I just… I'm so in love with you   I just don't know what to say."

"There's nothing to say, love. You already said the only word I needed to hear. All we have to do now is just *be*."

And that's exactly what we'll do. We'll spend our days being in love with each other, until we run out of love; something, I think is safe to say will never happen.

Let love BE

THE END

For more information on future works, be sure to sign up for my newsletter

www.melissacollinsauthor.com

*Melissa*COLLINS

ACKNOWLEDGEMENTS

When I started this series, I created Momma with the perfect "mother" image in mind — kind, caring, loving, understanding. Her story wasn't initially clear in my head. I knew she had lost her husband and I knew she deserved love. I just didn't know the in between stuff. Lucy (not Momma) started to come to life as I was writing Let Love Heal. She became more than a mom and I started to get really excited about her story. It was truly just some random strokes upon the keyboard that brought Lucy and Evan together — a momentary and fleeting decision that really brought this book to life.

Perhaps that's the most amazing thing about writing: you never know what the story is until it writes itself.

And then, there's Evan - oh, Lord. Where do I begin with Evan? He is perhaps the most true-to-life character I've ever written. I lost my uncle, Lt. David Halderman, on 9/11 and my father, also a Battalion Chief in the FDNY, spent the months following 9/11 sorting through the rubble at Ground Zero looking for his younger brother. Like Evan, my father also had to retire early because of the lung damage he sustained. For these and so many other reasons, Evan will always hold a very special place in my heart.

I have super amazing beta readers who help me so much. Pam Schaeffer, Jennifer Diaz, Jennifer Short - Benson, Michelle Stratton, S. Moose, Emily Minton and Kristy Bruno — thank you all so much for your feedback and for loving my characters as much as I do.

Let love BE

An extra special thank you goes out to Nasha Lama and Ashely Griffieth for some of the most beautiful teasers I've ever seen.

Carey Heywood — I love your friggin' face, wife! You are seriously my savior and often my voice of reason.

Michele Molitor — I wish there were words bigger than "I love you" to let you know how much you mean in my life. Thank you for writing the dedication line for this book and for just being you. I know you will always carry his heart with yours and I know you will always speak to him in the quiet hours of the sunrise.

Let Love Be would be a very rough version of the one you've just read without the wonderful talent of Becky Johnson and her team at Hot Tree Editing. Thank you for taking my words and cleaning them up. I promise you, I am not a Cyborg (though, that sounds an awful lot like what a Cyborg who doesn't want to be revealed as a Cyborg would say). Hmmmm?

Toski and Sommer — I love you girls hard! This cover is, simply put, utterly gorgeous. Thank you for bringing Lucy and Evan to life.

Tami with Integrity Formatting — thank you for taking this very plain and simple Word document and making it so unbelievably pretty.

There are just too many bloggers to list, but please know that every time you share something of mine, post a review, or just recommend me to a reader, I fall in love with you a little bit more. Thank you also to my street team. You are so much more than a group of fans. In the months that we've had the group, you've all become my friends and for that, I'm hugely grateful.

To my husband — I cried so many tears writing Lucy's story because, in short, it made me have to envision how I would feel if you were no longer a part of my life. I love you with everything that I have and I always will.

OTHER WORKS

Let Love In (The Love Series #1)

Let Love Stay (The Love Series #2)

Let Love Heal (The Love Series #3)

Let Love Shine (The Love Series #3.5 ~ a novella)

SOCIAL MEDIA LINKS

Web and Newsletter Sign-up –
www.melissacollinsauthor.com

Facebook -
http://www.facebook.com/MelissaCollins.Author

Twitter - @mcollinsauthor

Pinterest – www.pinterest.com/mcollinsauthor